FALLING STAR WISH

by

Betty Hanawa

Dedication

Thanks to Kristi Studts, publisher at Triskelion Publishing, for the original premise of Holly and Edan.

Thanks to my editor, Terese Ramin who always comes to bat for me even though sometimes I'm sure she wants to swing a bat upside my head.

Thanks to Tawny for nagging and pushing, yet again.

Thanks to my critique partner Laura who always helps me with my manuscripts by sending me such loving, supportive, constructive comments as "This Sucks! Fix it!"

Thanks to Purple and Greenie, our children's dragon familiars who brought so much to our lives.

Love always to my husband.

But especially this is for Allie Standifer whose phobia of frogs is legendary, but who faces everything else, including the possibility of cancer, with courage, strength, and a wicked sense of humor. Thanks, Allie, for being an inspiration to all of us Muses.

Published by Triskelion Publishing www.triskelionpublishing.com
15508 W. Bell Rd. #101, PMB #502, Surprise, AZ 85374 U.S.A.

First e-published by Triskelion Publishing
First e-publishing March 2005

ISBN 1-933471-52-2
Copyright © Betty Hanawa 2004
All rights reserved.

Cover art by Triskelion Publishing & Dragon drawing by James Troyer

CHAPTER 1

Holly Tate usually didn't hallucinate with a hang-over. But this morning, in front of her half-opened, bloodshot eyes, a royally pissed-off self-proclaimed elf straddled a ladder-back chair, his arms resting on the chair's back.

"Edan Fariss, Prince of the Elf Kingdom of De'erjia."

Okay, make that a pissed-off Royal Elf. As if.

Black eyes as cold as a Yule night regarded her. Winter frost coated his deep baritone. The sound reverberated though Holly as though she were standing in a bell tower.

He touched his fingertips to his forehead.

Holly's attention briefly focused on the thick mink-colored hair that fell in waves past his shoulders. Why did her hands hold a memory of that curling softness sliding through her fingers?

Holly wasn't sure how exactly he managed to end the open palm salute with a mocking bow while still straddling the chair. But bow he did, adroitly managing to make her feel like a total doofus.

His tone of *I-am-dealing-with-a moron-whom-I-must-humor* didn't help her self-esteem.

He also had the advantage of being fully dressed while she huddled totally naked under her favorite lilac sheets.

Holly still couldn't figure out why she wasn't screaming for the police. She could easily take him out and get to a phone. She knew *S-I-N-G:* sternum, instep, nose, groin. How many ti8mes had she seen that Sandra Bullock movie?

Maybe she couldn't do anything because she

couldn't open her eyes wide enough to find the phone, much less dial 9-1-1. Every time she cracked her eyes open a trifle wider, a hundred screaming demons sent light in to sear pain into her brain.

She doubted she could form a thought, much less talk on the phone. A multitude of monkeys were slamming cymbals inside her brain in an attempt to finish the complete works of Shakespeare in Morse Code. She figured her skull would explode before they finished.

Actually, much as she hated to admit it, part of her wanted to buy into this over-enthusiastic Lord of Rivendell wanna-be who was dressed entirely too early for the area's Ren Faire.   Fawn-colored pants outlined dancer-strong thighs tucked into calf-high soft boots planted firmly on the floor. It didn't help Holly's concentration one bit that the thong that was supposed to tie the linen shirt together was undone revealing honey colored skin.

Her body hummed with energy, imagining the friction of that silken flesh sliding against hers. Her breasts thought about the pleasurable flattening against hard muscle covering strong bones.

Holly shook her head, trying to shake away the erotic fantasy. She only succeeded in dislodging some of the monkeys in her skull who screeched and began pounding louder.

"And I..." her voice trailed off; she still couldn't believe what he said.

"You summoned me."

Disappointment flattened Holly's want-to-believe hopes. "I knew we were too loud in the bar."

"I beg your pardon?"

"You eavesdropped on us. You heard us talking about summoning and either followed me home from the woods or asked someone where I lived. I can't have you arrested for rape because I was obviously stupid and let you into my house. But I want you out of here. Now."

A sudden thought seared through Holly. "Please, please tell me I wasn't so drunk that I didn't make you use a condom."

Dark brows drew together in puzzlement.

Holly covered her face and moaned.

"Would 'condom' have been the sheath you insisted I must use as a covering?"

Holly peeked through her fingers at his face creased with an annoyed frown that matched his disgusted voice.

"Um, yes."

"Ridiculous. I told you there was no need. But you insisted. It greatly diminished my pleasure."

"Too damn bad," Holly snapped. She wrapped the sheet around herself and struggled to her feet. "Bad enough I was so stupid to lower myself to a bar pick-up, but at least I was coherent enough not to risk a disease or pregnancy."

Holly stood with the sheet draped around her and straightened her spine to her full height. Okay, 5'2" wasn't an imposing stature and even though she logged her food, did her exercises, and religiously went to the weigh-in meetings each week, she just couldn't get rid of that last stinking twelve pounds. Damn plateau.

Nevertheless, despite her apple-shaped body, she still had her dignity. She flipped the loose end of the sheet over her shoulder and kept the image of the proud Greek goddesses in mind. She pushed unruly mounds of hair out of her face and behind her ears, inwardly wincing at the thought of what bed head did to her curls.

"Please leave. Now."

What's-his-name, oh yeah, Edan — Holly still felt sick that she'd allowed a bar pick-up whose name she couldn't remember into her bed — Edan swung one booted leg behind him, effortlessly set the chair to one side, then looked down at Holly. With her nose level with that lovely hollow at the base of his throat and feeling the ghostly taste and soft texture of it on her lips and tongue, Holly figured she'd better pull herself together before she leaned forward to lick it.

"I am not a '*bar pick-up.*'"

Disdain twisted his full lips. Holly had a fleeting memory of those lips smiling at her in the moonlight, closing over her aching nipple, gently trailing down to her body to…

A hot shiver leapt through her. *Don't think about where those lips and that tongue went.*

"I am a Prince of De'erjia. And you summoned me."

Holly had the wild thought that maybe, just maybe, he really was a prince. He definitely had that chilly, haughty royal look in those glittering obsidian eyes down cold. Prince Charming, he wasn't.

"Right, right. I summoned you. So, go back to wherever I summoned you from and let me get dressed and try to forget this entire episode."

"I have no wish to remain any longer than you desire, but you must release me from the summoning."

"Fine, fine." Holly flapped a hand. "Shoo. Go away. I release you from whatever. Just go."

Holly's fingertips could still feel the strong corded muscles in his arms that she'd clung to as he thrust deeply into her. He now crossed those arms over the broad chest Holly remembered lying against, his skin gilded in the moonlight.

He tapped one booted foot, the soft leather barely audible against her hardwood floor.

"That is not how it works. You must use the proper procedures to release the enchantment. The way you did last night to summon."

"And how exactly did I so-called 'summon' you last night? 'Here, Prince. Come, Prince'." Holly whistled the multi-tone whistle that had called numerous dogs to her heels since she was a child. Just as she did then, Holly crooned, "Good boy, Prince. You were a very good boy to come."

The sticky, feel of her own hot honey pooled between her legs and reminded her just how good he had been, how she had come herself, bucking wildly against his body. Definitely not a boy.

She forced herself to the cold-voiced command, the way she had to when dealing with delightful, rambunctious puppies in her training classes. "Now...Go...Away."

Edan touched a warm hand to her forehead. "Remember the moonlight. Remember the forest. The trees."

Vaguely, Holly recalled the floating ride from the bar to the forest. She remembered the car and, in the butter yellow morning light, came the realization she and the other girls were damn lucky not to have had an accident as drunk as they'd been from all they drank and the adrenaline of exhilarated anticipation.

But they'd reached the forest, stumbling, cursing, and giggling as they made their way between the trees and through the underbrush to a clearing.

She could feel the moonlight drenching her skin as she danced with the other girls, sky-clad as though it were a Beltane evening. Words came from her throat, pulled skyward on the moonlight path.

The other girls had their own ideals of the perfect immortal being. Holly knew what she wanted.

An orthodontic-needy vampire didn't intrigue Holly. Besides, since her too-close brush with death, she gave to the blood banks regularly. Not a chance she'd let some dude suck blood she wanted used for saving lives.

Shape-shifters made Holly think of schizophrenics. She'd dated too many men who turned into animals she'd had to fight off to keep out of her bed. Granted they'd been in human shape, but still, she dealt with dogs on a daily basis. She sure didn't want to deal with some dude shifting into some critter while with her.

And a god? Not a chance. Until she became a full-time dog groomer and part-time trainer, she'd had a couple of bosses who thought they were gods. Entirely too high maintenance for her.

With the heel of Edan's palm against her forehead and his voice musically whispering "Remember," Holly remembered her song for an Elf in the silver moonlight. An Elf like those from Terry Brook's fantasy sagas who battled with humans using broadswords and bows and arrows, an Elf of Tolkien's that she'd loved years before the movies, although the movies reinforced her desire to be one with an Elf.

Holly stepped away from Edan's palm. The loss of his warmth cut as quickly as the ice shards still in her heart.

"It didn't work," she said flatly. "I came home with nothing. You followed me home from the forest after you heard me. You are not an Elf."

"Did you truly believe the song would work?" Edan's voice vibrated in her frozen heart, threatening to sear the healed scars open.

"Of course not." Holly wrapped her arms around her waist holding her sheet tighter. "It was a joke. A drunken playtime for me and my friends."

"And when you made a sincere wish, the summons invoked me."

"What sincere wish?"

"Think," Edan commanded.

Holly ignored the clamoring monkeys still pounding cymbals, closed her eyes to the sunlight that made her eyes tear. She thought it was the sunlight. Surely, the tears weren't coming from her heart yet again.

"There was a falling star in the dark side of the sky."

At Edan's prompting, Holly saw the star again, streaking golden red across the starlit splattered dome above her face.

"And you wished," Edan reminded her.

Almost unable to hear herself she whispered, "I wished that the song had worked."

Edan lifted the deep brown hair curtaining the sides of his head. Like Holly had done with her frazzled curls, he tucked its heavy weight behind his ears.

He lifted Holly's hands and placed them on his ears.

He placed his own hands against Holly's breasts.

Gently he rubbed her nipples into peaks.

Hot desire shot through her and Holly realized Edan's face reflected the same ecstasy she was experiencing as she gently rubbed her fingers over his ears' peaked points.

"Edan Fariss, Prince of De'erjia." Edan's voice slid through her ear channels as sweet as crystal chimes. "You summoned me with your sincere wish on the falling star. The song needed sincerity to work." Breathy pants made his voice seem hesitant. "I wish to return to my realm." He slid the sheet off Holly's body, baring it to the morning sunlight. His black eyes glittered with need and pleasure while his ears throbbed seductively under Holly's fingertips. "Later."

"No." Holly stepped away from his hands and dropped her hands from his ears.

Edan nearly staggered from the shock of interruption of pleasure. He reached for Holly to continue to pleasure her, for her to pleasure him. Once she was thoroughly satisfied, he would return to his realm. That she satisfied him was simply a bonus. However, he would insist this time that he not employ the sheath that detracted from the pleasure much as though he were walking through dewdrops wearing his boots.

To his annoyance, Holly pushed him away and

gathered the bedcovering around her body, once again hiding her sunlit rosy perfection from his view.

The absence of the coverings on the bed woke Holly's small dragon bedmate who'd tolerated him when Holly was lost in their joining. Holly, being mortal, obviously could not see and did not know a youngling had appointed itself her protector.

On some plane of her existence though, she must be aware of the dragon. Small green porcelain dragons cavorted on her bookshelves. A crystal dragon reflected and shattered the morning sun's rays into a rainbow across the mellow deep brown wooden floor reminiscent of Edan's own abode.

Edan watched the dragon mince its way across the rumpled bedclothes and land with a thump on the floor between him and Holly. The dragon, too young to have determined its sex, hissed a clear warning at Edan. Edan went no closer to Holly, well aware that even a young dragon would bite and possibly flare anything it perceived to be a threat to its ward. Instead, he bared his teeth back at it; both an acknowledgement of the dragon's right to its property and a warning that he would defend himself if need be. This was simply not the moment to take issue.

"There's no need to get snitty." Holly's voice detracted him from his eye-to-eye glare battle with the dragon.

"I beg your pardon?"

Edan shifted his view from the dragon to Holly's green eyes. He'd watched humans periodically throughout his life, had even befriended a few, but he still did not quite grasp the intricacies in the nuances of conversational speak. It didn't help that every culture in each different era had its own versions of words and even versions within versions, depending upon the tone of utterance.

Now Holly's face had twisted in a scowl, her brows

furrowed. Her eyes no longer held the softness of summer grass, but bore the yellow spark of sun blazing in the desert.

"Just because I don't want to have sex with you, there's no need to have a snit-fit."

The vibrations in Holly's voice enthralled him as tightly as the Sirens of Antiquity. His ears wanted to hear her voice as much as his body wanted hers against him, around him. He wanted – no, he realized with a shock, he *needed* – to hear her voice rise in songs of pleasure as he entered her body, as his own pleasure spiraled upward to merge with hers until they both crested in the cosmos only available to joined lovers.

"Snit-fit? What is 'snit-fit'?"

"That ugly pouty feeling you're obviously experiencing because I don't want sex with you right now."

"As much as I would enjoy joining with you again, I assure you I do not *pout...*"

"Then why the sneer?"

Due to the annoyance underlying Holly's vocal vibrations, Edan managed to hide his smile at Holly's lovely full lips twisting her mouth in mimicry of the traditional teeth baring used in dealing with dragons. He glanced at the chartreuse dragon leaning against her calf that obviously shared his enjoyment.

Holly might not be consciously aware of her dragon, but her hand reached down to rub the side of her knee. The dragon preened under her stroking hand.

"Ah," Edan held up his hands, partially cupped in the traditional sign of promised silence to dragons with his index fingers straight upright and his thumbs pointing outward yet curved to his palms to indicate a dragon's horns, "that was not directed at you nor at the cessation of joining, but at the situation in general. Particularly at the problem that, until you release me, I cannot return to my own realm."

With a slight bow to the dragon, Edan retrieved the

thong tie for his shirt from under the dragon's rear paw. Ah, there was his hair tie under the pillow on which the dragon had been sleeping.

"Do you have to talk like a college English prof? I mean, you've got a cool accent and everything, but, gag, every time you talk I feel like I'm back in college."

"'Prof?'"

"Short for professor."

Edan couldn't decide whether his fascination came from Holly's voice or the way her emotions flickered across her face. He had not blinked, yet her face changed from annoyance to amusement to the softening of someone well loved as the dragon imparted its contented hum against her calf. Those wonderful ivy-colored eyes of hers enchanted him like no Elf woman had in millennia.

Unlike other Elves, he'd never had a mortal lover before. It seemed futile to him to spend such a fleeting time with a lover who would pass to the beyond where he could not follow.

But Holly was different. For the first time, he realized the attraction of a temporary liaison with a mortal lover. Perhaps he'd simply enjoy these moments and not press Holly to release him for a time. Eternity did have its moments of boredom.

Plus a human who'd attracted a dragon without invoking it or even realizing she had it was not your average run-of-the-mill human.

"Ah. Professor. A teacher at a school of higher learning. As for the formality of my speech, you must…" Edan allowed himself to be distracted by the sunlight shining on Holly as it turned the pale purple bed linen translucent. He saw the darkness of her nipples in hard peaks and the shadows of her curls that cushioned her deep secret joys at the apex of her legs.

He cleared his throat and forced himself back to his

explanation. "You must remember that the language in which we are speaking is not my natal language. I learned the formal version of this language and must be educated in the more casual delivery and words."

"Yeah, right."

"Of course, some forms of communication require no speech."

Once again, Holly evaded his overture and the dragon hissed.

"I said 'No' and 'No' doesn't mean 'Maybe' in my book. Go away. If we can't send you back to your *realm* right now, at least go to the kitchen or something. Go get some coffee. There's cereal and bread for toast. I'm going to take a shower and get dressed. Then we'll figure out how to click your heels and send you home."

Understanding only a few words of Holly's chatter, Edan allowed himself to be pushed from the room. He heard the click of a lock, knowing if he truly wanted in, a pitiful mortal lock would no more keep him out than the closed door kept the dragon from materializing through it and coming to stand at his feet.

"Kitchen?" he politely asked the dragon. It wasn't worth his while to annoy a dragon, even a youngling.

Behind him, Holly's bedroom door muffled the sound of water falling with the roar of a nearby waterfall or sudden summer shower. Ah, shower. Now Edan understood. Mortals had learned to direct water into falling in a 'shower' to cleanse themselves. When last he'd been around mortals, it took several people carrying buckets of hot water to fill a tub in which to bathe. Excellent. Much easier on everyone by this new shower device. He'd have to experience it himself. With Holly.

Anticipating Holly's wet skin sliding against his during a joining, feeling the individual drops of water hitting his skin while he enjoyed Holly's innermost fluids embracing him in the most intimate of holding, Edan felt his hardness throb against the tightened cords of his breeches. Yes, he should definitely stay a few days and enjoy Holly's body before he helped her release him from her summoning.

Unlike the dragon, he couldn't phase through the doorway off the dining area to which the hallway from Holly's bedroom led. Not seeing a handle, he gave a gentle push and saw the kitchen. Hmm, no woodpile, no bustling servants.

But there was the deep, rich smell of brewed coffee. He remembered coffee; the tasty bitterness, the increased zing of his brain synapses as his body ingested the fluid.

He crossed the room to where a full glass carafe of coffee waited on a platform beneath brown container. No servants, but the coffee was ready. Hmm, perhaps in addition to the 'shower,' mortals had learned to utilize a minor form of magic to brew coffee without the servants they'd previously used the way House Brownies helped out amongst Elf. Quite a bit of time had passed since Edan had last been in the mortal plane.

A sharp bark distracted Edan from his re-acquaintance with coffee.

In a metal cage stood a large rat. No, wait. It was not a rat. Rats did not bark or wave their long tails. This animal's tail waved like a curled rope above its body. This animal had a round head with a small, sharp nose, and round, large, dark eyes. With its dark fawn coloring, it resembled a minute deer, but the head was as round as an apple and the smell wasn't right for a deer.

Edan thought about the scent. A dog? A miniature dog? The only dogs Edan knew were large dogs, used by hunters, but this did smell somewhat like a dog. It did not have the pungent odor of the hunting dogs. However, underneath the slight floral scent, Edan caught the musky whiff of dog glands.

The dragon moved to the cage where the dog barked again. The dragon looked at the dog, then at Edan. Then it phased through a door. Through the door's window, Edan could see wooden fencing enclosing a wide grassy area, shaded by two large oaks.

The dragon phased back inside the kitchen, went to the dog's cage, gave Edan a command gaze, then phased back outside.

Ah, Edan understood. The dragon wished Edan to release the small dog to the outside. *Very considerate of the dragon,* Edan thought, *to think of Holly's dog's comfort in needing to be outside so as not to soil Holly's living area.*

If he were not here, the dog would have to wait until Holly came into the kitchen. But since he was here...

"Open," he commanded the cage. A latch released and the tiny dog bounded out and came to Edan.

Remembering the hunters with their dogs, he placed his palm upward to the dog that was busily sniffing and licking his stag-skin boots. Distracted by his hand, the dog imprinted Edan's scent on its tiny brain then returned to the more interesting odor of his boots.

The dragon phased inside again and hissed at the dog, which promptly followed it to the doorway and scratched a metal plate fastened on the wooden door.

Edan followed, futilely twisted the round handle, then huffed in disgust at himself. "Unfasten."

At his command, a latch above the handle twisted itself. From the middle of the round handle, a small button, as hard as Holly's nipples beneath his tongue, popped against Edan's palm.

Ignoring the cat, sunning itself on the porch railing, the dog ran down the cottage's back steps to the furthest portion of the yard from the building.

For a moment, Edan thought he looked into one of the gardens that embraced Elf abodes. In addition to the ancient oaks, dark ivy climbed the wooden fence on one side. He took a deep breath of the morning air and looked at the hollyhocks marching along another side of the grassy area and jasmine twining a trellis near the porch. In one corner, Edan saw a small plot containing the gray-green of bay leaf, the deeper green of basil, a rosemary bush, and other herbs thriving in deep, dark soil.

The cat landed with a heavy thump on the wooden porch and loudly called to Edan. Obediently, Edan held open the door and bowed the cat into the kitchen, according it the same dignity as he gave the dragon.

In the kitchen, Edan began a search for a cup to use to enjoy the pleasure of coffee. The cat called loudly weaving to and fro in front of a small door beside the cabinets. The dragon phased back into the kitchen and the dog scratched on the back door. Edan opened the door again and the dog joined the cat in front of the small door.

"What *is* it?" Edan snapped the cupboard door closed on plates and bowls and turned to the dragon that hissed like a container of boiling water. The dragon phased through the small doorway before which the cat continued its complaint.

Stifling his irritation and beginning to miss the House Brownies from his own home or, at the least, the servants from his previous visit to the mortal plane, Edan followed the commanding dragon and opened the door. Beneath the scents of cinnamon and dried thyme, the sweet aroma of sugar, and the cool dusty odor of grains finely ground, Edan smelled an odd scent. Not quite meat. Not quite fish. Not quite vegetable.

Yowling with happiness, the cat bumped its head on a clear container that emitted a slightly fishy smell. Fish. Cats. Edan studied the container. He flipped opened the flimsy latch and spied a small cup. Filling the cup, he carried the dry fish-smelling pellets to a small bowl with a drawing of a cat in the bottom, placed on a portion of the cabinet far away from the food preparation area.

He returned to replace the cup and spied the dog sitting before yet another container. With a sigh as he realized there would be a further delay before he could enjoy his coffee, Edan filled a cup of meaty smelling pellets and emptied it into a bowl near the dog's metal cage.

"They are both eating," Edan told the preening dragon after he'd shut the small door. "May I have coffee now? Or must I perform more morning rituals? Perhaps slay something for you to break your fast?"

With a pop, the dragon returned to its own plane for its hunting. While Edan kept careful control not to annoy dragons, he still resented the way they would order one around when they had self-appointed themselves to someone's care. On second thought, Edan realized when he finally found cups for the coffee – several of which sported dragons either painted on them or shaped into part of the cup – it wasn't the orders that annoyed him so much as the indulged amusement the dragons released when one obeyed their commands.

Edan still smelled the sweet vanilla of dragon laughter. He hated to be laughed at. To be the center of a joke, even a dragon's idea of a joke, held no dignity.

Bossy creatures, dragons were, no matter what shape they took. Just because they'd been around the planes and realms longer than even Elf and others, they thought everyone needed to be at their beck and call. Obviously, they knew what was best for everyone. Or thought they did. He'd had enough of dragons for the morning and finally found a plain green cup, one without dragons decorating it. .

Edan lifted the carafe of fragrant coffee and began to fill the cup. His mouth salivated at the realization of tasting coffee again.

The door from the dining area opened.

Edan forgot about the coffee when Holly's ripe body glided across the floor. He noticed how her round rump molded itself into the breeches she wore as she bent to pat the rat-dog. All his senses focused on Holly, Edan overfilled his cup, sending coffee streaming down his hand and across the cabinet.

"Ef'ken ho'ser," Edan cursed at the hot splash across his hand.

Before the last syllable died on his lips, Holly had taken the coffee cup from him and immersed his hand under a stream of cold water from a metal pipe curved over a sink.

"Are you okay?"

The cool water relieved the sting, but his body heated at the touch of Holly's hand. His senses began to spiral out of control at the scent of lemon verbena floating from her damp hair. She had braided the sides to meet at the back of her head in a bright red band, from which her hair curled in waves and ringlets to her shoulders.

"Edan? Your hand? Does the burn still hurt?"

Burn? Burn? Yes, he burned for her. He needed to take her again. Now.

The straps holding up the bib attached to her breeches kept her skin from him. He pushed the straps down her arms and reached for the scrap of blue cloth of the under blouse. Holly knocked his hand away and pulled the straps back up onto her shoulders.

"Obviously, your hand doesn't hurt *that* much." Even sarcasm could not stop the Siren pull of her voice. Its sweet cadences slid across Edan's ears and hummed into his very being, stringing him tight.

"Look, Edan, we had our fun. I acknowledge you're an Elf. Elves and humans have no future together. I can't become Elf. You want to return to your realm, which means you don't want to choose a mortal life. We've had a fun night. Let's just leave it at that."

She detached white paper lightly sprinkled with multi-colored flowers from a tube of papers standing on a wooden column and wiped up the spilled coffee, then discarded the paper in a container under the sink. Reaching into the cabinet, she drew out a dragon emblazoned cup and poured coffee into it.

Edan watched the hips he'd gripped last night sway under her pale blue breeches as she walked across the kitchen to stop at the cat and rub between its ears. He could still feel the resilience of her skin under his fingers and the lovely softness that covered her bones and pleasantly cushioned his body.

"And if I choose to remain in this plane for our pleasure?"

Edan watched in enchantment while lust, wonder, and delight flittered across Holly's mobile face. Then her round jaw firmed and the sparkle left her peridot eyes, turning them the flat, muddy gray-green of pond scum.

An odd sensation began to grow in Edan. What was it? He could only equate the uneasiness to the long, tiring days of winter with its slate gray skies and continual chill.

The chill deepened as Holly said, "I want more out of life than just momentary pleasure. I thought I wanted an Elf, but – as great as last night was – um, what I can remember of it – I guess I need a human. A mortal. Someone who will be a companion and a helpmate, give me more than just great sex."

"I can be a companion. A helpmate. I fed the dog and the cat this morning." No need for Holly to know the dragon and the animals instructed him in how to do it.

"Oh." Holly looked at the animals' bowls as though suddenly realizing they'd been fed. "Well, thank you. I appreciate that."

A bit of the chill eased in Edan.

"But there's more to being a life-long companion

than feeding the animals."

Edan crossed the room and eased the curls on Holly's shoulders through his fingers. "Must you plan a life at this moment? We could simply enjoy the next few moments."

Holly stepped back from him. The sadness in her eyes increased the chill within Edan.

"I can't," she whispered so quietly that a mortal would not have been able to hear her. "I've merged fantasy and reality. There's an old saying: 'Be careful what you wish for, you may get it.' I wished you here and my fantasy became reality. But it's not really reality. I have to live in reality. I can't live with the fantasy that you might choose to stay with me. I wish you'd go back to your realm before I break my heart wanting you to stay."

Holly's face began to dim from Edan's sight. He smelled the De'erjia fields with the familiar scents of violets and clover. His being began to be drawn back into his own realm.

CHAPTER 2

With a wrench of power, Edan gained control of the summoning spell. Or rather, in this case, the anti-summoning spell Holly had unleashed with her wish.

Holly's face came back into sharp focus. The scents and sounds of De'erjia disappeared, leaving him standing firmly in Holly's sunlit kitchen, the dog still crunching those meat-scented pellets although the cat was watching him with wide eyes.

With satisfaction, Edan once again smelled the lemon verbena softly floating above Holly's dark curls, cutting through the tang of fresh coffee. Holly might have summoned him to her against his will, but he had his control back now. He would return to De'erjia when *he* decided, not at Holly's whim.

In addition, he needed to examine this odd pull Holly had on him. A mortal being such as Holly should not have been able to overcome his own power to summon him to her, even if she had attracted a dragon. Dragons and cats were renowned for their curiosity, which was probably why the dragon had decided to spend time with Holly. Edan had to admit he had his fair share of the attribute himself, especially – for some odd reason – since Holly had injected herself into his life. Ah, well, curiosity kept boredom at bay.

The cat gave an indifferent shrug Edan knew was too subtle for Holly to see, then returned to its own crunching of the fishy pellets.

"For a minute there, I thought I had wished you away."

Was that subtle pleasure at failure underlying Holly's statement? Edan briefly considered giving Holly affirmation the wish had not been successful. He realized immediately the cat would relay everything to the dragon.

The dragon would then proceed to make his life miserable for lying to its gifted one.

"Your wish worked." Edan picked up his coffee cup and sipped the still hot brew. "I chose to remain."

Holly's eyes narrowed to green-lightning slashes. "I thought you wanted to go back to Detergent."

"De'erjia."

Surely the amount of frost in Edan's voice had iced his coffee. But, no, Holly watched wisps of steam rise from the top of his cup. She could almost see matching wisps of steam coming from his ears, those lovely pointed ears above his rigid, angered jaw.

Good, she was glad she annoyed him. Maybe if she got him mad enough, he'd leave.

Leave. She looked at the clock ticking merrily away on the wall above the doorway. Oh, great stars. If she didn't leave quickly, she'd be late. She'd have to deal with Edan after work. Hastily, she dumped coffee into a thermos and grabbed a couple of granola bars from the pantry.

"Rat. Come."

"Appropriate name for a dog that looks like a rat."

"I didn't name him. His former owner did. The dog's ancestry came from Mexico where they were bred to hunt rats."

Obediently, the Chihuahua she'd inherited came to heel.

"Bred to hunt vermin." Edan sounded as though he were reminding himself of something. "Just as other small dogs were bred to sit on laps to keep people warm during the cold winter months."

"Yeah, Miniature and Toy Poodles, Yorkies, Bichons, Pekes, and the like." Holly scratched Crush between her ears in farewell, then rummaged in her bag for her keys.

"Looking for these?" Smugly, Edan swung her key

ring around one long forefinger, his legs crossed in front of him as he indolently leaned against her counter, the morning sunlight sparking undertones of burnished gold in the depths of his mink hair.

Holly snatched at her keys. With a grin as mischievous as her younger – and taller – brother's, Edan held them out of her reach. He sipped his coffee as his smile deepened with satisfaction.

A moonlit memory of the same deep smile hovering over her flittered through Holly. He'd come hard and shouting in her, leaving her limp with her own pleasure. Once again hot moisture flashed through her inner core.

"Give me my keys." She needed to go to work, not strip here in the kitchen and wrap herself around him. He wasn't going to stick around and she had her dignity, even if she did have her panties sticking to her.

Edan's smile drooped with mocking hurt. "You wish me to return the first gift you gave me? You shall break my heart."

He held the keys firmly against his chest. Dark eyes glinted with black stars, mocking the unhappiness he tried to keep on his face.

"I did not give you my keys," Holly hissed between gritted teeth. "Give them to me. Now. I'm going to be late for work."

"I beg to differ with you. Last night, when the moon was full, and the falling star wish had been invoked, you gave me your keys. You were laughing at the moon. Giddy that I had appeared to service your pleasure. You could not open the door properly. You gave me the keys. These keys." Edan held them above his head as Holly lunged for them again.

Blasted man, er, elf didn't even spill his coffee.

"Then, after I unlocked the door – the key, by the way, was completely unnecessary as I can unlock any mortal door with but a simple command – you insisted I lift you and carry you into the house."

Holly remembered how the moonlight had swung in circles about her head when he lifted her into his arms and carried her into the house. He'd lifted her as lightly as dandelion fluff floating in the breeze. She remembered the heavy strength of his arm under her thighs, the firm brace of his arm supporting her back. Laughter filled her mouth, just before his tongue had, a tongue that promised to divulge hot, wet secrets.

While he unlocked the door, he held her tightly and his hand cupped the slope of her breast. The hand on her thigh had slid up her skirt to stroke the silken material between her legs. All the while, she grew more drunk on his probing, hungry tongue than she had all night on the drinks she'd had with the girls.

"You insisted all the locks be shut before you allowed me to remove your clothes."

Vaguely, Holly remembered Crush's orange body sliding outside, her fur sleek glowing in the moonlight. Holly had drunk far too many margaritas. Along with too much tequila was the giddy exhilaration that her wish had come true, even if it had been only a drunken erotic dream.

But now in her kitchen, stood the reality of almost six-feet of solidly built Elf – an *Elf*, for pity's sake. And he still held her keys out of reach while he poured himself a second cup of coffee.

"How do you summon your House Brownie?"

"Huh?"

"Your House Brownie," he repeated. "You poured most of the coffee into that container." He regally inclined his head toward the thermos Holly clutched. "I wish more coffee. I've seen no indication of servants like the ones I knew in my previous sojourns to this plane. You have mastered the technique to summon an Elf."

Once again he graced Holly with his bow, his mouth twisted in a mocking smile. Edan continued, "I assume humans have also learned how to summon a House Brownie to help with household needs in lieu of servants. Please summon it to refresh the coffee."

"Listen, bud, I didn't think summoning an Elf would work. Elves are fantasies in this world, not reality. I have no clue how I 'mastered the technique' to summon you. Elves don't exist in this world and neither do Brownies. I make the coffee around here. This," Holly shook the filled thermos at Edan, "is for me to carry to work. Now give me my keys and let me get to work. I've got a picky client coming this morning and the last thing I need is to be late."

"I wish more coffee." There was nothing plaintive about Edan's voice. The Prince was commanding her.

"Then give me my car keys and you can have some from my thermos while I drive to work." Holly lunged upward once more. "I need my keys. Now."

Edan looked sharply at the doorway then handed her the key ring.

"I will go with you for coffee."

"Oh, joy. Thank you. Let us away."

Holly unlocked her silver Volkswagen Beetle doors and flipped the driver's seat forward. At her whistle, Rat jumped into the back and scrambled into his seat. She harnessed Rat securely into his pet seat and slid into the driver's seat. She set her cup in a holder and tossed the wrapped granola bars onto the console. Her beloved George hummed sweetly as usual when she turned the ignition key. She rolled her neck to ease the tension. The tight muscles loosened as though a hot water bottle had settled itself against the base of her skull and draped itself across her shoulders.

Feeling a bit of the frivolous joy that had infused her last night, Holly lowered the passenger side window and whistled. "Here, Prince. Come, Prince, get in the nice car."

Edan opened the passenger door with annoyance. His eyes not on her face, but looking at the back of her neck rest, he bowed almost formally even as he folded himself inside.

Holly shrugged and put the car into Drive. "Seatbelt."

"I beg..."

"Your pardon," Holly said in chorus with him. She grinned at his glare, which made her giggle. His eyebrows drew together and his eyes darkened like ominous thunderclouds, but Holly just giggled more.

Edan folded his arms across his chest. "Do not laugh at me."

"Yeah, yeah," Holly managed to struggle out. It was hard to talk when trying to control giggles. He sat so straight and solemn as though he was a judge in a courtroom. Or a dignified Elf coping with irrational humans.

"'Seatbelt?'" Edan's voice still held frost.

Holly tugged her own seatbelt. "Put on your seatbelt."

Edan looked at hers, properly fastened, then twisted around to find and pull his across himself, then latch it.

Holly finally had her giggles under control and looked at her Elf Prince from the corner of her eye as she turned from her lane onto the road. An Elf Prince, who'd have thunk it?

Elf. Oh, drats. The ears. Those lovely, glorious peaks. Her inner thighs tingled at the memory of those tactile points sliding across her sensitive nerves while his mouth suckled her innermost center.

"You need to cover your ears." Holly resolutely kept her eyes on the country road making sure she'd see any deer out for early morning grazing. She needed to be alert to stop just in case a deer took it into its tiny brain to jump across the road. She hoped her voice didn't betray the heat flushing through her body.

"Yes, I know I must cover my ears. I have been in this plane before." Edan untied the thong around his hair, shook it loose, then retied the thong so his hair covered all but his lobes. "Coffee?"

"Your addiction?"

At Edan's silence. Holly glanced at him. His mouth was set in a straight, firm line.

Whether he was annoyed at himself or at her, Holly wasn't sure, but he patiently said, "Please explain 'addiction'."

"Um," Holly stopped the car to enter the main highway, "something you can't live without. Something you have to have to function."

"I do not have an 'addiction' to coffee. I have not had coffee in many years. I enjoy coffee."

Holly pulled to the end of the road to wait for a gap in the highway traffic. She indicated the thermos. "Help yourself, but pour it quick before I get on the highway. And if it spills and burns you, you can't sue me."

"I do not care to know what 'sue' means. Do you wish more coffee in your cup?"

Still watching traffic, Holly shook her head. "No, thanks." She tried to remember the last time a man she'd been involved with had offered even that much of a nicety.

Realizing he'd placed his filled cup in the holder and was tightening the lid on the thermos, Holly accelerated into the traffic.

"Why did you stay? You said my wish worked, but you didn't leave."

"I chose to stay and be with you longer. It has been many of your human years since I last visited this plane. I do not visit often and I rarely stay long. I prefer to be in my own home. But I have much curiosity. When last I visited, vehicles were pulled by horses, not this magic key you used. There were servants to prepare food and drink. And women..."

Edan glanced at the blue material snugly outlining Holly's round thighs, thighs that had hugged his body fiercely to her when the wildfire of their joining ripped through him. The material snuggled against her glorious breasts that had overfilled his palms like ripe sweet fruit. Underneath the straps of the breeches' bib, a darker blue material further covered her peach skin, but enhanced the lift and swell of her breasts.

"And women?" Holly's eyes remained on the smooth stone road, watching other vehicles. Wrapped around her neck, the dragon she had no conscious knowledge of twisted its neck to look at him.

Edan shifted uncomfortably in his seat, secured by the seatbelt. He wished Holly would look at him, but then again that might be a mistake. Just looking at her made him yearn to loosen the lacings on his breeches.

But why was her dragon glaring at him? He had not stroked himself in public for relief. Oh, yes, Edan realized at the dragon's silent chastisement, he had been speaking.

"The women wore dresses, with multiple under-dresses, so fully covered that a man could not enjoy the loveliness of their differences to a man's body."

"I'm fully covered."

"Yes, but your covering enhances all the differences that make a woman unique and the lovely differences that make you unique from other women. In my realm, when women wear clothes they wear clothing that enhances their uniqueness compared to other women. It is interesting that women of this era now show men the pleasures men might enjoy should the men please them and they choose to honor the man with their bodies."

What a lovely color Holly's cheeks had become,

almost as deep a rose as the petals between her legs must be. Next time they joined he wanted to see her in the full sun or at least a brighter light than moon glow.

"So, you decided to stay because you're curious?"

"Yes. It is an interesting world that you humans live in. I wish to study the differences between my previous visits and this time."

"I wish I could go to your realm."

Edan shrugged. "I do not believe that will be possible."

"It was just a wish."

"One must be careful of wishes. One might get what one wishes for."

Despite his solemn repetition of Holly's earlier comment, Holly laughed.

The joyous sound shimmered through Edan's ears bringing him joy. But it was not simply the sound of her laughter. Edan knew from experience that his sense of humor was considered defective by most beings. His humor brought him pleasure, but Holly enjoyed it also. With contentment, he drained the coffee and debated opening the container for more.

No, that would not be kind. He had indulged in three cups and Holly was just finishing her first. Perhaps her Brownie at her work could be induced to make more. But wait...

"You said you do not have a House Brownie to prepare your meals?"

"No, Edan." Holly's voice filled with the patience of dealing with a simpleton. "The only brownies I know are little chocolate cakes or else little Girl Scouts, an organization of young girls and women," she explained before he needed to ask. "Brownies are fantasies."

"In your world," Edan explained to the other simpleton in the car, "so are Elves."

Holly's laughter flowed from her again, sending joyous ribbons of happiness through Edan.

Watching the round curve of her cheek, his hands itched to fill themselves with the round curves of her rump, Edan knew he should keep the conversation to minimal topics and not reveal just now how very much he wanted her nude again.

"In my realm, if we are polite, kind, and treat them with proper and due courtesy, House Brownies will prepare our meals and other Brownies quite often help us with our work."

Holly shot him a startled glance, then returned her eyes to the smooth road – highway, she'd called it. "You work?"

"Of course, I work. All sapient beings work. Proper work done with enjoyment brings pleasure. I am a cobbler. In particular, I make boots such as these." He extended his leg as far as he could in the cramped space.

He saw Holly take a quick peek, then return her attention to the highway. Yes, that was the word.

She took a paper wrapped package from the area where the coffee cups rested and clamped the end of a paper-wrapped package between the straight, pearl white teeth that had nipped so delightfully down his naked body. She gave a jerk and the paper tore open filling the car with the scent of honeyed grain and sweet fruit.

Edan watched in fascination at the sensual pleasure that flooded Holly's face as she chewed on a piece of the plank of grain. His groin twitched heavily yet again at the memory of the same look on her face each time he'd thrust into her.

"Are you hungry? There's another granola bar." Holly nodded in the direction of the small area where their coffee cups rested.

"Thank you." Edan resisted the notion of explaining

to Holly how hungry he was for her. He settled opening the package as Holly had. The oil taste of the wrapper abated as the plank of honey grain dissolved in his mouth.

Edan watched Holly's hand motions on the hard round circle at the end of the long shaft and noted how they somehow kept the vehicle straight. Her feet manipulated flat plates, making the vehicle move faster or slow down, much the same way he'd learned to use reins to indicate to horses when to proceed and when to stop when they pulled a carriage. Carriage. Edan's brain made the connection between 'carriage' and 'car.'

Edan studied her actions in maneuvering the car between and around other vehicles, noted she flipped a stick protruding from the shaft that held the circle. A clicking sound occurred, the same sound as when she'd left the road to the highway. That time she'd pushed the level downward and turned left. Now, with the stick upward, she turned right. The clicking once again stopped as she turned.

Edan decided he would ask permission to drive this car. Perhaps he would take it apart and discover how it worked.

Holly stopped the car in front of a building, turned off the magic key, and released her seatbelt. Edan followed suit, noting the lever Holly pulled to open the door.

The white building in front of Holly's small silver car was painted with various dogs and cats playing and sleeping. "Aunt Holly's Grooming and Boarding" was stated at the side of the doorway.

The dragon flowed smoothly into the building, leaving Holly and Edan to make their way more slowly. Feeling much like Rat following at Holly's heels, Edan carried the thermos and his coffee cup and climbed wooden steps into a white building smelling of animals.

Unlike the outside, the air in the building held a chill and didn't contain the moisture of the outside air. As she had done when she left her house, Holly flicked a small rectangle in a plate on the wall. This time, her thumb pushed it upward and smooth glowing lighting came on above their heads. When she'd pushed it downward at her house, the lights had gone off. She pressed small disks in a cream colored metal box and the box began to hum, then a picture formed on a flat box. Holly nodded at the changing pictures in the artificial window, then briskly led the way from the entry room to a back room.

"You can set the thermos down there." Holly tilted her head to a table where a carafe such as she'd had in her kitchen sat on a metal tray. Edan poured the last of the coffee from the thermos into the cup she'd carried from the car and set it on the table.

"And, since I don't have a House Brownie and you'll probably want more coffee." Holly's eyes sparkled like dew drops on the new leaves that arrived in the Spring. She opened a cabinet and removed a can and some papers. She placed the papers in a bowl then opened the lid of the can. The rich aroma of coffee promptly filled the room. "Watch and learn, so you can make the next pot."

Edan found himself mesmerized by Holly's dancing movements as she performed the ritual to create coffee; placing scoops of coffee in the bowl with the papers, pouring water into the top of the box, and pressing buttons.

"Got it?" Holly winked at him when coffee began to gurgle from the bowl she'd placed above the glass carafe.

"I..."

"Beg your pardon."

This time Edan smiled with Holly as she chorused his standard answer.

"In this case 'got it?' means do you understand how to make coffee now?"

"It is a simple ritual. I believe I have 'got it'."

"Groovy."

Edan refused to rise to the bait of Holly's mischievous grin. He would translate the word as an affirmative.

"Come see my office."

Reluctant to leave the fresh brewing coffee but enchanted by the lovely movement of Holly's swaying hips, Edan followed as she crossed the hallway, opened a door, and illuminated another room. He watched while she again performed the simple magic to start another metal box humming and a picture again lit in another artificial window. Ensconced on a cushion beside a desk, Rat chewed a cloth squirrel.

Holly lifted a jacket from a hat stand constructed in a style Edan recognized from his last mortal sojourn. When she draped the jacket around herself, Edan nearly winced at the bright hues coloring the gamboling animals on it. He knew he didn't see much of this plane the rare times he came, but surely those colors were never intended to exist in nature.

Holly looked solemnly at Edan. "Did you mean what you said about being willing to help me? Because my assistant Carrie quit and I haven't found a replacement yet. I do need some help."

"Certainly," Edan said with a half bow.

"Thanks." Holly's smile was a lovely of a band of sunlight through dark clouds.

"Let me show you the dog boarding area and I'll introduce you to my part-time helper, Jon. He'll show you where the bathing and grooming area is."

Holly patted Rat, who was still occupied chewing his toy before she left the room. Edan stepped into the hallway beside her to keep pace with her. Much as he enjoyed the view when she walked in front of him, he was her equal, not her subordinate. Additionally, he wanted to touch her again.

Edan placed his palm against the soft arc of Holly's

back, the area just before her rump curved outward. Holly
sent him a startled glance but didn't say anything. Edan had
no idea where the dragon was, but he could smell cats
through one door. He assumed the dragon was probably
with the cats. Holly opened a different door.

Barks, yips, and a deep mournful bay reverberated
from the room. Edan managed to restrain himself from
clamping his hands over his ears at the cacophony that
assaulted his hearing

Holly set her now empty cup on a table, then went
from spacious cage to spacious cage, stopping to pat and
stroke each dog, calming them with her soft voice.

The door to the outside banged open. Edan watched
a young man, still with the long bones of rapid growth
uncovered yet by the muscles of manhood, lead a large
golden dog into the room. Seeing them, he came to an
abrupt stop, then grabbed a cage to keep his balance when a
small boy with a white puffball dog secured by a leather
leading strap ran into the backs of his legs.

"Good morning, *Holly*." The young man glared at
Edan.

Edan saw her eyes widen slightly at the mulish look
the young man sent him.

"This is my friend Edan Fariss, who'll be visiting for
awhile. Edan, Jon is my right-hand man. He's a pre-vet
student and helps out here between them. And this," Holly's
wistful smile twisted Edan's heart with the urge to give her
whatever she wanted in order to ease the pain hidden behind
it, "is his youngest brother Rob who helps Jon and me
whenever he can."

Jon ignored Edan and spoke to Holly, "All the dogs
have been walked, the cats fed and watered. I'll clean the cat
cages after I take Rob to school and get back from my
classes."

Paying no more attention to Jon than Jon did to him,

Edan knelt to greet a dog that wanted his attention.

"Thank you, Jon. I'm glad to see you, Rob." Holly smiled at the youngster while Jon began to fill dishes with the same kind of dry, meat smelling pellets Edan had found at her house. "Will you be back this afternoon?"

"Today is Cub Scouts," Rob said, helping the older boy dole out the dog kibble.

As Jon passed by Edan the young man bristled as if he felt his territory had been infringed on. Edan knew that unlike the dragon, this youngling had no right to claim Holly as his territory. He had no qualms about asserting his possession, however temporary, of Holly.

Edan effortlessly rose from his squat in front of the cage where he had been stroking the long nose of the dog whose ears almost reached the ground and whose soulful eyes could seduce an Elven Queen.

Although the youngling was taller than he Edan saw the youngling's face shift from challenge to reluctant acceptance at the realization he was but a callow youth next to Edan. Edan casually lifted a long curl from Holly's shoulder and draped it behind her back to demonstrate his claim of her to the youth.

The youngling shrugged and turned back to his duties.

"Why are you here?"

Edan looked down into a small face with suspicious brown eyes and saw a small mouth pressed into an angry line between his apple-round cheeks. The child might be young, but he was still male. Like his older brother, he apparently regarded Edan as a challenge for Holly's affections.

Holly moved from Edan's reach. "He's a friend of mine and he's going to help out today. I still haven't found a replacement for Carrie."

A bell rang in the entry room. Edan winced as a high pitched "Yoo-hoo!" lanced his ears. Holly and Jon grimaced and young Rob's face screwed up like a gargoyle's. The shriek was accompanied by multiple sharp yips to which the caged dogs added their complaints.

"Quiet," Holly commanded the barking dogs. "Jon, could you please show Edan where the equipment is before you leave?"

"Holly?" From the front room, the shrill voice caroled, "Darling, my babies and I are here."

"I'm coming, Mrs. Johnston," Holly called back. With her hand on the doorknob, she sent a wry smile at Edan and the boys and softly muttered, "And may I keep my mouth shut and my opinions to myself."

After the door closed off his view of Holly's round hips, Edan turned to see both boys studying him.

"If you hurt her, I'll hurt you," Jon promised.

Edan inclined his head in acknowledgment of the youngling's sincere warning.

"Why are you dressed so weird?" Rob's small face tilted from one side to the other.

"I beg your pardon?"

Jon's face creased with a smile that was not the least bit pleasant as though he were thinking of playing a prank on someone. "A couple of months ago that outfit was fine for the Ren Faire, but it's going to get ruined when you wash dogs. You should have worn jeans and waterproof boots. We wash them in here." Jon opened a door and gestured inside.

Edan stepped past Jon so he could enter a room lined with cabinets and an odd tiled area.

"Shampoo, conditioner, bluing, eye wipes." Jon pointed at various containers set inside a cabinet beside the tiled area that had odd-shaped silver knobs and a long silver hose with a multi-pierced flat base on the free end. Edan noted a railing surrounded the three tiled walls, from which hung several lengths of colored ropes with various harnesses attached.

Edan could smell water, both fresh and stagnant, although the stagnant smell emanated from a multi-holed circle in the center of the tiled area. Perhaps this was a "shower" such as Holly had used at her house earlier. Edan's penis gave a leap at the idea of Holly naked on the tile with water streaming over her soft curves.

"Towels and smocks are here." Jon opened another door to show Edan shelves of neatly folded drying cloths and more of the eye-wincing colored jackets hanging in a small area beside the shelves.

"This switch," Jon touched a lever on a large circular metal oddity facing several cages in differing sizes, "turns on the dryer."

"Used towels go in the hamper here." Young Rob smacked the top of a white container so the lid swung around. "Smocks go in the brown one."

"I do not believe I shall use a smock." The word tasted as odd on Edan's tongue as the colors felt to his eyes.

"Your choice, but that Ren Faire costume will be shredded by the time you get all the dogs washed."

Edan once again ignored the "Ren Faire" reference. He would ask Holly to translate the phrase for him later. He needed to keep reminding the youngling that he was both older and wiser and, consequently, more appropriate for Holly, despite the youngling's clear desire for her.

"Hey, Jon, maybe he should use that apron Holly doesn't like."

"Good idea, short stuff."

Jon opened a door revealing implements Edan recognized as cleaning tools used by servants during his last trip to this plane. A harsh pungent odor was only slightly masked by an odd fragrance that wasn't quite the scent of flowers.

From a hook, Jon lifted a cloak of some kind and

tossed it to Edan. The brown material had the same slickness as the skin of his Selkie acquaintances when they were in their seal forms. The scent it held wasn't animal, however, even though various dog odors permeated it. The main scent was oily, much like the chairs in Holly's car.

"Here's a vinyl apron, if you don't want to wear the smock, but you'd better wear something over that outfit. If you're not worried about ruining it, that's one thing, but some of these dogs get scared when they're being washed. If they bite at you, they're liable to tear those fancy sleeves. And the boots."

"My boots are safe if covered with water," Edan informed him coolly. "I have worn them in the rain."

Jon flashed him a grin that could only be described as wicked. "You'll find out."

"Yep." Young Rob's cherub face mimicked his brother's grin.

A momentary qualm shuddered through Edan. Surely these younglings did not possess a sense of the future he could not see. He knew they but were attempting to make him the center of a joke. He hung the vinyl cloak on its metal peg.

"I shall have no need of such covering."

"Hey, dude, don't say we didn't warn you. Come on, short stuff, let's get you to school."

With laughter that left Edan feeling uneasy, the brothers departed.

Holly waved good-bye to the boys as they headed off for their day. She almost envied them their school and classes as Mrs. Johnston continued her litany of instructions on the proper care of Precious and Sweetie.

A warm breeze with the sweet smell of summer stirred through Holly's senses. It warned her of Edan's presence behind her. The door to the dog boarding and grooming area shut with a soft click Holly wouldn't have thought she'd be able to hear with the Shih Tzu's' yipping.

Edan lifted her hair and placed his hand against the back of her neck.

Holly shivered with the flash of intense heat as though Edan's hand had cupped her between her legs. With no more than a gentle stroke of one finger across her neck, Holly could feel her nipples tighten as if he'd touched them instead.

"Oh." Mrs. Johnston breathed deeply to lift the assets her ex-husband had paid for and smiled at Edan. "Hello there."

Holly knew she didn't stand a chance against Mrs. Johnston's frontal assault and the woman's daily use of a personal trainer's for further body sculpting.

"Good morning." Edan's voice rumbled through Holly turning her to liquid.

She glanced up hardly daring to believe the indifference his voice held for Mrs. Johnston. The happiness within her began to glow as his fingertip continued its sensuous stroke up and down her vertebrae.

"Hush, Precious. Be quiet, Sweetie. Let Momma talk to the nice man," Mrs. Johnston purred to the continually yipping dogs.

Holly took the leashes from Mrs. Johnston's lax fingers. "Sit. Quiet."

Both dogs, a credit to their trainer, sat down and shut up.

"They never behave like that for me." Mrs. Johnston's mouth formed the come-hither-and-kiss-me pout Holly had seen work on many a male during the activities in the dog show circuit. "You're so good with *dogs*, Holly."

Holly had known plenty of women like her client who hid their own insecurities by tearing down other women. She'd learned years earlier to ignore unspoken implications that she couldn't attract a man.

Honest with herself, Holly admitted silently it was easier to ignore twice-divorced Mrs. Johnston's veiled sarcasm with Edan's palm sliding down her back to cup her rear and shoot fire between her legs.

"Holly shall take excellent care of your animals." Edan breath fanned sweetly against Holly's cheek. "When should she return for her dogs, Holly?"

One long finger slowly slid up and down the seam of her overalls between her butt cheeks.

Dizzy from the heat flushing through her, Holly managed to leash the dogs with her own leashes and hand the rhinestone encrusted collars and leashes back to Mrs. Johnston. At least, she thought they were rhinestones. With Mrs. Johnston, there was no telling.

"After one o'clock. I'll phone you if we finish earlier."

"All right then." Mrs. Johnston swept a hand under her hair, flicking the strands in a flirty come-see-my-hair-spread-on-a-pillow gesture. Her bracelets jangled and diamonds flashed in the entry room's fluorescent lighting. "Behave for the nice man and Aunt Holly, my darlings. Momma's going to get her own hair done and we'll all be so pretty this afternoon."

With a gust of perfume, a final pretty pout flashed at Edan, and a quick narrow-eyed glare at Holly, she took herself out of the building.

"Now that we're alone." Edan unsnapped Holly's smock, pushed it apart, slid Holly's coverall strap down one arm, and eased his hand between the bib and her tank top to cup her breast.

Fire shot from the nipple as he rubbed a finger across it.

"Perhaps you can show me how to use the shower and the solutions young Jon pointed out to me. I should enjoy drinking water off your bare skin."

CHAPTER 3

Holly looked into Edan's midnight eyes. She imagined that the secrets of forever looked back at her. She felt the desire they both had for each other and the moment flashed through her with joy.

Edan's long fingers immediately slid under the cotton tank top to stroke her skin. Her breast lifted and swelled under the pads of his fingers. Hypersensitive skin felt each fingerprint whorl, the slightly thicker texture of small scars, the roughness of calluses.

His eyes held hers with promised pleasure and delights beyond her imagination. Her nipple tightened unbearably under his fingers. Then he slid the breast free of the tank top and bent his head.

His mouth suckled her wet and strong. He drew her breast deep to be pleasured by tongue and teeth. The hand cupping her rump moved around to stroke her belly, then nudged down between her legs to rub the seam against her crotch. Her knees weakened and she clung to his shoulders.

Her panties grew wetter with each caress of his finger. She tried to grind herself against his hand, but he gave a low laugh and continued the light strokes. Shivers slid through her. She moved her legs further apart to give him more access. Instead, he kept his touch elusively light and suckled harder as though he was starving and her breast was a piece of succulent fruit.

Holly lifted her free hand off his shoulder and tangled it in his hair. She found his ear and began to lightly rub up and down his ear lobe. His nuzzling grew more frantic, but just as he teased her now soaked crotch, she teased his ear only occasionally touching the point.

The dogs whined at their feet. Holly twisted their leashes tighter in her fist and concentrated on the heat and moisture flooding through her.

Edan groaned heavily against her breast and tilted the side of his head toward her face. He quickened his hand on her crotch.

Holly responded by gently flicking his ear point with her fingers. Then she leaned over and pulled the top of his ear into her mouth. The tip of his ear pulsed hard against her tongue, more responsive than any human lover's flat male nipple.

With Edan's thumb pressed against the top of her pussy and his fingers cupping her crotch, his mouth sucked her breast to nearly unbearable pleasure sending waves of delight shot through Holly.

Firmly supported by Edan's hands, Holly surfed to the crest of the stars and briefly touched the suspension of time and matter. At this moment, this instant, nothing mattered but the energy of soaring as one with everything.

Gradually, Holly swam back to the reality. Her hand was cramped from her stranglehold on the Shih Tzus' leashes. The countertop dug painfully into her spine.

She drew in a shuddering breath, then a second as she fought to ground herself. She realized if she thought about it for awhile she could still remember how to breathe.

With a final lick and soft kiss on Holly's nipple, Edan slid her breast back into her tank top and pulled up her overall strap. He folded the front of her smock back together and snapped it shut.

Holly could still feel his shaft pulsing hard against her thigh.

She reached a hand to touch him, to share with him the pleasure he had given her.

He caught her hand before she touched him.

"Later. I hear a car on the outside." Edan untangled the leashes from her grip. "Shall I take these two to the grooming area for you?"

How dare he try to pretend everything was normal when she'd just had a mind-blowing orgasm with her panties still on? *How dare he!*

On second thought, that might be a good idea. He wasn't going to stay around and she didn't want to get too attached to him. Despite of, or because of, any more out-of-body orgasms., she needed to think ahead to when she would be alone again.

Holly gulped more air into her lungs. Feet were planted firmly on the floor. Another good sign of reality.

Her panties were soaked.

Holly looked down at her crotch.

Thank goodness, her overalls were dark. They didn't appear to be soaked through. She'd rinse out her panties and toss them in the dryer.

Later. For now, she had to return to the real world. She chose this job. She needed to remember the importance of this stinky, smelly job in her life. She couldn't fixate on an elf, no matter how much he blew her away.

She released the dogs to Edan. "Um, yeah, just put them in a cage for now. I'll check in the next client and then I'll wash all the dogs."

"I do know how to bathe dogs."

"With all that long hair, they need to be brushed before they're washed. "

Holly glared at the Shih Tzus. The two spoiled dogs firmly reinforced the reality of her world. Despite Edan's ability to send her to new orgasmic heights, her reality would not include him for any length of time.

"These two are the local equivalent of the Hounds from Hell. They're champion show dogs in their professional lives, but privately, without the correct commands, they're spoiled rotten and want their own way. You saw how they behaved with their owner. You have to keep a firm hand on them."

Edan looked down his nose at the dogs. "I can take care of two little dogs. I will use firm hands with them. You certainly enjoyed my hands. You will pleasure me later."

Holly watched Edan stroll down the hallway to the grooming area. Edan might be an elf, but he still had the cocky, annoying male I'm-such-a-stud-and-you-are-such-putty-in-my-hands mind-set.

She knew she'd have to deal with that attitude. But first, she'd have to get over her own body's I'm-melting reaction to watching his butt going down the hallway.

Then Edan did more. He turned sideways when he opened the grooming area doorway and gave her a full view of his jutting erection. Bastard had undone his pants' laces as he walked the dogs to the room.

With a wicked grin, he winked at her, stepped through the doorway, and shut the door behind him.

Holly leaned heavily against the countertop and closed her eyes. She had to get herself under control. She had work to do. The door chime sounded.

"Holly?"

Holly opened her eyes to see one of her favorite clients with her predominately Cocker Spaniel, but who knew or cared what else mixed into the dog's gene pool.

"Are you okay? You look flushed. Are you coming down with something?"

No, but she definitely wanted to go down on something and have something, or rather, someone go down on her. She tightened her inner muscles, her imagination racing into overdrive at the thought of Edan's mouth on her, his tongue in her. Sexual heat whipped through her and made her catch her breath.

The musty tang of dogs caught in her nostrils and hung in the back of her throat reminding her of where she was. She bit the inside of her cheek. The twinge of pain helped bring her back into focus.

Her client still stood in front of her and wore a concerned look. "Do you want me to bring Rags back another day?"

"No, no. I'm fine. How ya doing, Rags?"

With practiced eased, Holly looped one of her own leashes around Rags, returned the collar and leash to the owner, and avoided Rags' enthusiastic tongue trying to lap 'hello' across her face. Doggy breath tongue laps didn't have the appeal of Edan's tongue.

Damn it. If he hung around her much longer... oh, God, the word 'hung' led to the memory of the quick peek at the way Edan hung which meant her panties had now gone beyond stuck to her to practically dripping.

"Holly?" Once again her client's concerned voice brought her back to the here and now. "Are you sure you're alright? Your color's so bright. Are you sure you don't have a fever?"

Hot. Oh, definitely, she was hot.

"I'm fine. Don't worry."

A crease still puckered her client's face. "If you're sure, then. But, truly, if you get to feeling lousy, don't worry about Rags. I'll just come back and get her."

"Thank you, but it's not a problem. I'll see you this afternoon. Have a good day."

Nope, Holly didn't have a problem with Rags. She had a problem with soaked panties. She'd need to use panty liners if Edan didn't go back to his realm soon.

Holly had to be honest with herself. She knew she didn't want him to leave, but he would leave eventually. He didn't belong with humans. Sooner or later, he'd get bored with her and head back to his own life.

She'd just have to keep a lock on her heart. But for this time, however long, she was determined to enjoy Edan while she could.

And *enjoy* him she would. She knew she'd even

soak through panty liners the way Edan had her flowing with a touch, a look, and, heaven help her, when he put his hands and mouth on her.

She took Rags back to the grooming area. She had one more client to arrive for this morning's session, then she might indulge Edan in his pleasure with a quick wham-bam-thank-you-ma'am. It would have to be quick with four dogs to groom, plus all afternoon to be devoted to the Komondor. Getting the Komondor's white mop-looking coat cleaned out and making sure all the cords lay properly was a job and a half.

Holly grinned at the memory of the large, prancing mop dog the last time he was in Show. His win in Best of Class made him hyper. But it definitely made all her work worth the chore. Plus he was just a nice dog to work with. His owner had done a fine job of working with the handler in his training that the dog's sweet personality shone through.

The Johnston Shih Tzus on the other hand...

Before she even opened the door, Holly could hear the males growling at each other. Poor Rags began to tremble.

Holly poked her head cautiously around the door. She couldn't understand a word Edan said or the male Shih Tzu, either, but their body language and tone crossed boundaries of all species.

With Rags trembling at her feet, Holly leaned against the wall ready to enjoy the show. Already penned, the female Shih Tzu added her yips to the din.

One of Edan's flowing sleeves had been torn from wrist to elbow. Holly winced at the dark lines staining both of Edan's fawn-colored boots. She didn't know what kind of leather they were, but maybe the shoe repair shop on the next block would be able to clean off the dog urine stains.

Edan made a quick lunge at the barking dog staying just out of his reach and slipped in the urine puddle. The dog backed away more before Edan landed on him.

Holly filed the strange sounds Edan yelled at the dog in her memory. She might want to use them along with the swear words she already knew. She couldn't speak anything other than conversational English, but she was fluent in multilingual swearing.

"Precious. No," Holly commanded just half a second too late. "Sit. Stay."

Defiant, but obedient, the misnamed "Precious" sat well away from the once again peed on boots.

"Good boy, Precious. Stay."

From the floor, Edan snarled, "That is not a 'good boy.' It is not 'precious.' I will teach it to not piss on me."

"Did you get hurt? Is everything still in working order?"

"I am uninjured. But that animal." Edan picked himself up from his sprawl. As he stood, he seemed to grow taller and broader. Rage twisted his features into a menacing caricature of the handsome face that had already been imprinted on Holly's being since dawn this morning.

Had it only been hours since Holly awoke with Edan in her bedroom? She looked at the clock. Yes, less than three hours. Then why did she keep thinking she'd known him forever? She reminded herself that he was temporary in her world, a short-lived fantasy to be enjoyed while she had it.

Joy filled Holly. The joy was comprised of equal parts amusement, lust, tenderness, all strung together with the buoyed confidence that this extremely virile male made it eminently clear he wanted to stay with her. Even if it was just temporary.

But everything in the world can change in heartbeat, which Holly knew to her everlasting regret.

Edan stalked toward her, his entire being set on doing damage, yet she had no fear he would hurt her or even the Shih Tzu clearly sneering at him.

Quickly, she pushed the Cocker mix into a pen then snatched up the loose lead hanging around Precious' neck much like a noose. Holly hoped Edan didn't have the same thought she had.

Edan had undone his laces at his crotch and was reaching into his pants.

"What are you doing?" she asked, while gaining control of Precious.

Somehow, Holly didn't think Edan's current goal was to get laid.

"Move away, Holly."

Edan took the dog's leash from her. He held his arm out straight, the leash hanging down tautly so Precious couldn't get to his boots, although the dog lunged in effort. Without taking his eyes from Precious, Edan pulled out his penis and took aim.

"No." Holly grabbed the leash and got herself between Edan and her high-paying client's dog.

Edan refused to release the leash.

"No dog pisses on me. I will show this animal who is in charge."

"Not in a pissing contest in my grooming studio you don't. Not when I'm going to have to wash and groom this dog."

"Holly. Move now."

"Not a chance. You're not in charge either." Holly pulled harder on the leash. "No, Edan, don't."

She locked eyes with Edan. She knew she didn't have a chance if he decided to exert his will. She certainly didn't have the strength to physically stop him. She had to make him see reason.

"Edan, you're not a dog. Dogs try to be dominant by fighting and by marking territory. That's all this dog was trying to do. It wasn't malicious behavior."

Although Holly wouldn't put it past this particular dog to pee on a human just to be malicious. Nevertheless.

"You don't make a dog obey you by getting into a pissing contest with it. You control it by commands and praise. Let go, Edan. Please."

Finally, Edan released the leash. Holly shoved the Shih Tzu into the pen with his mate. At least the dog was smart enough not to argue with her.

Edan still glared at the dog.

"Tie up your pants, Edan."

His attention shifted to her so fast Holly's head spun with heat and lust.

"Perhaps not." Edan stepped closer to Holly.

The pen's metal bars pressed into her back. Edan's rapidly firming penis pressed into the cradle of her thighs.

His hand drew her fingers down and wrapped them around his heated, smooth skin.

"I believe this is my turn to be pleasured."

His heartbeat pulsed strong in the hard shaft under her fingers.

He tunneled his hands through her hair and tilted her face up so he could consume her mouth greedily. He tasted of coffee, of male musk, of…of…

Taste wasn't enough to describe his mouth. She couldn't find words to describe the feel of his tongue, his teeth, his juices.

The kiss grew beyond the sensation of being kissed senseless.

All of Holly's senses heightened and merged. Color blended into sound. Touch gave off a fragrance. Her mouth filled with explosions that sent her reeling. She squeezed the firmness in her hand.

His pure masculine rumble of appreciation vibrated through her mouth.

Her tongue stroked his mouth in time with the

matched eagerness he plundered hers. All her focus drew to his tongue in her mouth, her tongue in his. His fingers massaged her neck and skull and pulled her closer as he angled his tongue to delve deeper with a hunger that wouldn't be denied.

She had to touch him more. She needed to hold him closer and tighter against her. She wanted to keep this moment. To burn it in her memory for the long years ahead when he would be gone and she could chuckle to herself while she sat in a wheelchair in a nursing home, "Ah, yes, I had such a lover. Once upon a time."

She stroked the full length in her hands, its firmness rivaling the metal bars against her back.

The male rumbling in her mouth grew to a satisfying roar.

Far, far away, she heard the tinkling sound of a running brook. A sour smell suddenly extruded itself into her consciousness.

Edan jerked his mouth from hers and Holly's hands suddenly lost their happy burden. A brief bit of stickiness, the first jewel of Edan's cum, was all that remained.

Edan yelled to the heavens.

"I shall roast that animal for my dinner!"

Startled, Holly followed Edan's enraged glare to the floor. A fresh pool of dog pee puddled at their feet. The ankle of one side of her overalls bore the stain of marking. Edan's boot, which had been firmly planted beside her foot, had been the main target.

Edan's erection pulsed once, twice, then began to lose its strength as his rage rode over the lust.

"You cannot tell me that was not deliberate. I shall piss on that dog."

"You will not." Holly quickly tucked his penis back into his pants and firmly laced shut the opening.

"Look at my boots! The dog intentionally pissed on

them."

"I've groomed this dog for years. He thinks I'm part of his pack. You were intruding into his pack and he was just marking his territory."

"He pissed on me. I am not his territory."

"You need to calm down. Don't take this personally."

"You have no knowledge of the length of time I spent crafting these boots. You have no knowledge of the spells I wove into them for protection."

Edan heard an odd sound and turned his glare from the worthless dog to Holly.

"What?"

Holly's eyes glimmered and she bit her lips. The entry room door chimed. Holly ducked her face away from Edan's view.

"Holly. Look at me. Now."

"Um, door." She eased past him and pointed to the entry room. "My last morning client just arrived."

"Holly, are you laughing at me?"

"Uh, no. Gotta go talk to my client. Um, excuse me."

Edan held Holly firmly by her upper arms. "You will tell me why you're laughing."

Holly's eyes sparkled. "You said you wove spells into the boots for protection?"

Edan inclined his head in acknowledgement.

"Well, any water-proofing spell you wove was obviously piss poor."

Edan's jaw dropped and his grip slackened.

Giggling wildly, Holly practically ran down the hallway to the entry room.

Edan enjoyed the view of Holly's round rump then turned back to his newly sworn enemy. "Some day, I shall have your liver for my dinner," he vowed.

******

Holly pressed her fists to the small of her back and stretched backward. Straightening up, she stretched her hands above her head and flexed her fingers. She twisted her upper torso first right, then left to work out the kinks in her shoulders.

Three dogs groomed, one to go. The monkeys who had been pounding cymbals during her early morning hangover had returned with a new symphony.

Holly glanced at the clock. It was close enough to lunchtime for her. The coffee Edan kept bringing to her sat in a sour puddle in her stomach.

"This little dog I like."

Yorkshire Terrier Champion Rose Quartz of Hart's Gold with a detailed pedigree tree of Champions that filled a 48" X 36" chart, known to home and hearth as Bunny, could have given Scarlett O'Hara lessons in wrapping men around her dainty paw. Not once had she taken her Bette Davis adoring eyes off Edan's face. He carried her in one hand, the inevitable cup of coffee in the other.

Holly's stomach roiled at the smell. She needed some comfort food. Screw the diet. She needed carbs to settle her stomach. Her single granola bar breakfast was long digested or dissolved by coffee acid. She needed a sliced turkey sandwich on a nice Kaiser roll, with some potato chips. Okay, she'd have a piece of lettuce on it for a veggie and a cold cola with ice.

Holly eyed Edan, no longer the pristine clothed male who watched her wake up this morning. While she bathed the ornery Precious, Edan stood over the procedure just waiting for a chance to drown the dog. When she started on the female Shih Tzu, Edan gently moved her aside, then brushed and washed Sweetie as though he'd been a grooming assistant for years. Edan's help gave her the time to double-check the few cats currently being boarded and walk the dog boarders while Precious dried.

Now he showed the results of cleaning dogs all morning. Edan had folded both the torn sleeve and the still-whole flowing sleeve past his elbows. Bunny's damp silken coat draped over one of Edan's bared forearms, but Holly could see the lift and ripple of muscles in the other arm as Edan raised his coffee cup to drink.

Not addicted to coffee, her little toe. Wryly, Holly realized if she wanted Edan to stay on this plane forever and not vanish back into his Elf realm, all she'd have to do was introduce him to one of the specialty coffee houses. Then he'd never leave.

In addition to the markings Precious had scored on the boots, the darker splatter stain of liquid stool from the stream of Rag's expressed anal glands marred Edan's trousers. Holly averted her eyes from the bulge at his trouser lacings.

If Edan caught her interest, he'd be on her in a second. Every time she'd been within reach, he brushed a palm across her breast or cupped her rear. She decided she didn't want a quickie here in the grooming room. She wanted a nice, long, leisurely exploration next time, hours she could hold in her memory. All she had from last night were brief flashes. Next session with him, she wanted something tro savor, to warm her on cold, lonely nights.

Dog hair liberally covered his trousers and the linen shirt. The lacing tied around his hair had worked its way loose and he'd tucked the freed tendrils behind those lovely ear peaks.

Her mouth salivated at the idea of suckling those tips. For the first time, she wondered if men looked at barely concealed nipples the same way she looked at Edan's ear tips. Her own nipples hardened at the thought.

No, don't go there, she reminded herself. She picked up Rags' back paw, prepared to file the last set of toenails.

Rags' stubbed Cocker-style tail wiggled frantically. She whined softly to get Edan's attention. Holly knew Rags, like Bunny and Sweetie, had fallen completely under the elf's spell.

Edan set his cup on top of the pens. Sill cradling Bunny, Edan ruffled Rags' skull and slid the dog's long silky ear through his hand. Rags, who'd been Holly's special friend forever, swiped a tongue across Edan's hand and arm and totally ignored Holly working on her toenails.

"You, Miss Rags, no longer look so scruffy."

Holly glanced up at Rags to see her grinning happily at Edan's croon. She loved to see a dog smile. They smiled with their entire bodies.

"Settle down, Rags," Holly cautioned with amusement while she focused her attention on the rasp of her file over the Cocker-mix's toenail. She definitely didn't want to be caught drooling over Edan the way the dogs were.

With the same casual gesture he'd used on the dog, Edan lifted a hank of Holly's hair and rolled it between his fingers.

Until then Holly hadn't realized hair had nerve endings of its own. Her hair seemed to have a life of its own as it twisted in Edan's fingers, hugging them and begging them to hold it closer, to stroke the strands harder. Shivers started from the tips of her hair and fired their way into Holly's brain sending lightning through her.

It took all her willpower to continue to file the dog's nails. She knew if she turned around to look at Edan, if she let herself think about the way his fingers felt, she would strip down to give him access to her shorter hairs.

As it was, each tendril received its own gentle stroke. With the sides of her head French-braided toward the back, Edan reached under the braid to grasp each strand at its root. He held it between his thumb and first two fingers to caress it all the way to the bottom-most tip of its length. Then he'd reach under the braid for another tendril of strands.

As he slowly made his way across Holly's head, her breasts swelled against her tank top and the bib of her overall. Her nail file slowed its progress on the dog's nails.

Her eyes drifted shut at the sensual massage. Her body grew languid and heavy, relaxing as though she slept in the warm sunlight at the lake with small waves lapping the shoreline.

Warmth stole over her. Edan's hand moved to the back of her neck. Talented fingers found and eased stress knots Holly wasn't aware were there until he released them.

The warmth trickled further down her body and settled in that favorite spot at the apex of her thighs. When Edan's mouth replaced his fingertips on her collarbone, she automatically tilted her head for him to move his lips up her neck.

Rags promptly slurped a loving doggy kiss across both their faces.

Edan cursed at the smell and taste of dog tongue instead of Holly's sweet skin. The dragon phased into the grooming area to see what the fuss was about.

The dog's ears drooped and her eyes filled with hurt.

"Rags, Rags, sweetie," Holly crooned. "It's okay. Did mean old Edan scare you? He's not mad at you. Are you, *Edan*?"

Edan sighed. No, he wasn't mad at the dog. He wasn't mad at anybody. He just wanted pleasure with Holly again. Yet every time he felt ready to ease into her, something interfered.

He rubbed his hand across the dog's soft head and gently tugged her ear again. "No, Rags, I am not mad."

If Rags was a cat, he would have apologized in Elvish to make it clear he was sorry he'd frightened her.

But, being a dog, the dog would understand tone more than words, so, like Holly, he simply patted the dog until her eyes sparkled again.

Little Bunny in his hand also forgave him for frightening her.

The dragon floated up to lean against Rags to help settle her hurt feelings, so Holly could easily finish the last of her chores.

Edan narrowed his eyes at the dragon. When he needed help with that wretched so-wrongly-named Precious and when that noxious liquid from Rags' anus squirted on him, the dragon was off communing with the cats. But let Holly say as little as "Settle down, dog" and the dragon promptly popped back into the room to soothe and calm the dog being groomed.

No wonder the dogs in Holly's care thrived. She had a dragon helping her maintain balance. Once more, Edan wondered how Holly had attracted a dragon.

Not that he was jealous. Elves didn't get jealous. Curious, that's all it was. He wouldn't want a dragon around anyway. Bossy things always tried to influence the beings on the realms and planes. Just look how they introduced cats to humans so they'd have continual communication with the human plane. No, Edan definitely did not want a dragon around. He was simply curious.

He needed more coffee.

"Holly, where is your cup? I am going for more coffee. I shall fill your cup, also."

Holly's face screwed up like a gargoyle. "No, thanks. I've had more coffee this morning than I can stand."

She reached her arms around Rags and unsnapped the holding leash. Edan handed Bunny to her and lifted Rags off the table himself. He placed the freshly groomed dog in the pen and snarled back at the so-called Precious, who flounced a black bow-tie topknot at him. Wearing a pink ribbon on her topknot, Sweetie simpered at him.

"Look, Edan, I'm hungry. If I give you directions, will you go to the deli in the next block and get us some food? Bunny won't take long. If you go now, by the time you get back, I should be finished with her. Then I can eat."

"Certainly. But first explain what is 'deli' and what is 'block.' Food, I understand."

******

Edan returned with a sack of delicious-smelling food, including something called 'cookies' that looked like small cakes. He also had a container of coffee made with cream and cinnamon that the young female called a latté. Even if Edan hadn't decided to stay in this plane to enjoy Holly for a while, he would have stayed for the latté as soon as he found out about them. He'd go back to that shop later and ingest some of the other flavors he could smell.

He opened the door and caught a brief whiff of something odd. The stench grew stronger as Edan walked down the hallway. In the grooming room, he could hear Bunny yipping. Rat was frantically clawing at the grooming room door.

"Holly?" Edan dropped the bag of food and pulled open the door. The foul odor of rotting fish and spoiled eggs crawled down his gullet. The Shih Tzus were gone from their pen as was Rags. In a pen, Bunny barked hysterically and Rat added his shrill barks to hers as he dashed to the washing area. Edan hastily set his cup on a pen and followed Rat.

The dragon stood on its back haunches hissing furiously.

Holly pressed against the wall of the washing area, her hand covering her nose. She was wild-eyed with panic.

On the drain hole sat the source of the foul odor, a nucklelavee who slavered at Holly.

"Get rid of the frog," Holly said hoarsely.

"Frog? What frog?" All Edan could see was the nucklelavee doing its evil best to frighten Holly and succeeding.

"That frog." White-faced, Holly pointed a shaking finger at the gruesome faery. "Get rid of the frog."

Edan advanced on the nucklelavee. As it jumped out of his range, its wings fluttered, sending off more of the noxious smell.

"Catch it. Put a bucket on it or something. Just get it out of here."

Catching it might be difficult. He needed something to fix its wings in place. Ah, yes. The fixative Holly used on some of the longhaired dogs when she fluffed them. What did she...?

There it was – hairspray.

He shook the can as Holly had done when she demonstrated it and cautiously approached the faery. The faery fluttered again just as Edan sprayed.

He could tell he caught part of a wing because the smell decreased slightly. Grimly, he stalked it around the small room, spraying it each time he got close enough.

"My, you certainly wield a mean can of hairspray. My hairdresser needs another stylist. Maybe you can get a job with him since you're in this plane for awhile." Muffled as it was by Holly's hand on her nose, her sarcasm came through clearly. "Would you just stomp on it on something? I hate frogs and toads. They're gruesome and slimy. Give me a nice snake anytime."

With Rat obeying the dragon's instructions to stay between Holly and the nucklelavee and the dragon herding the faery to him, Edan finally managed to coat the wings with the hairspray.

He focused his energies on the incantation and banished the faery back to its normal environment. The stench immediately dissipated with it.

Edan nodded to the dragon that emitted the satisfied odor of cinnamon before flowing to the other room to calm Bunny. Edan patted Rat in appreciation for his help then caught Holly as she stumbled away from the wall.

For several long moments, Edan ran his hands up and down her back soothing her trembling body. Rat leaned his small body against her ankles in comfort. The dragon flowed back into the washing area and wrapped its body around Holly's neck crooning to her much the same way she'd crooned to Rags earlier.

Finally, she lifted a tear-splattered face to his. "What happened to the frog?"

"That was not a frog. It was a nucklelavee."

"I beg…"

"Your pardon," Edan finished with her. To his pleasure, Holly gave a watery laugh.

"A nucklelavee is an evil faery. No, not really evil, just cruel. It wouldn't have hurt you. It simply likes to scare humans. It takes on whichever shape a human dislikes the most."

"An, ugh, frog."

"In your case, yes."

"But why did it come after me?"

"I will endeavor to discover that," he vowed.

His palms soothed up and down Holly's shuddering back. Gradually, her shaking eased and she grew warm in his arms. She lifted her head and smiled at him. Without thought, Edan slanted his mouth onto hers.

At the taste of her lips, wildfire whipped through him again.

CHAPTER 4

Edan's mouth covered hers with an intensity Holly had never before experienced. She'd had men kiss her with tenderness to make her feel special, to make her feel cherished. Never had she been kissed the way Edan kissed her now.

He consumed her with a hunger that made it seem his very being depended on her accepting and cherishing him. He laved her mouth, his tongue giving each tooth its own attention. He drew her tongue into his mouth and encouraged her to discover his unique tastes and textures.

The more she concentrated on his mouth, the quicker the fear of a few moments ago eased away.

A small, barely logical fraction of her mind still wondered why an evil faery had tried to menace her. Most of her, however, had no thoughts, but only marveled at the sheer wonder and joy of this man – no, not man, Elf – and the strength of his kiss.

After all that terrifying irrational fear, Holly delighted in the glorious taste and scents of Edan holding her, kissing her, making it clear with the rigid hardness pressing her belly that he wanted her.

Holly squirmed closer. She wanted to inhale his essence. Despite the scent of wet dog and the sharper stinks of more noxious dog bodily fluids that coated his clothes, Edan's skin smelled of fresh cut summer grass and the ozone of a building thunderstorm cut with the sharp breeze of cool rain.

His fingers tunneled through her hair. They massaged her skull with a heated touch that she'd only experienced before when a male's hands had caressed her breasts or between her thighs.

She rubbed the aching apex between her legs against

his thigh. His erection pulsed against her.

Headiness swirled through her. The giddiness of Christmas morning presents to unwrap, the exhilaration in the surging drop of a roller coaster, the silver shimmer of the full moon on fresh fallen snow, all joy wrapped in his kiss and scent spiraled her upward.

He slowed the kiss gently and brought her back to earth. He smoothed the hair he had loosened from her braids and tucked it behind her ears.

"Why did you stop?"

"Because once again, we are in your place of business and I heard a vehicle outside. There are two different dogs coming now. I can hear them bark. They are quite loud."

"Oh, damn. They're early." She looked at Edan in confusion. "Two?"

Holly had such a puzzled look on her face. It gave Edan joy to see it.

"It was only supposed to be one."

"No, there are two. Can you not tell the difference?"

Holly's face squelched up in concentration. "Yep, definitely two. Oh, joy. He must have rescued another Komondor."

She leaned her face against Edan's shirt. "I'm sorry we had to stop again."

"Tonight, when there are no interruptions, we shall continue this. You have my word."

"As a Prince of Dessert?" Holly's smile lit her face.

"De'erjia," Edan said with a frown.

"Mmm," Holly hummed, "Dessert. Because later tonight I'm going to eat you for my dessert."

With her laughter trailing behind her, Holly went into the reception room.

Edan adjusted his breeches, wishing once again that he'd had slightly more time for his own pleasure. The dragon hissed at him and released the scent of fresh basil.

Edan glared at it. "Do not act like I mishandled Holly. It was no more than a kiss. You did not mind watching our joining during the night. Now that I remember it, you actively encouraged it. I have done less today."

The scent of basil grew stronger. The dragon's chartreuse deepened to sage.

Edan raised his eyes at the dragon's displeasure. "Oh, now I understand. You wish me to join with Holly and are annoyed that we have not."

The dragon's color lightened slightly and the slightest hint of pleased cinnamon floated upward.

"Why?"

Hissing furiously, the dragon's anger deepened its color to dark pine.

"I simply ask the question," Edan told it. He knew he might be provoking a flare, but he would not be told what to do by a dragon. "I grow tired of dragons and their interference with Elves. Perhaps I shall simply return to De'erjia and not join with Holly again."

The dragon promptly returned to chartreuse and popped into another plane. It left behind the vanilla scent of dragon laughter.

Edan cursed. Not for a moment did the dragon believe his lie. The dragon, just as Edan himself, knew it was but a matter of time before he and Holly joined again. Despite his suspicion the dragon had a plan or was a helper in a Master Dragon plot, Edan relished the idea of Holly's soft skin against his, of burying himself in her tight wetness, of hearing her song of pleasure.

His stomach grumbled with the reminder of the necessity of eating despite the tightness pressing against his breeches' thong. He and Holly needed to eat before they cleaned the next dog. He lifted the tray with his latté and Holly's cold drink and went to find where Holly had carried the sack of food. When she went to greet her customer, he'd seen her pick it up from where he'd dropped it when he rescued her from the nucklelavee.

He found the food in the room with the coffee maker. Holly had called that a break room although he still didn't understand why. The glass carafe for the coffee was the only thing breakable in the room. Oh, and the window. Ah, wait – break room – as in a specific room in which to break one's fast.

He realized he was slowly beginning to grasp the nuances of this era's conversational language. Although there were still many times when he... What had Holly said? Ah, yes, he didn't quite 'get it.'

Not that it mattered, Edan thought with a shrug, after he'd set down the drinks and went to the entry room where he could hear Holly talking with her customer. He and Holly would not need spoken language when they joined again tonight. He did admit to a curiosity regarding Holly's statement regarding eating him for dessert. He knew she ate meat, but surely she was not of one of the few cultures that ate the flesh of other peoples, regardless of whether they be human or Elf. He would insist on an explanation of this 'eating' of another person before they joined.

Remaining in the hallway, Edan watched and listened to the tall man talking to Holly. While one of the strange dogs sat properly at his feet, the man's arm corded with heavy muscles while he continually kept a very grimy, bedraggled dog under control. Unlike the weedy young man who helped Holly earlier in the morning, Edan knew this man could be a threat to his possession of Holly.

The man had the solid build of someone who worked with large animals on a daily basis. His shirt showed the strain of deep muscles across his chest. His skin held the darkened hue of daily exposure to sunlight and wind. This man, like the hunters and fighters of De'erjia, had the physique that attracted females in ways unlike Edan's own slighter build.

By his speech patterns and vocal tones, Edan could tell he also had self-confidence without arrogance, another feature that attracted females.

But as he walked into the room, Edan scented the slight shift in Holly's pheromones. When he stood in the hallway, he'd only detected the sweet smell of her body's natural perfume. Holly had a very pleasant, friendly odor while she talked with the man. However, when Edan approached her, her body suddenly spiked with the mating aroma.

Edan placed a hand on her shoulder curious to discover how Holly would react. To his satisfaction, the tang strengthened into a bouquet of hormonal pleasure. He held Holly's attraction, not this stranger.

The odd dog at the man's feet had risen when Edan came into the room. While it looked like a very large mop, its stance clearly indicated Edan must come no closer to its master. The other dog bayed at Edan. Edan flinched at the echo in the small room, but managed to keep from holding his hands over his ears.

"Friend, Monster," the man said. "Sit. Stay."

The first dog promptly returned to its haunches. Despite not being able to see its eyes through the long cords of hair covering its face, Edan knew the dog still kept him firmly under watch and would defend its master should Edan make any threatening moves.

The man rattled the chain around the neck of the second, still baying, dog. "Quiet, Puff. Friends. Sit."

The man released the lead from Monster and placed a palm firmly on Puff's rear to push her to sit. "Sit." When the dog sat, he fed the dog a small meaty smelling pellet and praised her.

At the dog's bark, he repeated, "Quiet."

When the dog stopped baying, the man repeated the pellet offering and praise.

"Bright dog," Holly told the man.

"Yes, she is. Like I said, she just needs consistent training. I'll have to find someone with patience. The former owners let her run wild. Idiots. Got her from a puppy mill with absolutely no idea how much work a Komondor requires. Just wanted a large dog and thought these looked cute on the dog shows on TV. I suggested they get a mellow mix of Golden Retriever and Lab from the animal shelter and take obedience training. Probably won't do it, but at least I can control who takes on Puff next. Do you have time today to clean her coat? I'm sorry I didn't call sooner, but I got the phone call that she was arriving on an earlier flight just a short time ago, then I had to go to the airport and retrieve her with all the paperwork."

Edan looked at the mud, sticks, leaves and noxious smelling substances stuck to the animal's matted coat. She tossed her head and the matted strings flipped away revealing a deep brown eye.

Edan didn't understand what he felt when he saw that eye looking at him. He asked the man, "May I touch this dog?"

At the man's assent, Edan knelt in front of the dog and pushed the filthy locks from her eyes.

Edan held the dog's stare with his own eyes. Beneath the suspicion of the strangers, the fear of a new situation, the hurt of betrayal, the dog's eye held humor, hope, and a plea to be loved. A part of Edan that he never realized was empty filled with a hunger to have this dog in his life.

He shouldn't have anything to do with this dog. He would return to De'erjia. His sojourn on this plane was temporary. But this dog pulled part of his soul, the same way Holly had summoned him from De'erjia with her wish on the falling star. Edan could feel this dog's distress as easily as he could scent Holly's desire for him.

Stroking the dog's deep fur, he made a decision. He had to have this dog. His life would be incomplete throughout eternity if he could not have this dog. He would arrange a bargain with the Dragons and have them use their power to enable the dog to accompany him when he returned to De'erjia. If the Dragons would not bargain with him for use of their power, he would remain in this plane for the length of its lifespan. When it passed to Beyond without him, he would have the memories of his time with it.

Edan stood and wrapped his hand around the dog's leather leading strap. He met the man's eyes with the same firmness he used to make disagreeing Elves reach compromise. "I wish this dog to be part of my life."

The man frowned at Edan. "Do you know anything about Komondors?"

"No, but I shall learn. This dog shall be mine."

"Edan." Holly placed her hand on Edan's, still held wrapped around the dog's lead. "You'll be leaving soon. You can't take the dog with you."

"I will try to make arrangements to take her with me. If it cannot be done, I will remain here. This is my dog."

"This is not just a dog," the man said firmly. "This is a Komondor. They're herd guard dogs. Not herding dogs. They protect the herd from predators. They don't necessarily need a herd, but they need something to take care of even if it's only the people they live with. They can be aggressive with strangers, especially if they think their people are being threatened. They need space to run. This one is half-grown. She'll reach around 100 pounds at her full growth. This is not a dog for a small house with small yard in town or a home with everyone gone all day."

"I will arrange things for her comfort, even if I remain here. My usual job affords me the luxury of keeping her with me. She will have ample room to run and stretch her muscles. I will learn to clean her coat so she looks like Monster." Edan tugged the leather lead again. "This is my dog."

The man looked at Holly who nodded her head in the dog's direction. The dog had leaned her head against Edan's legs, her nose firmly pressed against Edan's crotch, claiming ownership of Edan.

The man shrugged and released the lead to Edan. "I've bred enough dogs to know when one has chosen its owner. And I've been a victim of the instant love syndrome myself. Take her. You want to make the Rescue Dog Donation now or send me a check?"

Edan sent Holly a questioning look for translation.

"I'll write you a check now and Edan will reimburse me," Holly said while she patted his dog's head. "How are you doing, Puff? I hope you get along with Rat and Crush."

"She will enjoy being with Rat and Crush," Edan said, fondling the dog's ear. "Her name is not 'Puff.' That is one of the reasons she has not been happy. She will tell me her real name when she calms more."

The man's deep laughter echoed through the small entry like the dog's heavy barks had. "Yep, she's got you good. This will definitely work out. Holly, you'll help him with a training schedule?"

At Holly's nod, he said, "I know you'll call if you want some advice. You get all the info for the hotel reservations for the Show next weekend?"

"Yes, and I appreciate you and Mrs. Johnston taking care of the bills for me."

"Hey, Beck and I don't have much in common, but we do like the way you prep our dogs. It's not a big deal. Happy to help. Y'all have a good afternoon with my Monster and this girl. I'll be here before you need to lock up for the night."

After their lunch, Holly trimmed the younger dog's forming cords to facilitate the cleaning, then showed Edan how to hand soap the forming cords, remove the debris, then rinse them clean. Although Holly did the handwork to shape the undercoat into the cording, Edan watched, learned and kept his dog calm throughout the procedure.

The dog slept with contentment in a pen with the dryers providing indirect heat. Edan's awareness of the dog's distress eased. Instead, he now found himself worrying about Holly.

"Holly?"

"Hmm?" she said quietly while she hand-soaped each of Monster's cords.

"I must leave for a time."

She turned questioning leaf-green eyes on him. "Why?"

"I do not like that a nucklelavee came to frighten you. I will return to my realm to endeavor to discover why it came."

"Oh. Okay. Um, you will be back?"

"Yes, of course. Not only have I promised to care for my dog, but I also gave you my word that we will join tonight without the constant interruptions that have plagued us today."

Holly's eyes did not lighten with the happiness Edan had come to enjoy. He lifted her curly hair and massaged the tight muscles in her neck. "I will return. I did promise."

"Yes, but... Oh, never mind." Holly bent back to cleaning Monster. "I'll see you later."

Edan shrugged. He'd never understood females, especially human females. Their logic patterns were totally incomprehensible. He had no experience with human females, but he did know how to cope with Elven females even though he didn't delude himself it always worked. The best way he had discovered to muddle through with females was to assure them they still held his attraction and to keep the promises he made to them.

He tilted Holly's face to him and kissed her. This time he refrained from releasing the hunger and massive desire he had for her. This time he gave her the gentle kiss of comfort and the kindness of friendship.

"I will return."

"I know."

Holly's smile still did not shine with delight. Her voice still held a hint of disappointment.

Ah, well, when he returned, he would make her smile again. She would be assured he kept his promises and he would be able to promise she would not be bothered by an evil faery, too.

Edan stepped back from Holly before he gave into the temptation of removing her clothes in the grooming studio. He absolutely did not want to be interrupted yet again.

He held his hand upward and palm forward in farewell. The vision of Holly's sadly drooping mouth stayed with him even as the washroom faded and his own abode formed around his being.

After he changed into more appropriate clothing and left his House Brownies gnashing their teeth at the state of his discarded clothing and boots, he made his way through the community to the King's Hall.

In his favorite of the entry halls, Edan stroked the cheek of the small, sweet face of his mother carved in mellow oak. His father had all phases of her face on the wall: maiden, woman, crone. Edan's memory held firm both the woman and the crone, although he'd lived in these Halls once the Elven Power had been discovered too strong in him to remain with his mother while he achieved maturity. He had visited with her on occasion, but she had died of old age before he had achieved enough maturity in his power to mimic the human aging cycle the way his father had while he lived with her. By human reckoning she'd been dead several thousand years.

Still, like his father, he touched each of her faces reinforcing and cherishing her memory. Unlike his father, he would not reproduce Holly's images as memory plaques. He would simply enjoy the short time he'd spend with her, then erase his memory from her so she would find contentment and children with a human mate. If he had to remain on that plane for his dog's life, he would live in a different area of the world from Holly.

His duty to his mother complete, Edan strolled into the King's Room.

The King nodded gravely to him and indicated he wait until he finished the current Audience. Across the Room, Edan spied Daffodil. Ah, she owed him a favor. He would ask for part of it in return.

Edan joined her on the padded bench. Daffodil's pale grey eyes glinted at him in amusement.

"What's her name?" Daffodil murmured beneath the conversations of the Audience.

Edan managed, just barely, to stop his jaw from dropping like a blithering fool.

"How did you know?"

Daffodil's mouth quirked with a smile similar to Holly's when she knew a joke she didn't want to share. Daffodil had always been one of the loveliest Elven females. Edan could not decide why Holly's smile sent tremors through him, but the same smile from Daffodil just irritated him.

Daffodil managed to muffle her laughter before it trilled through the Room. "We were joined for quite a long time, even by Elven time measure. I know when you smell of mating. Yet your scent is different, sweeter somehow.

"She is mortal," Edan replied. "It is but a temporary

liaison."

Daffodil leaned close to Edan's ear and, extremely quietly, blew, "Pppfffbbtt."

Edan glared at her. "I have never understood why an Elf such as yourself with untold dignity uses your normally sweet mouth to make that most rude snort. You sound nastier than even the most battle-scarred warrior's contribution to anal sound contests."

"Tell me about her."

Edan sighed. He had learned in his dalliance with Daffodil she was persistent. Nag was a better word. He'd end up telling her eventually, but for now...

"She has large brown eyes. Her hair is white and she wears it in long curls," Edan said with a smile of his own. He looked deeply into Daffodil's eyes. "She needs me as I have never been needed."

Compassion and understanding softened the mischievousness in Daffodil's eyes.

"And you must be the one to save her?"

"Someone else could, but she is my responsibility. When she leaned against my legs and pressed her nose to my breeches' thong, I knew I could not abandon her."

Daffodil's eyes widened with shock. "She...?"

Edan nodded modestly. "No female had even given me such immediate trust before. I must return to her soon. I can feel her through the planes missing me even now."

Actually, though he would not tell Daffodil, he not only felt the faint stirrings of his dog, his being and thoughts reached for and found Holly's essence even more easily. He reached through and sent her a reinsurance that he would return soon. He almost, but not quite, heard her hum of contentment.

Daffodil still looked at him dubiously. An amused quirk twisted through him.

"When I bathed her," Edan kept himself from

laughing at Daffodil's widened eyes, "she licked across my entire face in gratitude and love."

Daffodil's mouth opened, then she snapped it shut. Her eyes narrowed.

"You are not talking about a human."

Edan shook his head, unable to retain the amusement in his voice. "She is a dog. I'm considering naming her 'Daffodil' because humans call a female dog a bitch."

Edan could almost hear Daffodil's teeth grind.

"I do not believe you are mating with a dog."

Edan sucked in his breath. "Daffodil, how dare you say something as evil as that?"

"What is her name and how did you met her?"

"Do you like your slippers?"

Daffodil tucked the buttery yellow leather slippers inscribed with the flowers of her name and the symbols of her House and her Powers under her skirt. "You are not changing the subject. I wish to know with whom you are mating."

Edan met her eyes clearly. "It is none of your business. I have a boon to request."

"Should you tell me just a little about this human female," Daffodil's lips lifted with pleasure, "I will do this boon and still owe you the favor for my slippers."

"Why must you know every facet of my life?'

"I am simply curious. Your mating scent is delightful. I partly wish you had such joy with us. But I truly wish you much joy in the future. A name and a trifle bit of information, Edan, so that my Power can be enhanced when I grant this boon."

Edan thought. As magickal as Daffodil's workings were, he knew they were greater when she focused them to an individual.

"Her name is Holly. Her eyes are as changeable as the green of the summer leaves. I wish only a trinket for her to enjoy."

"Ah." Daffodil's brow wrinkled in thought, then it cleared. "I have a moss agate. Its green shade is the deepness of the underside of pine needles on a night of a dark moon to the clear green of a wave with sunlight shining through it before it crests. I shall shape it for you before you return to her."

Daffodil's sunlight smile lightened Edan's heart, filled him with joy at the thought of Holly's happiness.

"She is quite fortunate, for however long this liaison lasts. Ah, the Audience is ending. Now I shall discover if I shall be creating bonding bands with a possible new Life gift or consolation gifts."

Edan frowned at the couple in front of the counselors and King. "They are still trying to create Life? They disagree almost as frequently as they agree. I have had them in my court for arbitration multitudes of times."

"Sometimes it is great fun to apologize after a quarrel."

Daffodil's eyes sparkled with a shine that Edan had long ago resolved not to waste time trying to interpret. He had decided it was simply a female thought process beyond the keen of male logic.

"Ah, lovely."

At Daffodil's exclamation, Edan looked at the couple, who had taken their final bows to the Council and turned to face the Court. Their faces glowed almost incandescent.

The King did not bother making the formal announcement. It wouldn't have been heard in the babble anyway. There would be a joining at the Marriage Tree in the near future. Magick from all beings would be required to reinforce the Joining Magick and create a Life.

As much as Edan had enjoyed his sojourn with Daffodil, he knew they didn't have enough strength between them to go through the process to recreate themselves into a new being. His thoughts slipped to a nebulous vision of brushing hair with the texture of Holly's curls on the head of a small daughter. For a moment he saw a small son suckling at Holly's breast.

No. Edan shook away the daydreams. It would never happen. Holly was mortal. He would not risk having a child with her so magical he would have to remove it from Holly's care and place it in the care of Elves. Even worse would be to have a child who would go Beyond the way Holly would, leaving him to carve their images on his walls.

He could live with the memories of the dog in his life. He had no desire to be so committed to Holly he would have to spend eternity missing her.

He gazed over the crowd surrounding the future Life couple. The King tilted his head toward a doorway leading to a small chamber.

With a last look at the couple, Edan followed. He assured himself he did not feel jealous. It didn't work because all he could wanted was Holly's face looking at him with the same glow the Elven woman wore. But it would never be. He would just have to be content with protecting her from any future evil faeries. Holly was mortal. They had no future.

CHAPTER 5

In the King's chamber, Edan made the formal bow with both hands extended palms forward offering his service and allegiance to the King. Various attendants were helping the King divest himself of his ceremonial robes and chains of office.

Edan hoped like hell he was never appointed king. Each layer of robe, each chain, each bracelet, each ring, each band in the crown represented another acceptance of responsibility to House, Power, and Community. Edan touched his own simple leather band that showed his Power with nothing more on it than the small silver disk bearing the inscription of his House name. He and Daffodil had never bothered to exchange bond rings.

"It's rare these days you come to the Halls, young Edan." The King pulled a final band from his hair and massaged his skull. Although his face showed the image of a man in the older prime of life, Edan could see the invisible weight of a millennia filled with responsibility. Responsibility and duty still invisibly cloaked him even though the King had divested himself of the outward trappings of high office. The King smoothed his hair away from his face and pulled the silver-white strands into the same simple ponytail Edan wore.

"Come along, urchin," the King said, affectionately slinging his arm around Edan's shoulders. "We'll let these *toadies*," he waved a hand at the attendants straightening robes and baubles, "clear this mess. One of the few perks of getting stuck being King."

The attendants, who had fiercely competed for their privileged positions, as Edan himself had once competed and served, gave the King and Edan various comments of farewell. Edan found himself pleased at being included with the same level of affection the King received.

The King settled himself in his chair; the leather creaking with familiarity as it molded itself to his contours. Edan kicked the hassock to the King for him to set his feet on. From seemingly out of nowhere, a black and white cat flowed onto the King's lap. A House Brownie literally popped in with a tray of steaming cups. A second followed with a pipe rack and cured leaf.

Edan sat at the edge of his chair. "This is not precisely a social call, Sir. I have a request."

"Urchin, you grew up under my care. You did not request a formal Audience. Therefore, if it is within my power as your former guardian to help with whatever you need, I shall do so. If it takes more than what is in my Power, we'll have to take it up with the Court."

The King's eyes glinted with humor and acceptance of the vagaries of unknown years of dealing with life. "I'm guessing it involves a female."

"It always involves a female," one of the Brownies chirped and offered Edan the second of the steaming cups.

"Unless there's a female sitting on the edge of the seat in the visitor's chair–" The other Brownie held out the tray with the selections of pipes and leaf to Edan. "Then it's a male problem. See, Sha, we're as smart as the King."

As with dragons, one never knew and didn't ask the gender of Brownies at the risk of them taking offense and leaving one's abode. The return nicety didn't apply from Brownies to Elves and never prevented Brownies from commenting on interactions between Elven genders.

"Pah." The King's voice held an indulgent chuckle. "Any time you wish to assume the robes and other accouterments of Office, you may do so."

"Nope, not a chance," Pah said.

"That's because we're smarter than you and have seen what you and other Kings do. We're happy with our jobs." Sha beamed and turned to Edan. "Would you like us to remain and give you our advice? We've been around as long as Elves. She must be quite different. Ta and Weg are having fits about your clothes. Have you been rolling in a pig sty?"

Edan declined the offering of a smoke, but set the cup on the table next to his chair. "No, I have been in the human realm and have been cleaning dogs. Several very nice ones and one that is a canine reincarnation of The Great Beast That Eats Brownies."

At the Brownies' widened eyes over the thought of the actual reality of the mythical Beast of their night terrors, Edan had a sudden remembrance of the deep bliss on Holly's face while she chewed on the chocolate chip cookie and explained the difference between cake, cookies, and brownies. He wondered if he'd see that same gratification on her face when they joined the next time. And what *did* she mean by eating him? "She does, by the way, enjoy eating brownies."

Sha and Pah both looked at him in shock.

"No."

"That's uncivilized."

"She has much to learn about the faery ways. She is mortal."

"Bleech," the Brownies said together.

"Settle back down with an Elf, Edan," Pah advised.

"Elves are much nicer than mortals," Sha said. "We're needed elsewhere now."

"Eats brownies, does she?" The King stroked the cat and looked gravely through the pipe smoke curling around his head.

"She explained they are small cakes made of chocolate. Chocolate is very good."

The King nodded. "I know chocolate and the brownies she speaks of from my sojourns in the human plane. They are quite good. You need to eat one."

Edan twisted his mouth allowing his Sir to share his puzzlement. "She said something very odd about eating me."

The King choked on his smoke and started to cough. The cat shot off his lap.

Edan pounded the King's back, hoping he wasn't going to dissolve into the Mists right now, and wondered where the damn Brownies were when they were needed.

The King got the cough under control and waved Edan back to his seat. He sipped the hot wine and persuaded the cat back onto his lap.

He cleared his throat and sipped some more. Where that glint in his King's eye was coming from Edan didn't know. He had a sinking feeling it boded no good at all for himself, but the King simply said, "It's been many, many years since you've journeyed to the human plane, young Edan. You need to visit more frequently."

"All my needs are met here. Why should I go there?"

The King merely tightened his mouth. Edan knew *That Look*. *That Look* was the way Sir looked whenever one of the part Elf-blood children under his care did something he was trying not to laugh at.

"You are a small portion human. You should visit the human plane more frequently to know that part of your heritage."

"I am Elf. My home is De'erjia. As much as any Elf."

"Of course it is. You would not have been brought to maturity in De'erjia if you were not Elf. I carry human blood also. You know this. I serve appointment as King, but I go frequently to visit the humans. They are interesting."

"I find De'erjia, *my home*, meets my needs. I had *no* desire to go to the human plane."

"Then why did you go?"

Edan tightened his own mouth to hold back the anger, still annoyed at being ripped from his own abode at the whim of someone else. "Because she summoned me. She created a ritual and it pulled me into her plane."

The King blew a series of smoke rings. "She made a ritual for you specifically. Interesting."

"It wasn't for me specifically. It could have been any Elf. She just wanted an Elf. Some odd notion of joining with an Elf based on human so-called fairy tales and legends."

"Ah, but Edan. How many Elven males live in our Community of De'erjia? How many Communities are there? Yet, you were the one pulled into her plane."

The King's brows knit together. "Since you are here, she's already released you from her ritual. Did you not please her? And why were you washing dogs?"

"I pleased her." Edan would control his anger. He still felt the tremors of her body when Holly crested the cosmos. When he had joined with her joyous bucking body, he flashed into the gloriousness of being with her. Not that he'd explain to his King the details of her cries of happiness, the scented damp sheen of her bare skin against his, the touch of her hands, her mouth stroking him to hard gratification so many times.

"She enjoys my company. But she is *mortal*. She wants a mate and children. She knows there will never be such between us. She released me from her ritual. I spent the day cleaning dogs with her because that is her job and I wished to spend more time with her. As you said, humans can be interesting. I find her interesting. She has attracted a dragon."

At the King's look of astonishment, Edan tried – not as hard as he probably should, but he did try – not to allow the smugness filling him to show on his face. It always pleased him when he could surprise someone who'd been around for most of Eternity.

The King nodded gravely. "Yes, that would be interesting. Do you plan to return to her?"

"Yes, for a bit of time, perhaps. Plus I also have obtained a dog. She was lonely and rejected by her previous owners. She wants to be with me. When I think she will be comfortable crossing the realms, I shall ask the Dragons for help to bring her here with me."

"And this mortal woman?"

"I shall stay with her for awhile, should it continue to please her. But I will erase myself from her memories. She needs a mate and children. Eventually." Edan rolled the cup between his palms, felt the heated sting of the metal it was shaped from, and stared into its depths. He had no power to foresee the future in its darkness. All he saw was a dim reflection of himself.

He looked from the cup and sipped the heated wine. The King continued to smoke his pipe and rest his hand on the cat between sips and studies into his own cup.

"What do you need, young Edan? Do you require the coin of the current human realm? For that you could simply go to the Balancers. You have built a great store of favors and boons, easily converted by the Balancers to provide for your needs while you sojourn in the mortal realms for as long as you wish to stay. As I know from your previous visits, you will quickly find work to add to whatever you deduct from your current store. One thing I am most proud of is that the children in my guardianship have always discovered the means to be self-sufficient regardless of the realm in which they choose to reside. Tell me, Edan. What is this request you have from your former guardian, urchin?"

"Sir, there is something, as you say, 'interesting' about Holly."

"Ah." The King breathed in satisfaction. "I thank you for sharing her name."

Edan shrugged and finally sat back in the chair. "Not only did she overcome my Powers to summon me to her. Not only does she have a dragon familiar. Today, I trapped and banished a nucklelavee menacing her."

"A nucklelavee?" The King's eyebrows rose again in surprise. "Why would someone summon a nucklelavee to frighten a human?"

"I'm beginning to wonder about the Dragons. Her familiar seemed to be trying to encourage us to join in mating when I was trying to comfort her."

The King twisted his lips in consideration. "Always a possibility. They do have a pertinacious interest is Elves and mortals. If Dragons are involved with this Holly, that would explain why her ritual drew you from our realm. Do you wish me to discover why the Dragons have taken an interest in you two? That would be beyond my own Power. I would need to consult the Council to meddle in the affairs of Dragons."

"No." Edan drank some of the cooling wine. "As I said, I will return to the human realm and spend more time with Holly. Perhaps our liaison is but a trifle matter in whatever the Dragons are considering. But, as my former guardian, Sir, not as my Sire King, I do request you inform them I do not take kindly to them frightening Holly. To frighten a mortal for the sheer purpose of encouraging mating is cruel."

The King nodded at Edan's conclusion. Edan watched the planes of his former guardian's face settle into the lines of decision. Since Holly was now under Edan's care and Edan had once been under Sire's care, Edan knew Sir would now regard Holly as in his care, too. And, no one, not even the Dragons, ever frightened a child in his care.

"Yes," the already firm voice of the King of De'erjia

was further hardened by the determined protectiveness of the man, Sir, whose child was endangered, "I shall take this matter up with the Dragon Master."

"Thank you, Sir." Edan drained the last of the wine in contentment.

He felt the passage of time and reached through the realms for Holly. She was conversing with the young man, Jon – Edan remembered, who helped with the animals. They were feeding and caring for the animals that would remain overnight. He needed to return.

"I must take your leave now, Sir. I wish to visit briefly with my father before I return to Holly. Ta and Weg have certainly organized my clothing by now and made arrangements with the Balancers."

"You have quite devoted Brownies. You'll miss them in the human realm. They'll miss you. Do not stay away too long."

Edan rose and lightly kissed Sir's cheek, the less formal leave of his former guardian, rather than the protocol required of his Liege. "I shall not. I will request they assist my father while I am gone. They like him also."

"Like father, like son," Sir said in contentment. "In more ways than one."

Edan saw Sir's eyes gleam with amusement again. Damn it all. He hated that look. He knew Sir was just about to say something that he would find amusing, but Edan would not understand either the comment or the amusement.

"Edan, when Ms. Holly's ready to eat you, suggest chocolate."

Edan could still hear Sir's roaring laughter even after he quietly shut the door and walked down the hallway. He was proud he'd been able to maintain his dignity, not to mention remain politic, and not slam the door of the King's personal chambers.

It never mattered who did the laughing, Edan still hated

to be laughed at.

In his abode, he found not only Ta and Weg drooping beside a packed satchel, but his father waiting for him.

He raised his eyebrows at his father sprawled in a chair idly looking at his reflection in the blade of his knife. While he knew it was his father's way of contemplation, he also knew that on occasion his Father used his knife blade to scry.

"Father, will you house Ta and Weg while I am away?"

"Of course.   It will be my pleasure."   He straightened and bowed to Ta and Weg, both of whom looked noticeably happier. "I have several new commissions I must fulfill, new wards to help adjust to life, plus the King has asked me to take on your official duties while you are gone."

He scowled at Edan and pointed his knife blade at Edan. "Do not be gone long. I have served as Prince before. I would rather forge my knives."

"'We all would rather do our chosen jobs than serve the Community, but it is essential to the welfare of De'erjia we take our turns serving the Folk of De'erjia.'"

In a swift movement, his father sprang from seated sprawl to holding the tip of his blade against Edan's throat. His eyes glittered like the blade's point. "Do not quote my words to me, young Edan. I shall make you suffer."

Edan's own blade point touched just under his father's chin. "You and what Army?"

"If you get blood on the carpets, I'll be very unhappy," Ta said.

"If you are going to fight, can we contact the other Brownies? I won a great deal the last time," Weg chirped happily.

Ta sighed.   "I don't think they're going to fight,

Weg. I'm afraid it's one of those boring 'I'm going to miss you, but I don't want to admit it' scenes."

"Those are no fun," Weg whined. "I like it when they seriously try to maim each other."

"Too damn bad," Edan's father said.

"On three?" Edan suggested. He did want to discuss some things with his father who frequented the other realms much more often than many elves.

"I'll count," Weg offered. "One, one and a half, two, two and a fourth, two and three eighths–"

"Ta shall count," his father said, "or you shall go live with the shepherds while Edan is away."

Weg shut its mouth with a snap.

"Three," Ta said smugly.

Edan and his father withdrew their knives from each other's throats, touched the points together, and bowed before sheathing them.

Pure pleasure lit his father's eyes when he straightened from his bow. "You have been practicing, Edan. Not long ago I could disarm you before you even thought to pull your blade."

Edan grinned back. "Ta and Weg have been helping me practice. Under the tutelage of Costac."

"Excellent tutor. I trained him well."

"Pphhffttt." Edan repeated Daffodil's rude sound at his father's lack of humility.

His father simply laughed. "I shall arrange for you two," he nodded at the chortling Brownies, "to tutor some of the young ones in my care."

"I wish to visit with my father a few moments before I take my leave of you," Edan told his Brownies.

"One more thing," Weg said. "This is from the Balancers. They said where you are staying, in the current time period, that this will access your store of favors and boons. It must be a new form of magic."

Weg handed a flat rectangle of slick material to Edan, then it and Ta popped from the room. The disk was brightly colored and had raised numbers across one side with Edan's name also in raised letters. The backside held minute letters and numbers with a dark brown band.

Edan sat in his favorite chair, looked at the card, and handed it to his father seated across from him. "Have you seen this magic before?"

He glanced at it and handed it back. "Yes, that is called a credit card. Recently, when I have gone to Faires to sell my knives to mortals, they have used those magic cards in lieu of a favor or coins. I'm not sure how it works. I tend to stay with the coins of the realms, but this female…"

"Holly," Edan supplied.

"Thank you. Holly," his father repeated. "She will be able to explain how it functions. Females always understand how coins, and the current facsimiles, function better than males can understand. Also she will be able to help you choose clothes more appropriate for where you are staying. I would give you some of mine, but…" His father gestured at the differences in their body types. Edan not only stood taller than his father, but his father bore heavier muscles from hammering knives and swords at his forge. "Are you committing to Ms. Holly?"

"No. It is but a temporary dalliance. Some day she wishes a mate and children. I remain here in De'erjia. What is mizz? The King used the title also."

"Ms. is a current title to distinguish a woman who is no longer maid, but not committed to a mate."

"Thank you." Edan's brain made a sudden connection. "The Faires you attend to occasionally sell your knives – are these called 'Ren Faire'? Several people have mentioned the clothes I wore were appropriate for Ren Faire."

"Yes. Ren Faire – Renaissance Festivals. They are

costumed activities that celebrate various eras in human history. You will find them enjoyable. Many elves attend them, for legends and myths are celebrated also and humans think we simply have elaborate costumes." His father's teeth gleamed. "Including our ears."

Edan frowned. "There is much I do not understand about this current human plane."

"It always takes a while to adjust. Their world moves at a different pace."

"So you always say. You do go there frequently."

"Humans are interesting. Although I've never had another mortal lover since your mother, I still see the attraction."

"You still treasure my mother." Joy flowed through Edan at his father's statement. A longing to have known his mother better once again shimmered through him, but the years had passed and it would not be. It was an old longing easily shrugged back into the mists, much the way he easily ignored the scars obtained while learning knife and sword handling. The thought stung with as little pain as the nicks and pinches he obtained while creating the leather footwear that was his main source of boons and favors.

"Yes, of course. I see much of her in you, but I retain my memories of her for the joy she herself gave me."

A stab shot through Edan as sharp as his father's knives at the realization that when he left Holly and took the memories of his time from her, he would also lose most of his own memories of her. He would not again carry the sound of her laugh in his ears, the scent of her mating pheromones in his nostrils, the texture of her hair in his hands.

He reached through the realms and found the tendril that was Holly. It settled something tight in him to hear her contentment in dealing with the boarding cats, talking to Rat and Jon.

The sweet chime of requested entry came from the opening of his abode. Ta popped into the room. "Daffodil has come to call. Shall I allow her entry or do you wish more time together?"

"Father?"

"If you have further need of me, you have only to reach for me. I shall stay attuned for you."

"Thank you. Yes, Ta, please welcome Daffodil into our abode."

After greetings were exchanged, and Ta and Weg had brought drinks and food, Daffodil pulled a green velvet bag from her skirt pocket. "Your trinket, Edan."

Edan lifted a thin silver chain from the bag. Hanging from it was the moss agate Daffodil had described. Edan watched the reflection of light on the swirled greens now shaped with two rounded hills on the top that moved smoothly to a point at the bottom.

"What is engraved in the heart?" asked Edan's father.

"Heart?" Edan didn't understand. He had seen hearts. He had gutted his share of hunting animals. He knew from the healers that Elven and human hearts were not shaped as this stone was.

"It is called a heart. It is a stylized shaping of a symbol of affection between those who Join in the human area to which you will be returning. You shall see it frequently," his father explained.

Daffodil ducked her eyes from Edan's stop-interfering-in-my-life glare, but he saw the dimple in her cheek from her smile.

His father continued, "What is the silver on it?"

Edan turned the heart over. He met Daffodil's puzzled eyes.

"I had a sudden urge to inscribe a small dragon in it. It looked better filled with silver. I do not know why this happened."

"I do," Edan said grimly. Dimly he began to sense a disturbance in the connection he held with Holly.

"Holly has attracted a dragon. This," he swung the heart like a pendulum, "is simply further proof of the Dragon interference."

The dread grew more intense.

"Would you like me to make something else?" Daffodil's eyes flashed with the same annoyance at Dragon interference that Edan felt and that he could see in his father's eyes. "I have a very fine emerald. But if you want something simpler, I also have some lovely aventurine."

"No." Edan could not shake the horrid gnawing in his gut. He had not felt this shaking worry in years. "This will be sufficient. It is lovely, a tribute to your always high craft Power. Holly likes dragons. She has a number of dragon decorations in her home. She will like this. I thank you."

Edan reached for the essence of Holly. A blurred wave of exasperation and aggravation came through in addition to Holly's normal comforting presence. Still, he couldn't shake the concern something was wrong.

Edan stood suddenly. "I must return. Ta. Weg."

The Brownies popped into the room.

"I am leaving now." Even when he knelt beside them, Ta and Weg still did not reach the mid-point of his chest. He easily circled his arms around them and held them to him.

"You will come back?"

"Of course. Haven't I always?"

"We will miss you."

"I shall miss you two also."

What had been just unease now began to gibber wildly. "I shall bring you back something you will enjoy. I must leave now."

He released them and his father took their hands. He placed the magic card – credit card, he'd have to remember that – in the smaller packet holding other odd things Ta and Weg had accumulated for his use to pretend to be human in Holly's era. The smaller packet he replaced in the bag with his personal clothes and cleanliness items. Holding the bag with Daffodil's trinket for Holly, he lifted the satchel and raised his open palm in farewell.

A burst of terror sent him to his knees as though he'd been knifed in the heart. Gasping for air, he dimly heard his father and Daffodil's concerned voices, Ta's and Weg's shrill cries.

A shift of air and the smell of scorched eggs flooded Edan's room. On his hands and knees, Edan saw Holly's dragon. As dark as poison ivy in moonlight, it hissed frantically at Edan.

Daffodil and his father helped him to stand.

"You need our help?" Daffodil's voice chimed.

His father snarled at the dragon that left with a storm's wind force.

"Please." Edan could hear the shaking in his voice. He knew he didn't have the Power to reach Holly himself.

"Satchel." Weg wrapped his fingers around the handle while Ta wrapped the strings of the velvet bag around his wrist.

His father's hand held his with the same strength Edan could remember from the first days of his infancy. One of Daffodil's soft hands, with its small scars from nicks and burns from the Power of working her jewelry, took his other hand, while her free hand linked to his father's. Ta wrapped its hands on his and Daffodil's. Weg's spindled fingers twisted around his and his father's.

His home faded and with it, the concerned faces he loved. As he swept through the realms, the terror gave way to complete despair. Something or someone had destroyed

Holly's world and Edan felt her pain as his.

The last of the sense of De'erjia faded and Edan again stood in Holly's grooming studio. He dropped his bag and ran the length of the hall following the echoes of Rat's continuous barking.

The dragon phased through the closed door, hissed at Edan, then phased back into the storage room. A long handled broom with a wide brush had fallen across the doorway. Somehow, it had become wedged at an angle so part of it lay firmly against the doorknob preventing it from being turned. The top of the handle stuck against one side of the hallway, the other end firmly butted the opposite wall.

Even before he reached the door to remove the broom, he could hear Holly's soft crying. Edan had heard those types of cries before: when a child died, when a beloved passed Beyond, when something shattered a life.

"Holly, I am here." He wrenched the broom free and pulled opened the door.

Holly huddled on the floor, wiping away her tears. "You came back."

"I promised you I would." Edan helped Holly rise, then lifted her. He carried her to the break room and set her on the worn couch. "You need something warm to drink."

"No coffee," Holly said between gulps of tears. "Herbal tea. Bags in that metal box. Heat water in the microwave."

Edan followed the ritual Holly had used to operate the microwave, setting it for the number of minutes she told him. "Is there a blanket here? You are very cold."

Holly shook her head, her hands busily stroking Rat, crooning comfort to the shaking dog between her own tears. The dragon wrapped itself around her neck.

"I shall get some towels from the drying machine. I will return before the water is hot."

Edan wrapped Holly in an armload of clean towels

and had her drinking her hot tea before he finally could bring himself to address the dragon.

"What happened?" he asked in Elvish. He held Holly with one arm and her teacup in the opposite hand.

The dragon sent a burst of speech that flowed across Edan's ears in a burst of colors. Green clashed with off-key flute notes. The taste of rotted fish overlaid flowers spoiling in a vase. A discordant purple cast made the entire commentary shudder.

Edan cursed. Even the dragon, more attuned to Holly than he, was too incoherent to make sense. Not that he was fluent in Dragon Speak anyway, but he could frequently get the gist of it. Pity Rat was canine and not feline. Cats understood Elvish and Dragon Speak but then again cats did have an annoying tendency to not care to translate to Elves what Dragons were communicating.

Holly lifted her pale face to Edan. In a wobbling voice, she said, "Door slammed shut. Couldn't get it open. Hate being trapped. Awful. Thought I was stuck there…kept telling myself the building wouldn't fall down."

She shuddered Even with Edan helping her hold the teacup, it shook so hard the tea nearly spilled.

"Thanks for coming back." Her voice still quivered.

"There is no need to thank me. Not only did I tell you I would return, I heard your fear through the realms."

"You heard?" Holly's dark brown eyelashes were starred with wetness over frightened green eyes.

"Yes. We have bonded in some way. I could feel your emotions in De'erjia."

"Oh." Holly looked into the teacup much the same way his father had studied his knife blade, as though it held answers. "Couple of times this afternoon," she snuffled, "I turned to say something to you and then realized you weren't there. Thought I was losing it."

Edan nodded. "We have bonded for a time. We

shall see where it leads."

Holly lifted her face to look at Edan. "The future can change instantly."

"I have not a soothsayer's powers to see the future. But we have now."

Holly set the cup on the small table to the side of the couch. "Now is okay. I can deal with now."

She toyed with the thong of Edan's shirt. Her finger rippled across his chest. He could feel the single finger trace a path as heated as the flames from his father's forge even through his linen shirt.

Despite her dragon familiar beginning to hum and pulse with the blue of Power manipulation, Edan gathered her closer. She opened her lips to his hungry mouth.

CHAPTER 6

Holly shrugged off the towels and pressed against Edan. Instead of the cold concrete floor, his shirt fabric cushioned her hand while the muscle and bones beneath it gave her firm support to lean against. She could feel the steady thump-thump of his heart beating against her palm, the rise and fall movement of his chest while he breathed, the reminder of life still living.

No longer did she smell the artificial pine scent cleaner, the scouring powder's sharp tang or the mop's slight mildew. Instead her nose inhaled the sweet scent of a field of clover and buttercups, the woodiness of fresh rosemary and the power of male musk.

Edan held her tighter to him. Her breasts flattened against his ribs, the tight knots of her nipples pressed between her bra and his shirt, wanting to be freed and suckled by his mouth.

But his mouth was busy with hers. His tongue probed, twisted and demanded her full attention. He tasted like wine and apricots with just a hint of coffee.

The light leeched through her closed eyelids reminding her that she wasn't trapped. She was in the break room and could get away if she needed to. She kept her eyes closed to savor the wet darkness of his mouth, the steady feel of his arms around her, the scents of the aftermath of a summer thunderstorm of wet grasses, fresh air, and the remaining ting of ozone.

Holly's bones began to melt and her muscles grew slack. Edan's arms retained their hold while her body reclined of its own volition. His mouth followed hers, never letting up its assault.

Dimly, Holly heard the jingle of Rat's tags and the scrabble of his claws when he jumped to the floor. Material slithered off the couch with a soft rustle.

Then Edan's body covered hers, warming her more than the towels ever could. Unlike the weird screaming feeling she'd had in the closet, now Holly felt protected, sheltered by the sensation of Edan lying on her, pinning her to the couch.

She slid one leg from under him to prop her foot on the floor. His hip and thigh settled solidly in the open V of her legs only slightly easing the ache wanting him.

He drew her tongue into his mouth while he tunneled a hand in her hair. While she tasted and dueled with his tongue, he lifted her head slightly and stroked her hair from under the back of her skull. She felt a slight tug and, from the pressure released on her scalp, realized he'd untied the band holding her braids off her face.

She nipped his lower lip then drew it into her mouth to comfort it. She heard his chuckle, felt the vibrations of his laugh across her mouth, against her body.

Both of his hands were busy with her hair, releasing the French braids and easing the constriction of her scalp. She arched her body to rub her crotch against his thigh, to thrust her breasts against him. She wanted his hands on her body not just her hair and scalp.

His mouth never left hers as he continued to lave his tongue through her mouth as if the only thing important in life was the taste of her mouth, the texture of her hair. His hands found knots in the back of her neck she wasn't even aware hurt until he eased them.

Languidly she reached behind his head to release his ponytail. The heavy hair flowed of its own volition through her hands. Not static electricity, not the friction of soft threads, but the curling warmth of sweet life. If each silken strand could be woven into fabric, it would be the softest, most luxurious piece and she would hold it forever. For now, Edan's hair was Holly's to stroke, to slide through her hands, to feel across her body.

The thought sent shivers through her. As delicious as his hair felt in her hands, she wanted more. She wanted it sliding on her skin. She wanted his mouth suckling her as he had cherished her breast this morning. She wanted to feel his skin against hers, not just his hands, his mouth, his hair.

A memory flash gave Holly an idea. Although the temptation of continuing to run her fingers through his hair was great, she removed her hands. If she wanted more, she had to go after it.

Edan kept kissing her as though time stood still and her mouth was the only thing that mattered. Despite her rubbing her body against his, telling him wordlessly she was ready for more, he continued his focused assault on her mouth. His hands dipped down no further than her neck.

While she thoroughly enjoyed Edan's kissing, her jaws were beginning to ache. Could a person get lockjaw from too much kissing? Besides, her breasts wanted some of the action, too. Not to mention her soaked panties were already sticking to her.

She knew Edan was ready for her. Either that or he'd grown a third, shorter, leg. Its firm length dug into her hip with the same solidness as the thighbone pressed hard against her crotch.

Holly ran her hands across Edan's ears. His body trembled against hers. As lightly as she could she fluttered her fingers up and down the outside edges of his ears, almost but not quite touching the uppermost peaks.

For the first time without heart-wrenching pain, she remembered the lover who once made her come by no more than stroking her breasts. At first his fingers had circled the areoles, but had never touched the tips of her straining nipples. For a time she had thought she could simply lie there and let her sex slave caress her like that all night. She'd been half-asleep, practically hypnotized by the feathery strokes of his hands when his fingers started slipping against her nipples. By the time he'd started lightly rubbing them she felt the start of an orgasm. He'd added a few random tweaks and soft pinches, and her hips had started to undulate. When he licked his fingers and stroked her nipples into peaks, her mind had exploded. She'd screamed her throat raw before her orgasm crested.

With a mental kiss and thanks to her former lover, she now applied the same pleasurable torment to Edan's ears. Barely touching their outer shells, she slowly moved her fingertips in circles around his ears. From an old barely-passed biology class she remember ears were shaped much the same as conch shells, spiraling inward to take the sound to the delicate inner bones and membranes. Edan's elf body had the same attributes as other males Holly had known, both platonically and in the Biblical sense. If sound could slide in and tickle the ears, surely a light touch could do the same thing.

She slid her fingers around his ears first to spiral inward, then outward. Each time she went outward, she felt Edan tense as though just waiting for her touch.

The closer she got to his peaks, the more his tongue slowed its exploration of her mouth. When she by-passed the absolute peaks, his breath hissed into her mouth. She slid her fingers around the curves and cartilage gently moving to the inner holes, then brushed across the opening, being very careful not to insert her fingertip inside.

Edan shifted on the couch to twist both of them sideways. Holly's spine now pressed against the couch back, yet even without an obvious way out, part of her knew that if she felt trapped, Edan would immediately release her.

Holly hooked her legs over his hips angling against his hard shaft. Despite his own hips beginning to pump against hers, even though she continued to tease and tantalize him by not quite touching his ear points, Edan still didn't stop kissing her, he still touched her no further than her head, hair, and neck.

His scent increased to the heady smell of man holding himself back. The sandalwood smell of the sweat sheen on his body caught in the taste buds in the back of Holly's throat making her hungry to taste his skin.

She stroked his ears once more, this time barely touching the peak. Edan groaned into her mouth, but still limited himself to kissing her and tunneling his hands through her hair. Holly knew she hadn't been kissed this long with this limited contact since her first front seat of the car make-out session after the high school football games.

Kissing and being kissed by Edan was spectacular, but Holly wanted more. *Now.*

She slid a hand under Edan's shirt and across his back. Like the shirt he'd worn this morning, this one flowed over his slim hips rather than being tucked in. The part of Holly's brain that hadn't yet fuzzed out in hormonal overdrive made a mental note to take him shopping for some clothing more appropriate to her world rather than his.

He held her too tightly for her to be able to get her hand between their bodies to untie his pants. She wiggled her crotch closer to his penis. It throbbed with a pulse beat of its own against her aching core.

Her breasts crushed flat against his chest. One hand stroked up and down her back while the other still tangled in her hair.

Holly still didn't feel close enough to him. She was tired of just kissing. If Edan wanted to ignore what she damn well knew were less than subtle clues, then she would have to take charge completely.

He'd come to her at the beginning because she'd summoned him. They didn't have a future together, but he had come back to her from Delicious or what-ever-the hell-it was called. She knew the only thing they'd ever have would be hot and heavy sex. She would just make him her sex slave; starting now.

Holly used both hands to push him off her. As she thought he would, Edan promptly released her. He moved to sit up, but she pushed him onto his back and straddled his body. She ground her crotch against his shaft while she unlaced and pulled off her shoes and socks.

She reached for the clasps on her overall bibs, but Edan's hands wrapped around hers.

"I want this." Holly raised herself to her knees and put her hand flat on Edan's hard length. She began to fumble with the laces holding his pants together. "You want me just as much. Let's get naked instead of just lying here kissing like a couple of teenagers."

Once again Edan stopped her. He looked over her shoulder.

Automatically, Holly turned to see what he was looking at. Why would Edan glare at the back of the couch with the same disdainful look that the Schnauzer, the poodle, and the Pug gave the cat sitting beside them in the poster hung on the wall above the couch?

Edan said something in Elvish, then turned back to Holly. He rubbed his palms across her thighs and lightly pressed them until she again sat on top of him. Gently, he began to massage the small of her back, slowly easing her down until she sprawled across him.

Her cheek against his shoulder, her breasts snuggled against the hard planes of his chest, Holly began to feel more like the afterglow of hot sex rather than wham-me, bang-me, take-me-now. The hungry ache between her legs eased and she simply lay against him content as a cat asleep in the best chair in the house.

The coiled tension in her back began to ease at the pressure of his palms stroking against her.

"Holly?" Edan's voice gently soothed as sweetly as

his hands on her back.

"Hmmm?"

"How did you get trapped in the closet?"

Holly had seen hypnotists several times to help her with her fear of being trapped, especially in high places. Their voices weren't half as enchanting as Edan's voice. Anything he wanted to know, up to and including her weight program start weight, she'd tell him.

Heck, Holly thought sleepily, she'd even tell him where she kept her hidden stash of chocolate covered caramel bars. She might even share. Maybe.

"Holly, the closet?"

"Oh, um, not sure." Holly muffled a yawn against his shirt. He smelled so damn good; sandalwood and wildflowers with spring rain. "I'd just finished sweeping and wanted to straighten some of the closet shelves and check supplies before I put the broom away. Rat had one of his terrycloth toys and was running back and forth and barking playing some doggy chase game. He must have hit the door because it banged shut. When I turned around to open it, I realized the broom had fallen across it and it was wedged tight."

Momentarily, the terror of being trapped stabbed through her again. But at her shiver, Edan's hands smoothed along her spine. His heart beat firmly against hers. Her body rose up and down with his breathing.

"I'm glad you came back."

"I am glad also." Edan rolled slightly keeping Holly pressed tightly to him with one arm while he fumbled on the floor for the velvet bag. He still ached for joining, but he could feel Holly relaxing.

He refused to be part of a dragon project. When he and Holly joined it would be because they both wanted to, not because her dragon was enhancing Holly's and his pheromones.

Holly's dragon, still on the back of the couch, hissed softly at Rat who nosed the bag to Edan's hand.

"Thank you, Rat." In Elvish, Edan told the dragon, "You and I shall talk later."

The dragon's color still held the amethyst overtones of distress, with flashes of the plum of embarrassment. It flowed downward and settled itself against Holly's neck occasionally giving Edan's hand swipes with its dry tongue as though apologizing.

Edan settled on his side, giving Holly room to lie beside him on the couch. Still holding her, he held the bag in front of her. "I have brought you a gift."

"Really?" Holly sat up abruptly, but Edan managed to catch her before she fell off the couch. "You didn't have to bring me anything."

Hearing the pleasure in her voice, seeing her eagerness in opening the bag, Edan realized her statement was a null comment. Of course, he didn't have to bring her anything, but her pleasure gave him deep satisfaction.

The silver chain sparkled, but not as brightly as Holly's eyes. They held the same depths of color as the moss agate.

"Oooh, I love dragons! Thank you."

"Yes, I saw the dragons at your house." Edan sent Holly's familiar a warning glare.

Holly's smile contained enough joy to please Edan. But, not being a fool, he certainly didn't push her away when she pressed her lips to his.

Gentle and sweet, Holly's kiss touched a part of Edan he was surprised to find invoked by a human female. The protective part of him wanted to keep her safe forever. Yes, his body still wanted her, throbbed for her, but now he also wanted to take care of her, to keep her happy, and never again hear her heart-tearing sorrow.

With this kiss, Holly led the way. It didn't surprise

him when she ended it, then pulled away to lean against him. As he suspected, the emotional whirlwind of panic at being trapped, the extreme distress in the closet, and the giddiness of relief at being rescued had combined to leave her tired. Now she seemed quite content and happy to watch the moss agate heart glimmer in the light at the length of its silver chain.

Yes, Edan had regrets the sexual animal part of Holly had retreated. But it made him angry that the damned dragon had been the one to aggravate Holly into hormonal overload. She didn't really want to Join at this moment; she just didn't want to be alone. He'd suspected as much earlier which was why, despite the dragon's interference, he'd forced himself to limit himself to kissing her while he wouldn't let his hands move past her collarbone.

If he wanted he could have her naked or even take her with a minimum of her clothes off. But it would be a Taking, not a Joining. Being human, Holly would know no difference, but he would know. And he would not Take Holly's body. He would wait until she was ready to Join, and not when the dragon pushed them together.

Edan knew he wouldn't die of sexual frustration, he would just feel like it. But he was male and had enough sense of himself to want Holly to want *him*, Edan. Not just because he happened to be an Elf she summoned. Not because the dragon provoked the mating scents in them both. But because he was who he was, Edan, a Prince of De'erjia.

Rat put his paws on Holly's knees and whined.

"What's the matter, boy?"

"Perhaps he needs to go outside."

Holly looked at the large round clock on the wall. "It's time to go home. It's suppertime."

Edan rose and took Holly's hand to help her upright. "Would you like me to help you put that on?" He indicated her agate heart.

"Why?" Holly looked at the chain's clasp. "Does it need a special spell to unlock the clasp?"

"Um, no. It shouldn't. Daffodil knows you are mortal. She knows I will not remain. In all likelihood, she enhanced the stone's powers, but she would have made it easy for you to wear when I am not here."

Holly's eyes dimmed momentarily. She released the clasp and laid the necklace around her throat. She smiled as the moss agate settled into the hollow of her throat when she'd rejoined the clasp.

Edan could almost see the stone's resonance accept Holly's grief and send healing vibrations through her skin in synchronization with the pulse point of her throat. He knew Daffodil had picked the stone for its colors to match Holly's eyes, but some part of Daffodil's Power had sensed the tones of Holly's depression and enhanced the moss agate to help her.

"I'm not going to ask who Daffodil is. I can guess she's a former lover." Mischief danced in Holly's eyes when she touched the stone. "Please thank her for me when you see her again."

Edan bowed at Holly. "Of course. She will be pleased. What is 'suppertime'? The evening meal?"

"Yes, of course. Hmm, are we bringing your dog home with us?"

"Of course. How is she doing?"

"Come and see. I think I have a portable cage we can use to crate her until we can get a crate at the store."

"Is a crate like what Rat was in this morning?" With a shock Edan realized he had only been summoned by Holly's wish less than twenty-four of the human hours ago. His life had been so drastically altered in such a short period of time. He almost had trouble remembering when Holly wasn't been part of his existence.

No, he could not stay. He still missed his mother.

Thinking back to the nuances of his father's speech and body language, he realized his father missed her with greater intensity than he did. He would not spend Eternity missing Holly. He would leave before he bonded tighter with Holly.

Yet, when he looked into his dog's eyes, he realized he had to remain longer. Fear still shone in the deep brown orbs. The pain of betrayal and loss dulled eyes that should have been bright like Rat's. This sad, frightened dog would not yet be able to cope with the passage between realms.

"Holly," Edan fondled the dog's ears. He realized had to bond with her and learn her name. "Must she stay in the kitchen like Rat?"

"Actually," Holly knelt beside Edan rubbing the dog's shoulder. The dragon also leaned on the dog, although Rat had stayed in the doorway at Holly's command. "Rat's crate is usually in my bedroom. I'd put the crate in the kitchen while I was cooking dinner. When I got home, I left him in the kitchen last night because I was, um, a little drunk."

Edan raised an eyebrow at her.

Holly laughed. "Okay, I was a lot drunk. I was also horny and being carried by an Elf. Moving Rat's crate wasn't high on my priority list."

"Ah, good. I know the hunters in De'erjia sleep with their dog packs as they train them. I think she will bond with me sooner if she and I sleep together as a pack."

"Oh."

At the sound in Holly's voice, Edan looked at her. For a moment he saw intense disappointment, then she lifted her lips in a bittersweet smile. "That makes sense."

"I have to have her tightly bonded with me so she will trust me completely when we return to De'erjia," he explained. "I need to spend as much time with as possible with her before I take her back."

"Right," Holly said. "I understand."

Edan didn't like the forced cheerfulness in Holly's voice, but she needed to understand.

"Holly, do you remember your wish of this morning? That you wished I would return to De'erjia."

"Of course."

He would not touch Holly. He didn't know if this nearly overpowering urge to hold her and stroke her until she was wet enough so he could bury himself in her came from inside him or from the dragon yet again. He knew though, if he touched her, he would become inflamed with her and would Take her on this hard floor. No, until he had time to make it perfectly clear to the dragon that he would not tolerate its interference he would not touch Holly.

"Do you remember *why* you wished me to return?"

In a small voice, as reluctant as one of the small children in his father's care who admitted an error, Holly said, "Because I want a human to love me and marry me and have children with me."

"Yes, Holly. And I am not human. I am Elf. You wish a life-partner and children. As Elf, it expends much more magic than I have in my Power to command to father a child. Plus I do not want the responsibility of fathering a part-Elf child. I cannot stay and help raise a child that is mortal rather than Elf. My life-force runs at a different pace than mortals. If the child were to inherit Elf powers, I would not want to be forced to remove the child from you and take it to De'erjia."

Holly stood abruptly, her fists clenched in rage. "You would never take my child from me."

"If the child was Elf rather than mortal, I would have to," Edan informed her coolly. He knew for her own sake she had to know this. He would not risk breaking her heart. "Elf life-force is slower than mortal. If you gave birth to an Elf child, by the time the child reached the age of the child Rob, you would be a crone. By the age of the youth Jon, you would be long dead of old age. An Elf child cannot live with mortals, it ages too slowly. Mortals live short, fast lives. When they die, they move Beyond. Elves live longer, slower, but they do not go Beyond. They simply fade into the Mists of time and legend."

"We don't have to have a child. I'm not expecting you to stay forever. Like you said, we have now. And now is good enough for me. You promised we'd have sex. You used the word 'join' and said we would join again tonight. Buddy, there ain't enough room in my bed for you, me, and a Komondor."

At the thought of burying himself between Holly's legs again, Edan's body, already pushed almost beyond his control, nearly exploded. Then he saw the dragon begin to pulse with the blue tones of Power. No, he would not be subjected to a dragon's manipulations. Grimly, he held onto his few shreds of control.

"I will not be the life-partner you wish," he told Holly between gritted teeth. He absolutely could not give in to the dragon's enticements, to his own base instincts. He was Elf. He was strong. "I will not give you the child of your heart's desire. I am returning to De'erjia when this dog of mine is able to travel with me. We should not Join again."

"Yeah, yeah, you keep saying that. But I didn't notice you hanging back this morning. You did everything you could to have sex this morning. You made me come in the entry room of my studio. I nearly made you come in the grooming area. Why are you stopping now?"

Edan heard the raw hunger in her voice. The dragon pulsed to a deeper sapphire.

In Elvish, he hissed at it, "Do not use your Power. I do not know your motives, but I will not be a party to coercion of either her or me. If you want us to Join, you will stop interfering. We shall Join of our own free will or not at all. I shall return to De'erjia immediately, without the dog, before I will allow you to force her or me to be participants in whatever you Dragons are now contemplating. You were the one playing with Rat and made the broom fall and block the door to trap and frighten her. I will not tolerate this behavior. Go. Tell the Dragon Masters I have spoken my last warning on this."

The dragon faded to the pale violet of distress and left the plane.

"Edan?" Holly spoke so softly he almost couldn't hear her. But then again, he had such anger at Dragons roaring through him all his other senses were muffled. He almost wished he could flare like Dragons. He knew one he'd like to burn to a crisp.

Edan's anger faded as he looked at Holly's troubled face. "I am sorry. I am not angry with you. But the situation between us is difficult now. When I was in De'erjia, it took very little effort to reach you through the planes and realms. We have bonded. If we Join again, we will bond tighter. Then when I leave, which we both know I must do, it will be very difficult to remove the memories."

"Why would you take away the memories?"

Now that the dragon was gone, Edan could sense the immediate decrease in Holly's pheromones. He was pleased about that, he assured himself.

"Because I am Elf. I do not belong here. Your memories of me will be erased as will mine of you. Otherwise, the bonding between us will cause us both distress where we can only reach each other through dreaming. The deeper the bonding, the more difficult it is to purge the memories."

"Completely erased?"

"I think some residue remains. Much the same as when you think of, oh, memories of a childhood friend whom you have not seen in many of your years. You remember a few minor incidents. You remember the affection. But you don't remember details."

"Have you been through this before?"

"No, I've never had a mortal lover before. I only know what has been told me by others."

"Oh. Well." Holly shrugged as though she were no longer interested in the subject. She clipped a leash onto Edan's dog's collar. "Let's get the dogs settled at my place and eat dinner."

Edan led his dog while Rat followed Holly about the grooming and boarding studio. All the boarding animals had been settled into cleaned pens while Holly explained Jon would return once more to walk the dogs in the late evening.

He mentally cursed his body's still unassuaged hunger for Holly. Why he couldn't just give in and let the dragon manipulate them, he didn't know. He hoped Holly believed his convoluted explanation about bonding and sex. He should refer to the explanation by its proper name; a lie.

If they both wanted, they could Join without increasing the bonding. He just didn't want to give Dragons further satisfaction by acceding to the affair they'd manipulated. His life was his, not theirs to meddle in. Holly's life was hers. If the two of them decided they wanted more, then they would have it on their terms.

But until he either discovered why Dragons were so interested in Holly or that Holly truly desired him for himself rather than at her dragon's urgings, he would keep his distance from her. He told himself he could admire without touching. Maybe.

And maybe the Sun would rise in the West.

Edan wrapped his hand tighter around his dog's leash so he could not reach forward and stroke the soft roundness of Holly's rump swaying in front of him while they walked to the car.

Once again he reminded himself he would not fade

into the Mists simply from unquenched sexual frustration. He'd only feel like it.

Holly's rump stayed within inches of his itching palms when she leaned in and set up a harness system in the back seat of her little car. She showed him how to contain his dog in it then serenely moved to the other side to drive.

Glumly, Edan realized he would be throbbing with lust the entire time he stayed with Holly. It was not fair. Females could always compartmentalize their sexual hunger and ignore them. Males ended up putting their sexual hunger on display for anyone who happened to look at their crotches. It absolutely was not fair.

CHAPTER 7

It absolutely was not fair, Holly thought sourly. For most of two days and now two nights, she'd lived in a blur of hormonal frustration compounded with exhaustion from the last of the preliminary grooming for the show dogs. But did Edan show any of the aching agony she was experiencing? Noooo, he just calmly went about doing the jobs she assigned him and training his dog under her instructions.

After a second night of tossing and turning with Edan and his dog in the other small bedroom and just a wall away, she gave up and dug out her vibrator.

She used her fingers to prime her clit, then switched on her favorite. She separated her folds to insert the vibrator when Edan knocked once then entered her bedroom. Hastily, she scrambled for her sheets.

"You're supposed to wait until you're told you can come in," she snarled while she switched off the vibrator. He stood there entirely too calmly for her over-strung hormones wearing the boxers he'd chosen after he had examined the zipper in the blue jeans and decided its metal teeth might catch and hurt him. At the time, *she'd* wanted to catch him in *her* teeth. Now she just wanted to hurt him – um – maybe not, she realized when she saw the bulge against the soft cotton boxers silhouetted in the morning light.

"I didn't know what that noise was. I was concerned another bad faery had come to plague you." His hair hung in thick waves to his bare shoulders. He folded arms corded with muscle over abs that could grace an exercise machine commercial. What body hair he had tufted under his arms and curled softly, but sparsely, around flat nipples. But below his navel the dark hair pointed the trail to what the boxers only barely hid.

"Nobody here but me. Go away." *Or come closer and let me eat that bulge.*

He tilted his head and slightly furrowed his eyebrows. His dark eyes narrowed as though he would pull out her secrets as easily as he could pull the covers from her naked body. Her breasts throbbed at the thought of Edan seeing her naked again. Maybe that would finally push him to the breaking point.

She shifted slightly so most of one breast was exposed. She not quite casually caught the sheet just before her nipple popped out to say "Good Morning."

"But what was that odd hum?" He didn't move closer to the bed.

Damn it.

He stood just slightly inside the doorway as though she were an animal he wasn't quite sure he could trust. If he didn't come closer and strip off those damn boxers, she'd show him animal. She knew the way the bulge grew he was interested.

"Nothing. Go. Away." *If he wasn't going to fuck her, then she at least wanted to use her vibrator in privacy.*

Or maybe not.

"Are you all right?"

The deep concern in his voice touched a tender part of Holly's heart. The horny part of her just wanted to get boinked.

"I'll be fine," Holly said with sweet innocence. "Just as soon as I come."

"Come where?"

Holly adored it when Edan didn't have a clue what she was talking about.

"Come to orgasm," she explained with the kindness of dealing with an idiot male who obviously needed direct visual instructions. "Since you are the great strong Elf and too concerned about my fragile human emotions if we *Join and Bond too tightly...*"

Did he catch the sarcasm? Good, she saw a barely there flinch.

Holly continued, "I'm going to give myself some relief."

She flipped the sheet back from her body. She didn't care if all the fat bulges and cellulite showed. She wanted Edan and wanted him now. Only a very odd male gave a damn about hip saddle bags and pot-bellies as long as the woman was naked and willing.

Edan's eyes widened and his boxers developed an interesting tent pole. He didn't move any closer, but he didn't leave either.

Her nipples puckered tighter. She wouldn't need her fingers any longer. Her honey pooled between her legs at Edan's heated stare.

"This," she brandished her vibrator like a sword at Edan, "is my vibrator. Watch and see what I can do with it."

She switched it on. It hummed sweetly at her. Her nipples tightened into rocks, while her clit slid more warm wetness between her thighs. She'd never used her vibrator in front of a male before. A voyeur in the room with her made her light-headed with anticipation.

Rat whined in his crate.

"Quiet, Rat."

"Would you like me to let him outside for you?"

And have you leave the room and give me time to think about this and chicken out?

"No, he'll be fine. Watch, but no touching." Hell, as long as she was going to do this in front of him, she might as well make him truly miserable. "Straddle the chair there and keep your hands on the chair back."

Never taking his eyes from Holly's body, Edan did she commanded.

Holly started plucking her nipples with her free hand and slid the vibrator up and down her wet folds while Edan watched. She saw Edan's fascination with her body and triggered a mini-orgasm.

She rode its small quakes and realized she would be able to send herself into mind-blowing spaces she'd never reached on her own before, if she didn't wuss out and quit. Never would she have dreamed she was a total exhibitionist.

She parted her folds. The vibrator slid into her channel, hard and smooth. Advertise what they would, these never felt quite as good as when a man penetrated her. Or maybe it was that she liked her legs wrapped around a man's body while he thrust high and deep in her.

She watched Edan lick his lips, then swallow hard. His fingers flexed as though he felt her in spite of the chairback between them.

She spread her legs farther apart and thumbed up the vibrator's speed. She slipped it in and out. Her breath caught at the sheer pleasure of the machine's friction against her vaginal walls and clitoris. She stopped a moan then thought, why bother?

At the next crest of orgasmic wave, she twisted her nipple tightly when the vibrator shook against her clitoris. She sighed a moan of pleasure. She watched Edan's hands tremble and he exhaled sharply at her moan.

Her body began to shake in anticipation. She was going to come and she hadn't even hit the super-speed level.

Edan's lips pressed tightly together and he lifted his hands from the chair's back.

"Don't touch yourself," Holly ordered. Her body nearly had a spasm at the abrupt stop just before orgasmic surge. Damn, damn, damn.

Holly panted in frustration.

"Holly?"

"This is *my* show," she said between harsh breaths.

"You keep telling me you don't want to *Join* because you don't want us to bond more tightly. So you just sit there and watch what you're missing. Because you're not touching me *and* you're not touching yourself either."

"Holly, as much as I ache to touch you, I find myself anxious to watch you continue. However, your machine is hurting my ears and Rat's also. He is whining."

"Hell. Sit there," Holly ordered.

She switched off her vibrator, threw it on the bed, and stalked naked to Rat's cage. She released the latch and called him to heel. She went to her window, jerked apart the curtains, and opened the window. With a whistle to the Chihuahua, she patted the windowsill. Rat happily hopped up then jumped the foot and a half to the deck. In the back part of the fenced acreage, Edan's dog patrolled the perimeter. Orange Crush meowed a guttural "Good Morning" from the deck railing.

"Holly?"

"What?" She turned back to Edan who remained as rigid as a statue on the chair.

"Could you leave the curtains opened when you continue? Your body looks so beautiful glowing in the sunlight."

His whisper, husky with sexual hunger, stroked her skin with the softness of the morning breeze through the opened window. Her nipples tightened as though his tongue had licked across them instead of the wind. The admiration in Edan's voice floated across Holly's body as sweetly as the scent of the flowers blooming in the pots on the deck. She tightened her pectoral muscles so her breasts lifted proudly and shut the window most of the way so Rat wouldn't jump back inside.

She turned around to walk back to the bed. His eyes raked across her swaying hips and the tight curls over her mons with the same heat as the sunlight streaming across her backside. She could imagine his hands hot and wanting cupped around the globes of her buttocks.

No, she'd told him not to touch. Not this time. His hands remained empty and taut on the chair's back.

She sashayed past him. It had been a long time since she'd felt this confident, this pure joy in feeling sexy and desirable.

The unbridled lust and anticipation in his eyes, the tension in his body and his quickened breathing sent her into a mini-orgasm at the mere friction of her thighs rubbing together while she walked across the room. She was so wet she could almost feel the moisture sliding down her legs.

Hastily, she grabbed cotton balls from her make-up vanity.

"Here," she held them out at arm's length. "Cram these in your ears to block the sound, but don't put your hands over your ears. I've seen what happens to you when those tips are touched."

"Perhaps you should put this cotton in my ears so I am not tempted to touch them myself."

Hot fudge topping sliding, melting down a mound of ice cream couldn't be any sweeter than the moisture heating and pooling between her own thighs.

Time slowed as Holly took the cotton balls from Edan's fingers being very careful not to brush his skin. She twisted one side of one ball thinking of her nipple being toyed with by Edan's long fingers. She watched Edan's face while she did it, fully aware of his eyes level with her breasts.

Her nipple knotted at a cool breeze. Edan had blown across its heated throbbing.

At her glare, Edan said, with the mocking innocence of a child snitching a cookie, "You told me not to touch. You didn't tell me I couldn't blow."

Holly pushed the cotton ball plug into Edan's ear

canal. She leaned over and delicately licked the outer shell and swirled her tongue around the tip.

Edan gave a deep groan. "You said you wouldn't touch."

"I said *you* couldn't touch. I didn't say *I* wouldn't."

She brushed a nipple across his lips and didn't quite pull away when his tongue darted out to wet it.

"May I?"

"Only your mouth," she qualified.

Edan suckled her nipple deep into the dark wetness of his mouth. Holly began to regret her rule of no touching. She slowly, patiently twisted the second cotton ball, then offered him her other nipple while she inserted the cotton ball into his other ear.

That done she gave herself up to the pleasure of his mouth suckling her nipple. She grasped a rung of the ladder-back chair. The solid oak gave her something to hold onto while her legs turned to rubber.

Her pussy throbbed for the same attention. Maybe. Maybe.

No, first she'd take herself with Edan watching her then she'd offer herself to his mouth.

And, if he was real lucky and asked pretty, please, she'd take the solid length of him into her own mouth.

Languidly, she moved away from his mouth and to the bed. She lay back and pulled her knees up and apart. Keeping her eyes on Edan's avid gaze, she switched on her vibrator, and pulled apart the lips of her labia. Her fingers slipped in the sticky wetness. The vibrator slid in with a purr.

She slid it in and out and thumbed up the power. There were times she wished she could just lie here and slide the vibrator back and forth for hours. It felt so damn good. The solid width and length hummed against her inner skin and sent jolts of pre-orgasm from her clitoris. Yes, sometimes she wanted to do this for hours.

This wasn't one of those times.

Her wet nipples still ached for more of Edan's mouth. His eyes raked hot across her body from her head to toes beginning to curl with anticipation. The thought of his mouth on her, those ear points rubbing the tender skin of her inner thighs while his hair brushed against her sent her hormones and brain into overdrive.

Within moments, the orgasm began to shake through her. She thumbed the power to super and thrust it higher and deeper while her legs shook.

Dimly she heard Edan's breath grow harsh and panting in rhythm with hers. She was close, so close. The pleasure from her G-spot focused all of her attention on that one center of her physical being. The head of the vibrator pressed solidly against it. The pulses slammed into her until the thrusts of her hips bounced against the mattress. Everything blurred into the slick heat and intensity of pure energy.

She flashed to the top of the crest and knew Edan was with her, aching, burning, throbbing, but still not giving into his own body's demands. She knew she had only to say the word and he would bury himself in her. But he would keep control until she gave him permission to join her.

The hot fire consumed her and the essence of herself flew along the crest propelled by the knowledge that Edan watched and thrilled with her body even though his own body strained to accompany her.

She exploded into flames and became one with the center of everything, pulsing with life, shaking with joy. She shrieked at the pure ecstasy of creation and willingly accepted the little death.

When her body stopped shaking and her screams had mellowed to muffled moans of pleasure, she switched off the vibrator. She withdrew it from her vagina and tossed it to the end of the bed.   She stretched with contentment and smiled at Edan.

Strain etched Edan's sharp cheekbones and tight lips. His eyes glittered with barely restrained energy. His hands white-knuckled the chair back. Through the ladder back rungs, Holly could see his penis throbbing against his boxers.

"Edan," Holly could barely breathe, much less talk. "I'm not as fragile as you think. Yes, I'll miss you when you leave. Yes, it'll probably break my heart. But, you know what? Part of living is dealing with the pain that happens in life. I'll take the joy of being with you now and deal with the pain when I have to."

Edan watched in fascination as Holly stretched, damp with the heady scent of satisfied sex. He glanced at the dragon. Its chartreuse held no tints of the blues of Power.

While he knew the dragon hadn't enhanced Holly's aroma and wasn't actively trying to force them together, he still felt somewhat uneasy about Joining with Holly. The Dragons had some plan in motion and Edan still didn't want to be a part of it.

Stiffly, he rose from the chair. Much as he wanted to join Holly on the bed, to join with her body, this was not the time.

He left the bedroom and shut the door.

"You asshole!" Holly shrieked. Something hit the door with a bang then a crumbling shatter of pottery.

Edan supported himself against the wall as he made his way to the bathroom. He hadn't realized how much pain it would cause for him to leave Holly. Not only could he barely walk, something in him had twisted in agony at the sound of Holly's ranting. He drew a bit of consolation that she wasn't weeping.

Edan saw his rueful smile in the bathroom mirror as he shut the door behind him. There had been a few times when he made an Elven woman so angry she'd cried. He'd ducked and run at that point. Furious females held danger in their tears.

He started the shower, discarded the cotton plugs in his ears, and stripped off his under shorts. His penis throbbed, hot, red, and angry. He stroked it with one hand, trying to soothe himself. Yes, yes, he could have slaked himself in Holly's happy body, but he still wanted to know why the Dragons were manipulating them. Why did Dragons believe they had the right to meddle in the affairs of Elves?

Edan lifted the slippery drape that protected the floor from the shower's water and stepped into the tub letting the drape fall into place behind him. He twisted the shower's nozzle to send the hard, pulsating beads of water across his skin.

He poured some bathing soap into his palm. The soap wouldn't be as hot and slick as Holly's welcome woman-passage. However, his hand slid slowly around his penis giving it what little succor the slick soap and warm water could offer.

He heard a click, then the creak of the bathroom door opening. Puzzled, he reached for the drape just as Holly opened it.

His penis throbbed viciously in his palm. It demanded Holly's body, not his hand with nothing more than soap and water.

"Hi," Holly said with a smile. She sat on the edge of the tub and crossed one leg over the other.

Edan caught a glimpse of the deep, brown thatch of curls covering her mons. Holly firmly tucked the dark blue terrycloth robe around her legs hiding herself from his view.

She had the robe firmly tied around her waist and only a small portion of the creamy V between her round breasts showed. At the hollow of her throat, the moss agate heart with its silver dragon rose and fell with her breathing.

"I figured since you watched me come, I could watch you."

Edan swallowed hard and his penis twitched in his hand. Dignity, he still had some dignity. He thought.

"You invited. No, you ordered me to watch you. I did not ask if I could watch."

Holly's smile changed to a smirk worthy of a smug Dragon. "I ordered you to sit in the chair and not touch either me or yourself. You are not a slave. You don't have to obey anything I say. You chose to sit in the chair and watch me.

"Now I choose to sit here," the underside band of the silver dragon ring she wore on one index finger chimed on the porcelain tub, "and watch you jack off."

"Jack?"

"From ejaculate. Slap the weenie until it pops. Wring yourself out. Hand wash until you hose the wall. Get to it, Edan. You watched me. I want to watch you."

Not understanding the majority of Holly's babble, Edan decide to seize on the few words that made sense. She really did want to sit and watch him pleasure himself the way he had watched her.

"And you will not touch yourself or touch me unless I give you permission."

Edan watched Holly swallow. A bead of water trickled down the side of her face. Whether it was from the hot water's steam or Holly's own moisture, Edan did not care. It took reserves of strength he didn't know he had to not lean out and trace the droplet's path with his tongue.

"Yeah. Right," Holly said. Her eyes held a mischievous sparkle Edan had learned boded no good for him.

Edan eyed the sash holding her robe together. Quickly, using Elven speed, Edan untied the sash, wound one end around Holly's hands, and looped the other end over the drapery rod above the tub edge.

"Hey," Holly's indignant tone had her dragon in the bathroom to see what the problem was. "How did you do that?"

Her arms now stretched over her head. The robe gapped open and revealed Holly's body with its soft muscles and glowing skin. Looking at her, Edan had a sudden vision of a blue china bowl filled with the first summer peaches in a pool of fresh cream. He wanted to eat her the way he savored the sweet fruit.

"Oh. Eat. I finally understand what you meant by wanting to eat me," Edan said with pleasure, adding to himself, *and why Sir laughed.* "I didn't realize you meant to pleasure one another with our mouths."

"Duh," Holly stuck her tongue out at him.

Edan's shaft pulsed at the thought of Sir's suggestion that Holly use chocolate when she ate him. The look on her face whenever she ate chocolate was almost as glorious as the look on her face when she crested as she pleasured herself. He stroked down his shaft imagining it dripping with chocolate and Holly's tongue licking it clean.

Perhaps he would coat Holly's body with the coffee ice cream she'd bought him. Then he could have both coffee and Holly's cream. It would be as good as a latte.

"How'd you tie me up so fast and why? I didn't tie you up. It's not fair."

"I tied you up because this way I know you will not touch yourself. I did it quickly because I used Elven speed. You can easily get loose should you choose. It is only a slipknot and just looped around the bar. But if you choose to stay and watch me, you will not remove the ties. I sat in the chair. You can stand like that."

Edan continued his slow strokes up and down himself while the water added its caress against his skin. He looked at Holly's dragon humming in contentment. In

Elvish, he commanded, "You go away. I will not have you influencing her or me. This is our pleasure not yours. I can still return to De'erjia."

With one last head rub against Holly's knee and colored with a trace of amethyst embarrassment, the dragon popped into a different plane.

"What did you say?" The breathlessness in Holly's voice sent tremors through him.

"Just reminding myself of the pleasure of remaining here rather than returning to De'erjia."

At Holly's widened eyes, Edan stroked himself again. He stifled his groan when his first bit of cum surged slickly onto his palm.

He heard Holly's breath hitch and saw her shrug one shoulder. The robe snagged on her nipple, just keeping Edan from seeing the fruit he wanted to suckle.

He could wait. Maybe.

He stroked himself harder. His penis pulsed with its own life.

He wanted Holly's smaller hands on him, her mouth sucking him instead of just his soapy hand rubbing.

But Holly had taken herself to the crest with her machine and his eyes on her. He had ridden the flash wave with her. It would only be fair for him to take her with him on his solo flight.

Edan could feel her hungry eyes devouring him. He rubbed harder and faster, wanting the crest, wanting Holly with him.

"Slow down." Holly's voice slid through his ears as sweetly as her hands had slid through his hair and across his skin the first night they'd joined after her wish. "You're moving your hand too fast. I want to watch."

Obediently, Edan shifted his psyche from Elven back to human normal. Holly's hair curled in tight ringlets around her damp face bracketed by her upraised arms. Her face glowed with passion and want.

What if he found something more sturdy to tie her arms to? Would she allow him to Join with her while she hung from it unable to touch him?

He would sew strips of the softest leather he had into a bundle. He saw himself lightly stroking her body with the ribbons of leather from the crown of her head to her pretty toes curling under the robe's blue hem. But in his vision she would wear nothing but the moss agate heart.

He could see the leather slide around each breast stopping long enough at each peak to coax it to a tight knot. He would trace the globes of her backside with the soft leather occasionally letting the ribbons slide into the parting of the two and underneath her, between her legs.

Holly's gasp of pleasure shot through him as though she could feel the leathers sliding and cradling her. But no, she still hung there in the bathroom devouring him with her eyes.

He would slowly, deliberately brush the feathery strips against her tight hairs and slide them between her legs until her own moisture dampened them. Then he would kneel and suckle her until she began to crest with her orgasm. As he joined her on the crest, he would lift her and Join into One with her.

At the thought of Holly's body, tight, wet, pulsing with life around his shaft, his own crest caught him. He shot into the bright blue skies, then into the stars. He knew the brightness that was Holly pulsed and joined with him while the spasms of his orgasm pumped and arced his infertile cum against the tub's tile work.

His cresting began to spiral downward as the shower washed his spray down the drain. Once again he momentarily mourned his infertility – no, not infertility – just not able to sire a child. He would not sire a part-Elf child. He knew no Elven females with whom he could form or even wanted to form a bond to endure the long tenure to go through the trials and tests to create the Magick to form a New Being from Two.

As he once again left his own introspection behind, he dimly became aware of a deep blue spot of sorrow in Holly's joy. He probed cautiously, not wanting to startle Holly and break the threads that formed their One. They would unravel soon enough for his cresting had begun to spiral downward to the final spasms. He had to know if the sorrow originated because of his actions.

No, the regret in Holly came not because they were not Joined physically. She sparkled and soared along his crest with almost as much joy as he did.

Holly's blue sadness threaded throughout her being. Something in Holly's past had left its grieving mark on her. It was permanently imbedded in her and would forever be part of her soul. It mattered not what anyone said or did, she had learned to live with it and she would always mourn; much as the knowledge he would never recreate himself always ached within him.

Gradually, he became aware of Holly's life threads sliding away from him and back into her own being. He felt the shower spray sting his skin with cold water.

"Well," Holly said with a tug on the robe's sash. As he'd told her, the sash promptly uncoiled and released her upright arms. "This has been fun. Kind of. Sort of. Definitely interesting. Unfortunately, we have to get dressed and be on our way or we'll be late."

Holly's lips quirked and her eyes sparkled. "Maybe sometime you can get over your asinine attitude about *Joining* and we can have a little fun together."

"Perhaps tonight." *If the damned Dragon stays away,* Edan added silently.

"Do you mean that?" The moss agate heart bumped against Holly's throat with her quickened breathing.

"I said *perhaps…*" The last of his crest shuddered though him. Or might it be a new crest wanting to arise? Absent-mindedly, he stroked himself once more, already firming at the thought of being One with Holly. Still drifting in the aftermath and anticipation of the future, he said, "Before we Join, I must have surety of some plans in the making."

Abruptly, he heard his words hang in the steamed air. He could not erase them or back up a few moments and not say them. He did not have that Power.

Holly narrowed her eyes at him. "What plans?"

"They are not plans of mine," he tried to reassure her. "Something else is making plans. I am trying to prevent their affairs from meddling in our lives."

"Who?"

"Now is not the time I can tell you. I can tell you only this, these beings are normally benevolent. Their intercession caused the success of your wish to bring me here."

"I wondered why I got a brunet elf. I had a yen for a long-haired blond elf. Guess we don't always get what we wish for." With that, Holly danced to her bedroom and firmly shut the door behind her.

Edan cooled the steam from the mirror with his breath. He looked at his damp, dark hair and muttered the drying phrases. He reached to pull his hair back in its usual band then looked again. With a word, he transformed his hair so it was wheat-colored like Daffodil's.

No, absolutely not. He looked pale and sickly. He turned his hair back to its natural color and nodded.

Yes, that was his image. Not that washed-out likeness that bore a striking resemblance to Daffodil.

Now why would Holly wish him to be blond? It was a puzzlement.

But if he could understand the female mind, he

would be more powerful than Dragons. He did not need to waste his time with Holly trying to understand her. He just needed to enjoy her.

Carrying his boxers, Edan went to his bedroom to pack the last of his belongings and collapse his dog's sleeping cage for their trip. Perhaps tonight, in the sleeping quarters they were assigned for the duration of the Dog Show, he and Holly might Join.

He gave a resigned look to his stiffly rising penis. Whether they Joined or not, he was going to ache all day. Then again, he thought with a disgruntled sigh as he tugged the boxers over the hard shaft and then coaxed it down so he could zip the blue jeans, why should today be different from any other day since Holly had summoned him?

Damned Dragons.

As if summoned, Holly's chartreuse dragon popped into the room holding the green velvet pouch Daffodil had used for Holly's necklace.

CHAPTER 8

Edan looked at Holly's dragon, the puce tinges of embarrassment still on its wingtips and around its muzzle. "Thank you for leaving us alone. For once. What are you doing with Holly's pouch?"

The dragon hopped onto Edan's bed. It nudged his elbow with the pouch. Edan took the limp bag from the dragon's mouth, avoiding its teeth.

The dragon gave a slight shimmy and scales scattered across the bed, catching in the sheets and blanket still wadded up from Edan's restless night. The dragon began to nose the small green scales into a pile. It pushed its muzzle against the bag in Edan's hand, then the scales.

Obediently, Edan scooped up the scales and dropped them one by one into the bag. Since the dragon was small, its scales were also small, the largest just half the size of his littlest fingernail.

But the sheer number staggered him. Dragons only gave up their scales occasionally. Elves and other Beings valued them greatly, not only for the protective magick they invoked for the wearer, but for their sheer beauty. One of the crown bands worn by the King was shaped from the single scale of a Master Dragon.

Edan knew the few times Daffodil included dragon scales in her work she rarely used more than one scale per jewelry design. Usually jewelry that included a dragon scale went to a Council member or the King or another member of the Community who had sacrificed much for the good of all.

Now Edan placed nearly two dozen scales in the small bag while the dragon rummaged through the bedclothes to confirm it had retrieved all its scales. Careful to keep his grin off his face, Edan decided to annoy Holly's dragon.

"I thank you for these." Edan bowed to the dragon. "I shall treasure them all my life."

The dragon hissed and darkened into emerald. The room filled with the odor of burnt basil indicating the dragon's ire as much as its color and noise did.

"Oh," sighed Edan with mock disappointment and inward chuckling, "these are not for me?"

The dragon flashed a quick, bright yellow much like the aura that surrounded Holly then returned to the chartreuse Edan associated with it. Edan realized that Holly's dragon's color would probably be predominately green except for its contact with Holly. Its affinity for her was what made it chartreuse.

"All of these are for Holly?" Edan didn't bother to keep the disappointment out of his voice. He would have liked one for his memory well of Holly and her familiar, as annoying as her dragon was. Without Dragon intervention, he would never have met Holly.

From a crumpled wrinkle in the sheet, the dragon nosed two more scales to where the mound had been. Edan picked them up and opened the pouch. Before he could drop them in with the others, the dragon hissed and darkened to the color of pine on a fine summer morn.

Holding the two scales in his fingertips, confusion and daftness warred within Edan. He had no idea what the dragon wanted to convey, other than the scales didn't belong in the pouch with the others. He really needed to become more fluent in Dragon. He needed to acquire the skill in case – Edan shuddered at the thought – he was ever elected to Council and trained for a tenure as King. "Ah...what shall I do with these?"

The dragon placed its forepaws on Edan's arm, unfurling its wings to help maintain its balance as it raised itself on its back haunches. Keeping its eyes locked on Edan's, it used its dry tongue to scrape the two scales into the center of Edan's palm. Its tongue roughly wrapped around each of Edan's fingers pushing them closed until it had shaped Edan's hand into a fist.

"Mine?"

The dragon returned to its chartreuse state in affirmation.

"I thank you."

The dragon placed its muzzle on the pouch, looked intently at Edan, and exuded the scent of daffodils.

"Do you wish me to give these to my friend and have Daffodil shape Holly a piece of jewelry so she might wear these?"

The daffodil scent deepened.

"Shall Daffodil take her choice of these," Edan shook the bag, "in exchange for her favor of making Holly's jewelry for you?"

The dragon gave off the scent of cinnamon that Edan had come to realize meant agreement as well as pleasure.

"Then I shall take care of it for you."

The dragon hissed, faded out, then back in.

"I cannot go immediately. I must help Holly with the dogs."

The dragon's colors changed rapidly, its scents mingled from floral to fresh breads with the aroma of cooked meats.

Edan puzzled through all the colors and scents. "You will help Holly with the dogs?"

Again the dragon gave off the scent of cinnamon accord.

He shrugged. "Let me make sure she will be willing to make the drive by herself."

At the dragon's mixture of colors and scents, Edan soothed, "Yes, I realize you will be in the car with her, but she will not know that, will she?"

Edan took his dog's sleeping rug from her crate, glad

he'd earned her confidence enough to learn her name was Pook. He collapsed the crate and carried it, Pook's blanket, and his own pack to the kitchen where Holly was drinking coffee and eating breakfast grains.

He poured his own coffee and, unable to resist, lifted Holly's hair off her neck, and kissed the vulnerable skin, inhaling the fragrance of lemon verbena and sweet Holly. He traced each of her neck bones with his tongue then slid his lips across her jaw line to capture her mouth.

She opened to him, giving him access to her breath, her life force. She tasted of coffee and oatmeal with cream and strawberries. She tasted of womanpower, strong enough to send him to his knees to worship her body.

He could feel her joy encircle his tongue. The happiness showed him a brief glimpse of a future that would never be.

They would not have a future with Holly round with his child. They would not share a future of learning each other's nuances so they could communicate without words, but only with eyes and body language to express their pleasure in each other and their children. He would not be able to join her in the infinite Beyond.

Gently, Edan removed his mouth from Holly's, no longer wanting to feel the ache for what would not be. It was good the dragon wished him to immediately take the scales to Daffodil in De'erjia. He needed time to center himself, to remind himself he was Elf and De'erjia was his true home. He would not remain with a mortal.

"Holly–" He pulled a chair from its spot beside the table and sat facing her. "–would you be distressed if I were to return to De'erjia for but a short time? I promise I will return this afternoon."

A frown wrinkled Holly's forehead. "But I have to check into the hotel this afternoon and then go to the Arena to set up my grooming table for the first of the events in the morning. You won't know how to find me."

Edan stroked his thumb over the deep V between her eyes. "I came to you through the mists of time and the planes and realms the first time. I shall be able to find you again wherever you shall be."

Edan sipped his coffee, still cradling one of Holly's hands in his. "Can you drive to the city where the show is being held with both dogs in the car?

In Elvish, he said to the dragon bristling at him, "I know you will help her with the dogs. Quiet."

"Why do you talk Elvish sometimes? It's almost as though you're talking to someone else," Holly complained.

Despite Holly's surly tone, her fingers remained relaxed and secure within Edan's grasp. Edan decided she perhaps wasn't annoyed at his speaking Elvish. Perhaps she was but disappointed he would not be accompanying her this afternoon.

"I apologize. I was giving morning greeting to Orange Crush. Cats understand Elvish." The large marmalade-colored cat and the dragon looked at him with equal disdain at his dissembling.

Edan mentally shrugged. What was he supposed to do? Tell Holly about her dragon? As Holly was fond of saying, "I don't think so." Should the dragon wish Holly to be more aware of its presence in her life, rather than simply as a vague sense of being loved and protected, it must tell her. He did not have the right to inform her.

"Holly, the trip? You will not have problems in the vehicle with the dogs if I am not with you." Although he thought Holly would regard it as a question, he meant it as a promise and a reminder to the dragon.

Holly shrugged and finished spooning the last of her cereal into her mouth without releasing Edan's hand.

Edan drank his coffee while she chewed and swallowed then drank some of her own coffee.

"No, the dogs and I will be fine. You'll meet us at the hotel then?"

"Yes. I will help you load your car now then I will go. If all goes easily, I shall be at the hotel approximately at the same time you arrive."

They rinsed the few dishes, then packed the car with the dogs' necessities, their packs, and Holly's grooming tools. Crush had ample food and a clean box for the long weekend, plus Jon would come by to retrieve the mail and assure Crush he wasn't forgotten.

After Edan had placed Pook's security strap around her, reassured her he would return, and admonished the dragon to keep her calm, he turned to Holly. "I shall return."

Holly's arms came around his neck. Her warm, round body cuddled against his. He slid his arms around her, his hands cupping the globes of her denim covered rump.

She pressed herself tighter to him and his penis throbbed hard against her soft belly. Through the softness of his cotton shirt, her shirt, and breast bindings, he could feel the hard knots of her nipples straining for his hands, his mouth.

Her mouth devoured his, promising dreams and pleasures he'd never before experienced. Every female was different and Holly had a sweetness about her that Edan didn't want to lose. Perhaps this was why his father still mourned for his long-gone-Beyond lover who had been Edan's mother. This joyful, eager acceptance of life in its limited time span that Holly shared with her kiss, with her body undulating against his, might be the reason so many Elves took a mortal lover for a time. Holly showed him how to experience life, not just exist in it. Edan knew he would never be able to return to his Self as he had been before Holly summoned him to her. Part of him had changed and looked differently at how to live.

When Holly pulled away, Edan lowered his mouth

back to hers. He needed more. He couldn't let go of her now. He hungered for her. He burned for her.

He felt her hand rub his swollen crotch through the blue jeans. He pulsed against her small palm and reached down to undo the button and lower the zipper.

Now. He had to have her now. He wanted to Join with her here in the grass with the sun beating down on them, before the morning dew totally dissolved in the day's warmth.

Holly stopped his hand and spun from his arms. In a brief moment, she was in her car and reaching for the safety harness.

Still in a slow haze of lust hunger, Edan took the few steps to her car door. As he reached for the handle, Holly rolled down the window.

"You just make sure you come back, you hear? Perhaps we will continue this tonight." Holly mimicked his speech with laughter in her voice. "You do what you need to do in Derringer and I'll be waiting for you. Figure out whatever the hell is going on, because I'm getting awfully tired of not *Joining*. Kiss me good-bye?" Her rosebud lips puckered up.

Edan leaned down and Holly thrust her tongue in his mouth once more. Just as Edan began to reach for the car door determined to pull her from the vehicle and Join with her in the damp grass, Holly pulled her face away.

"More where that came from," she said with a giggle that chimed in his ears. "Come back soon."

She started her car and drove down her driveway to the small road that led to the highway.

Carrying the items he needed in a pack, Edan faded out of Holly's plane and into his own realm secure in the knowledge of the bond-threads between him and Holly. However painfully he throbbed, Holly also burned for him.

He took a deep breath outside Daffodil's abode. He

needed to regain control. He certainly didn't want his former partner teasing him about his sexual hunger.

When he had centered, somewhat, even though he knew he still reeked of frustration, he touched Daffodil's arrival notification. One of her Brownies immediately welcomed him into her home. Leaving his pack at the entry, he took a seat at the visitors' grouping of chairs and tables. He had barely sipped the warmed fruit juice a Brownie brought when Daffodil came into the room wearing a robe of translucent materials in shades of pink.

The layers of the robe floated around her. First it rounded over her thighs, then draped around her buttocks, to catch and outline each round handful, ripe for a male's grip as he thrust into her. The material fluttered in such a way that an onlooker caught a momentary glimpse of a deep rose nipple before the tantalizing display modestly disappeared once again. A glimpse of peach skin shimmered beneath two ribbons of robe revealing the soft juncture where her thighs met her body just before she sat in her chair.

And yet, as ripe as Daffodil's body was, as skilled as Edan knew her to be, he had no desire to Join with her. Instead, his memory sent him Holly's body covered in opaque denim and cotton that barely hinted at her curves beneath it. His mind's eye gave him the vision of Holly's body gleaming with the sheen of heated pleasure as she crested with the use of her machine and his eyes wanting her.

"How may I help you this glorious day, Edan?"

Edan withdrew Holly's velvet bag from his pants pocket, untied it, and poured the Holly's dragon's scales into his palm.

Daffodil's eyes widened with enchantment. "Oh, Edan."

She stirred through the glimmering pieces with the tip of one finger. "From Holly's dragon?"

"Yes. It wishes you to make Holly a piece of jewelry to wear. You may have your choice of these for doing this favor for it."

Daffodil's face had already taken on the distant visions of her Power gathering strength. Leaving the scales on Edan's palm, she continued to stir them with her finger.

The thin, remaining threads of their past Joinings gave Edan a slight knowledge of her thoughts. She collected the emissions of the dragon's thoughts through the scales: thoughts of Holly, itself in her life, of Edan in Holly's life, and of him in its life.

"A crown? No, not worn daily. It wants her to wear its offering daily. A ring is inappropriate, plus it would mar their shape and texture to shape them into a ring and there are too many. It would be too large for daily use. A necklace? No."

Daffodil looked at Edan with a delighted smile. "I am pleased she enjoys the necklace so much that she wears it daily."

Edan smiled back. "You added great power to the moss agate's vibrations. It brings her comfort. There is a thread of pain in her life that the moss agate eases."

Daffodil shrugged. "I put little into it that it did not already have. It bears her comfort because you gave it to her. Ah, a bracelet. I shall design a bracelet for Holly. When she sees it, she will think a dragon has coiled itself around her wrist."

Daffodil cupped her hands and Edan poured the scales into her palms.

"Gold? No, silver will accent these beauties more. Plus it will match her necklace."

"Her dragon wishes it done as soon as possible."

Daffodil hesitated. "I have some pieces I must finish."

"The dragon will not mind if you take some extra

scales for your trouble to explain the inconvenience to the others."

Daffodil stirred through the scales again. "Perhaps I can offer to set a scale in a piece for them. I shall inquire, but the primary problem, Edan, is it takes much Power to work with dragon scale."

Edan had seen Daffodil become gray after over-extension of Power. Her skin had turned the texture of badly cured leather with the clammy chill of fish ready to be cooked. Limp and exhausted, she had lain passive on their bower.

He would run his hands around her breasts until they warmed under his palms. He would kiss her skin and suckle her nipples until they'd pinked with life.

He'd separate her legs and lay his face against her most hidden, sweetest part of her body. He learned to start slowly to not cause her pain. First he simply breathed on her. As she warmed, he occasionally slid his tongue across her folds to soften the texture. He always enjoyed the sweet skin where her legs joined her torso, but more he enjoyed the taste of her female creams when they finally began to flow. Then he would suckle and nibble, caress and tease until her hips bucked wildly. Her Power would resurge then with a flash that shook her body and began her spiral upwards.

If she asked, he would Join with her, her spiral taking him upward with her, his pushing hers higher. If she didn't ask, he simply sent her to her crest knowing when he was exhausted and drained, she would service him with equal fervor.

But Edan hesitated. As much as he had enjoyed Daffodil, as much as he knew Holly's dragon wanted this done quickly, he could not bring himself to promise to help revitalize Daffodil's Power. Even now he could feel the threads of Holly's life entwining with his. He didn't want to bond fully with her, but he also didn't particularly want to get involved with Daffodil again.

Daffodil's face creased with laughter. "You're such a fool, Edan. I am not asking you. But I do want you to please go to Efran and inform him of this project."

"Efran?" Edan's thoughts scattered.

"Yes, Edan, tell Efran. Sometimes you are absolutely transparent. I am not expecting you to help me, but I do wish you to explain to Efran what I shall be doing. He is not planning to shape knives today, but please ask him to reserve his Power to help me."

Stunned at the thought of his father and Daffodil together, Edan tried to decide why it bothered him since both were full Elf and had known each other longer than his own life. They'd possibly joined before. But it just sounded – what was young Rob's word when describing his brother Jon kissing his girlfriend?

No, not a word. A sound. Icky. That was it.

It sounded icky that his father, *his father*, and Daffodil, *his former joined partner*, were together. Edan had participated in fertility ceremonies such as the one to occur in the near future. It mattered not with whom or how many joined in celebration, only a fertility couple would be able to create a new Life. Edan knew this. But *his father* and *Daffodil*? Ick.

Still, that was his opinion, not to be shared with either Daffodil or his father. Edan shuddered at the vision again.

Instead, he handed Daffodil his two dragon scales. "These are mine. I ask that you consider making a piece of jewelry for me with them."

"Mmm, lovely. A ring? No." Daffodil studied them the scales. "Give me your wrist band."

Edan removed the leather band showing his House insignia and his Power affiliation.

"Fo?"

One of Daffodil's House Brownies popped into the room.

"Could you please bring me some silver wire and my small pincer tool?"

The Brownie disappeared to rematerialize a moment later. It handed the items to Daffodil, then leaned against Edan's knee, watching with the same curiosity as he.

Daffodil took the velvet bag from Edan, poured the scales back into it, and handed it to her Brownie. She hummed to herself and focused her attention on the silver wire. In a short time, she'd pierced first one scale, then the second. Swiftly, she slid the silver wire through the scales and anchored one on the side of his House disk, the other on the side of the Power and handed the wristband back to him with a tired smile.

Knowing Daffodil, Edan knew it was not coincident that the darker of the two scales, the one closest to the deep green of Holly's eyes, had been placed next to his House. If Holly were Elf, he might consider the situation. But now, she would just be a part of his memory well.

He bowed at Daffodil's skill and Power. "Thank you. You will send your fee to the Balancers?"

"Give me a kiss for past joys and I'll consider it even."

Edan blinked at Daffodil's request, then she flowed into his arms. Her mouth tasted of crisp apples. His tongue slid around hers with long familiarity and a tinge of regret for times past. He heard and felt the deep hum of Daffodil's contentment. Her hand slid under the cotton t-shirt he wore. Her long fingers stroked across his abdomen, then went up to tweak his nipple while her other hand toyed with his ear.

His hand unerringly found its way through the streamers of her robe to catch and cuddle a ripe breast. Her nipple beaded in his palm with tempting possibilities.

The memory of Holly's fuller, rounder breast

interjected itself into Edan's mind. His thoughts strayed to the apricot lushness of Holly's nipples glowing in the morning sunlight.

Daffodil's height, more equal to his, made it difficult to cuddle her the way he did Holly. His fingers glided over the smooth skin of her rump, but he missed the soft roundness of Holly's.

Daffodil ended the kiss and lightly pulled away from his body. She readjusted her robe and then lightly patted his cheek. Her eyes once again held the mischievous sparkle that always gave him equal parts joy and exasperation.

"Thank you, Edan." Daffodil floated from the room. At the doorway to her workshop, she paused and looked over her shoulder at Edan. "I certainly hope Holly appreciates you. When you return perhaps you, Efran, and I could have an evening *together*."

Edan walked to his father's abode trying to erase that particular thought. He'd had multiple groupings before, some with Daffodil, others without her. In the Elf world, Joinings were a matter of pleasure given and received. But, ick, on the thought of Joining in a grouping with *his father*. No, definitely not something he wanted to do.

He passed along Daffodil's message to his father and managed not to flinch at the thought of his father and Daffodil together. After checking with Ta and Weg, he left his house Brownies happily devouring the chocolate chip cookies he'd carried in his pack for them. They planned to return to the practice field to help Efran train younglings in proper knife use after their treat.

His own abode smelled of its usual cleanliness and the tang of leathers he used for the footwear he designed. But a sad air hung about it as though the abode itself missed the bustle of living within its walls. He could not help that now. He needed to return to Holly. He had promised her and Pook.

The finished slippers and boots he had completed in his days at Holly's he gave to the Elves who had requested them. Ta made sure the Balancers placed the proper amounts in his account. He gathered his equipment and the necessities to complete more requested footwear.

He found it pleasing to include some of his leathers for the man who had rescued Pook who had requested boots for himself and his wife. Since the Balancers manipulated his favors and boons into the coins of Holly's plane in the "bank account," he had no doubts Holly could explain to him how to put the man's payment into "the bank." Then the Balancers performed their magic to manipulate it back to a form of exchange he understood. He had been surprised the man had a House symbol he wanted inscribed on the leathers, but Holly explained ranchers put such symbols on the animals they raised for consumption.

He had just completed the last of his preparations when Daffodil's Brownie popped into his workshop. Edan accepted the green velvet bag without opening it. He trusted Daffodil's skills and Power. The Brownie disappeared and Edan's own Ta and Weg appeared in the workshop.

"Are you leaving now?" asked Ta.

"Yes. You are enjoying your time with my father? I thank you for watching the abode."

Weg smiled around a mouthful of cookie. "It's our abode, too. Will you bring us back more cookies?"

"It's fun working with the younglings," Ta said. "Do they have other kinds of cookies?"

"Yes, there are other kinds of cookies and I will bring you more." Edan knelt for their hugs. With farewells given, Edan moved from De'erjia to Holly's world.

Just before he materialized, he paused to sense the area. He could feel no humans in range, so he entered the human plane by Holly's car, which was parked in a large area with other vehicles. Most of the other vehicles either had dogs waiting in them or bumper stickers or door plaques indicating kennels.

Edan used a simple phrase to unlock Holly's car doors, then leashed both Pook and Rat, leaving his pack in the vehicle. He picked up the thread of Holly's essence and walked with the dogs through the doors of the hotel.

The noise level from the melee of humans and dogs made Edan sincerely sorry he had the dogs' leashes in his hands. However, he also would have looked odd with his fingers in his ears. Perhaps Holly had some cotton balls in her purse.

Edan saw Holly across the entry hall. Her back was to the throng in the room, her dragon in its favorite place around her neck. She had her cell phone pressed against one ear and her finger plugged in the other. He could feel her distress before he reached her.

"Holly?" Edan switched both dog leashes to one hand to touch her. "What is wrong?"

Holly held her palm up, the signal Edan learned meant "Stay." In this case, he took it to mean "wait and be quiet."

The dogs also knew "wait and quiet." Both of them obediently sat. Edan held up the heavy velvet bag so the dragon could see he had returned with its jewelry for Holly, then tied the bag's drawstrings through his belt loops.

Holly concluded her conversation with despair in her voice. Her dragon rubbed its muzzle against her cheek. "I can't find another hotel. Every one that accepts dogs is booked. This one wants to put us on the seventeenth floor."

Edan shrugged. "I do not understand."

"Do you know how high up seventeen floors are?"

Edan thought a moment. "If the ceilings in the rooms are similar to your home," he looked at the ceiling, "and adding in higher ceilings for larger areas such as this entry, plus areas for plumbing and air-conditioning, then I would estimate approximately 180 feet in your measurement."

"Too far to jump." Holly's mouth drooped.

"Why would anyone want to jump?"

"I don't want to die in a fire."

"I beg your pardon?" Edan refrained from stomping his feet in frustration. Just when he believed he had a grasp of the current language Holly said something he yet again did not comprehend. "Fire? You have a premonition of a fire occurring?"

"No, it's just..." Holly's voice trailed away.

She knelt down to lift Rat into her arms. Edan released Rat's leash to her. When she straightened, Edan saw the shine of tears in her eyes. Abruptly, he remembered her tears and terror when she was locked in the closet.

"Do you fear being trapped if something were to happen?"

Slowly, she nodded, biting her lip.

Edan placed his arm around her waist and held her so she could hear his heartbeat. "May I remind you of the bathroom this morning? How quickly I tied you?"

He felt Holly's nod against his chest.

"If something were to happen, I will get you to safety. I move quickly when I wish to."

"And the dogs?"

The dragon twisted its body from Holly's neck. It flashed several colors with the scents of cinnamon and roses, darted its head from one dog to the other, hissing and clicking.

"Yes, the dogs will also be taken safely away." The dragon would help. At least, Edan thought that's what it had been conveying.

The dragon settled back onto Holly's neck, once again its normal chartreuse, with the faint odor of agreement cinnamon assuring Edan he'd properly deciphered Dragon

Speak this time.

Holly's tight muscles relaxed against Edan's body.

"Okay. I didn't cancel the room because I was afraid I couldn't find anything else."

"Then shall I remove our packs and the dogs' things from your car?"

Holly set Rat down and put him to heel. "Let's check in first and get the key cards."

Edan stayed in the larger waiting area with Pook while Holly, with the better-trained Rat, joined the registration line snaking through the lobby.

Edan felt eyes watching him. He turned to see a small girl, younger than young Rob, watching Holly's neck, then looking at him curiously.

Holly continued to move forward in the registration.

The little girl left the woman she was standing with and came to Edan. She crooked her finger downward and Edan knelt to her level.

She tangled her hand in Pook's fur. "I like your dog."

"Thank you. Yours is quite well behaved." Edan nodded at the toy Schnauzer cradled in the child's hands.

"This is a toy," she said scornfully.

"I apologize."

She nodded her head in acceptance of his apology as regal as an Elven female. "Could I pet your friend's dragon?"

CHAPTER 9

Edan blinked at the little girl. Despite the occasional dog barks and the conversations of the milling people, Edan knew he'd heard her correctly.

In his previous visits to this plane, he'd little to no contact with young mortals. He knew the younglings in De'erjia played various games. Perhaps she was simply playing an imaginary game. Perhaps he could distract her.

"How do you know she's my friend?"

"You were hugging her over there." She nodded in the direction of the area where Edan had been standing with Holly. "Can I pet her dragon?"

Edan didn't have the authority to grant her request. He also couldn't quite believe she saw the dragon. Though young Rob had come several times to help at Holly's grooming studio he'd never mentioned the dragon. Edan needed to know positively this young one saw it.

"Sit. Stay." Edan tugged the leash and placed his hand on Pook's rump to keep her in place. "Why do you think my friend has a dragon?"

The girl child gave him a withering look more scornful than when he'd complimented her stuffed toy. "I can see it. It's wrapped around her neck. Her hair covers most of its body, but I can see the head and tail."

"Do you know what color the dragon is?"

"Your friend's dragon looks like brand-new baby leaves. That lady's over there is bright yellow."

Edan looked in the direction of her pointing finger. A woman slightly older than Holly and pulling a dog carrier strolled confidently down a hallway. As the little girl said, the dragon riding the woman's shoulder was as yellow as an egg yolk.

"There's another lady with a purple one and here

comes a man with a big blue dragon," the child whispered in awe.

The dignified blue dragon, as tall as the gentleman it shadowed, bobbed its head in acknowledgement of Edan. Edan rose to bow in return and caught the sudden vanilla scent of dragon laughter. He straightened from his bow to discover his new companion coming up from a curtsey.

"That was quite polite of you. Dragons appreciate courtesies like that."

"I know," she gave him another exasperated look. "Please, can I pet your friend's dragon? I've never touched one before."

"Why not? You see dragons. Why have you not asked someone else if you could pet one?"

The little girl bit her lip. "I tried that a couple of times."

"And?" Edan knelt again to be on her level. There were tears in this small, young female's voice. He never liked it when a female cried. Female tears made his insides twist as though someone reached a massive hand into his chest and tried to rip his heart out.

"Does your friend know she has a dragon?"

"No, she does not," Edan said. "But how did you know I could see the dragon?"

And how do you – a mortal child – see dragons? Edan wondered.

The child watched the blue dragon go around a corner of the hallway and disappear, then she turned to watch Holly's dragon again. "The thing is people don't know they have a dragon and they laugh and pretend like it's there. That hurts the dragon's feelings and they go away. And the people look so sad when their dragon goes away. I don't want anybody's dragon to go away. You're an Elf. You can see it and talk to it 'cuz Elves can do that. Can you can ask the dragon if I can pet it so it won't go away from your friend?"

"Since I'm an..." Edan took a deep breath. Momentarily, his world shifted. He placed a hand on the floor to keep his balance.

"You *are* an Elf. I know you are." Her hands rolled into fists and she stuck them on each of her small hips. Her little mouth flattened to a white slash between round pink cheeks. Angry females of any age definitely struck fear in a reasonable male.

"Yes, I am," Edan decided he didn't want her angrier than she was. "My name is Edan. May I have the privilege of addressing you by your name?"

"I'm Dora. You sure talk funny." Her mouth still pursed in an angry pout.

Edan knew he spoke concisely, but he also still hadn't mastered this time era's jargon. "I speak differently because I am an Elf. But, Miss Dora, how did you know?"

Dora's focus drifted back to Holly, or rather to Holly's neck. Holly had finally reached the registration desk. Rat still calmly sat at heel beside her, unlike Pook to whom he once again had to show and state the commands so she would behave.

"Please?" Edan asked again. "How did you know?"

Without taking her eyes off Holly's dragon, Dora shrugged. "You look like an Elf."

Edan looked around at the other males in the hotel lobby. He resembled the other males in clothing. One male had longer hair than his. "How do I look like an Elf?"

"I dunno. The way your eyes look. You stand different. I dunno. You're just different. Please? Can I meet her dragon?"

"I shall ask."

Holly and Rat came toward them, her dragon flying in lazy circles around her head. The strain on her face softened when she reached Edan and Dora.

Edan stood again, draped his arm around her shoulders, and held her close to him.

"Everything will be fine, Holly. I will take care of you."

Holly lifted her face, her eyes again showed the hidden grief she normally concealed. "I know you'll try."

Holly took a deep breath and forced her memories back into the portion of her mind that would never forget. Life went on. She had to keep going. She smiled down at the little girl who knelt to pet Rat.

"Holly, this is my new friend, Mss Dora. Miss Dora, my friend, Holly Tate."

Friend. Hurmph. We're a bit more than friends, Holly inwardly grumbled, *but then again, he couldn't tell a little girl we're horny for each other.*

Maybe she ought to make Mr. Friend book his own room. That credit card he carried had a higher limit than hers.

But the thought of being that high up in the building by herself made her stomach clench. If Mr. Friend stayed with her, at least she'd have someone who'd talk with her. She'd keep her horny thoughts and hands to herself and make her *friend* sleep on the floor.

She didn't want to move out from under his arm right now, despite being a *friend..* She put her own arm tightly around his waist, wanting to lean on his strength and support, despite her irritation.

Controlling both her panic and her annoyance over the downgrade to 'friend' status, she smiled down at Dora. "Hi."

"Hello." The girl looked at Holly.

Holly looked into eyes that held a sweet, innocent joy. She vaguely remembered her own days of believing in Santa Claus, fairies, and – oops – Elves. The child smiled back at her, then looked at Holly's Elf.

"Please?" Dora asked Edan.

"Please what?" Holly asked.

Again Edan did that annoying thing of talking in Elven as though someone was there with them who understood him. Then he waved a hand to Pook.

"You may touch now," he formally told Dora.

The little girl's face lit as though it were Christmas morning and the one thing she wanted most was under the tree. "Thank you. Thank you," she whispered. She hugged Pook as though the dog was the one thing able to keep the monster from under the bed away.

"Dora?"

"Daddy," the little girl shouted, "come look."

"Hey, punk." Her father scooped her into his arms. "You scared me and Mommy. We didn't know where you were."

"I didn't leave the lobby just like you told me to."

"There are so many people here. We couldn't see you." Dora's daddy lifted her to his shoulders. "See if you can spot Mommy."

He circled slowly until Dora called, "Mommy! Mommy. We're over here. She's coming, Daddy."

Dora's daddy turned his head to look at Holly and Edan. "Elliot Fields. You've met Dora." His eyes sharpened on Edan's face. "Edan?"

Edan's smile warmed Holly even though it was directed at Mr. Fields. He and Mr. Fields grasped each other's right forearms. "It is wonderful to see you once again, Elliot. This is my friend, Holly. Holly, this is my friend Elliot."

Holly whispered, "I thought it had been a 100 or more years of our time since you were in my plane."

Edan saw the confusion on her face.

"Excuse us a moment, Elliot." He took advantage of Dora's mother arrival and exclamations over her daughter to pull Holly to one side.

.   "It has been," Edan said quietly in her ear. "Elliot and I were raised under the tutelage of the same Sir."

"This is your *brother*?" Holly's jaw dropped.

"Not brothers, but we were raised as such in De'erjia," Edan told Holly. "Please do not mention this to Elliot. He does not remember he is part Elf, but believes we were close friends in grade school and through college."

"That's weird."

"He's chosen to live as a mortal with his wife."

"Chosen?" A spark of hope flared in Holly's heart. "He's given up his Elf life?"

"Temporarily."

"Would you consider doing it?"

"It is a complicated situation. Elliot's situation and mine are different."

Holly's hope crashed. He had never promised to stay. At least, he promised to stay while she was stuck in this hotel. Holly shoved the thought of being up so high away again. If she thought about it, she'd be a gibbering idiot.

She needed to think about something else. Okay, she could do that. What was going to happen to Dora?

"Then Dora is part-Elf? How come Elliot didn't take Dora from Madeline like you were taken from your mother?"

"She is not a child of Elliot's loins. It is quite difficult for an Elf or even a part-Elf to have a child. Dora's father was a human. He went Beyond before Dora was born."

"That's sad."

"Yes, but Madeline and Dora have Elliot now. Elliot has them. They are happy. We should return to them now."

"Can you explain this whole thing later?" *And*

maybe give me something else to think about other than the fact that I'm stuck on the seventeenth floor?

"I don't know if I can. It is the Elven way. I shall try."

"You bet your boots you *shall try.*"

Edan looked down at his boots and then back at Holly. "Why would I want to bet my boots? I told you I will explain."

Holly felt a trickle of amusement further push her panic away. "I'll explain the phrase later."

"You bet your boots you will."

Elliot had one arm around his wife who kept a hand on Dora's ankle to keep it from drumming against Elliot's chest. "Madeline, do you remember my friend Edan? And this is his friend Holly."

"Daddy? You know Edan?" Dora leaned over and to look upside-down at Elliot.

"Yes, he's an old friend."

"Cool." Dora gave Edan a glorious smile.

"I apologize, but I met so many of Elliot's friends and family that day," Madeline said with a smile. "Our wedding day is still a blur."

Edan released Holly long enough to bow over Madeline's outstretched hand. "I remember you quite well. You were the one in the long dress with flowers on your headpiece."

"That's one of the reasons I like you, Edan, you have such a great grasp of the obvious. Hi," Holly said, extending her hand. "It's nice to meet you. Don't expect me to bow over your hand."

Madeline's light blue eyes twinkled with her smile. "Lovely to meet you, Holly."

"So, Edan, what are you doing here besides making friends with my daughter?" Elliot set Dora down. She promptly returned to hugging Pook who calmly leaned against Edan's leg.

Holly saw an odd expression filter across Edan's face when he looked from Elliot to Madeline to Dora. It contained equal parts envy and hunger then his face cleared and returned to its normal enthusiastic interest in his surroundings.

"Holly is a groomer by trade. She is also training to be a handler. I am here to help her with her job. She tells me it is also my job to applaud when she shows Bunny who is the loveliest Yorkshire Terrier."

Holly managed, just barely, to keep from snarling at Edan. Bunny is 'lovely' and she was regulated to 'friend?' Edan was so going to sleep on the floor.

Part of her knew she was blowing this 'friend' thing out of proportion, but part of her used the annoyance to keep from thinking about having to be in an elevator and going up, up, up.

"Madeline raises Welsh Corgis," Elliot said with pride. "This is Grand Champion Guinevere Heaven Skye, known to us as Candy. I'll be handling Candy plus a dachshund and a whippet for other owners. We haven't seen you at the Regional shows before, Holly. Is this your first one to handle?"

"Yes." Holly hoped her panic attack at staying in a room so high up didn't aggravate her already jangling nerves over handling Bunny. Bunny's owner and the usual handler had a great deal of trust to allow her to handle Bunny in this larger show.

She knew Bunny enjoyed being in the ring. She'd focus on Bunny's enjoyment and pride and do her best to keep Bunny from getting hyper and blowing her chances. She'd done it before, just not on this scale. She straightened her spine. "I've shown in locals."

"Just stay loose and cool," Elliot said. "The only difference between this and the locals is the size of the audience. If you'd like, I'll give you some pointers."

"Let's all get together for dinner," Madeline suggested. "We've promised Dora some swimming pool time before dinner."

Hours later, after walking the dogs one last time before bed, Holly and Edan returned to their room. As usual, on the way to their room up the elevator, Holly kept her eyes on the bank of lights.

At least, she thought grimly, they were only on the seventeenth floor. She cuddled Rat close taking comfort in the thump of his heart against her palm.

She followed Edan and Pook off the elevator and down the hall to their room. She focused on the mundane tasks of settling down for the night while she avoided looking out the windows despite the drawn drapes. She ironed the few wrinkles from the pantsuit she planned to wear when handling Bunny.

Edan lay on the bed and, just like an American man, flipped through the television channels. On the extra sink area in the bedroom, the room's coffee maker began to gurgle. He untwisted the lacing around his ponytail and ran his hands through his hair while he massaged his scalp. Then, he tucked his long hair behind his ears.

Holly turned away from the temptation of touching those sweeping ear peaks framed against the dark brown strands. She unplugged the iron, hung up her suit, and carried her nightclothes into the bathroom. There, she refilled water bowls for the dogs, then arranged her cosmetics and other things on the bathroom cabinet.

She glanced at her reflection in the mirror. Even in the less than perfect lighting in the bathroom, the deep green moss agate heart Edan had given her glowed against her skin. It felt almost as though it were pulsing with her heartbeat. She ran her thumb over the silver dragon set in it. She'd managed to get down over fifty stories, through terror packed stairwells, and live. This was almost a third that distance. As her fingers slid over the smooth stone and touched the silver dragon, she grew calmer and realized she could get down again if she had to. Resolved and at peace, she removed the necklace, took her shower, and fitted the necklace around her neck before she put on her pajamas.

When she left the bathroom, she looked down at her pajamas. If she'd brought her heavy flannel ones and her thickest robe, maybe then her nipples wouldn't show.

The only sign Edan had moved while she was gone was that the coffee pot had been emptied. Edan rubbed Pook's head balanced on the edge of the bed. Rat curled in a sleeping circle next to Edan on the bed.

"You're sleeping on the floor with Pook," Holly informed him.

"Holly, please come here," Edan invited and patted the bed.

Holly sat gingerly on the bedspread she'd folded and placed at the edge of the bed. She wanted Edan and, yet, now that they were here, part of her hung back. She didn't understand why she wasn't jumping his bones and, right now, didn't want to think about it.

Holly glanced at the drapes hiding the windows. She didn't need to think about it. She was high in a building for the first time in years. If she was lucky, she'd be able to remember how to breathe. No way could she even think about sex. No matter how hungry she'd been for him earlier, now she just wanted to get out of this building and go home. She couldn't do that. She had too many obligations to others. Maybe she could just sleep in the car. It'd be uncomfortable, but at least it'd be on the ground.

She rubbed her thumb against the moss agate heart and felt comforted again. She'd get out if she had to. Plus Edan said he'd be with her. Now she planned to make him suffer for that 'friend' comment. Why didn't he call her his 'very good friend' or even use 'girlfriend'?

Edan moved Rat, who grumbled and walked to the end of the bed where he huffed and curled up to sleep on the folded bedspread. Edan gave Pook the "bed" command then praised her after she settled herself on her blanket in her crate.

"Rat. Bed," Holly said.

"He wishes to sleep with us."

"Since you're going to sleep on the floor, that isn't a problem, is it?" Holly said sweetly. "You can sleep on the floor beside the crates."

"Holly…"

"Off, Rat. Bed." Rat gave Holly a sorrowful look, but Holly was impervious. "Now, Rat. Bed."

With a jingle of tags, Rat jumped down. Instead of going into his own crate, he curled up next to Pook in hers. Holly let it go. He was crated and with his friend. Rat thumped his tail at Holly's praise, then tucked his head back into his circled sleeping position.

Holly pushed a pillow to the floor and glared at Edan. "Get off the bed. You're sleeping on the floor. You can have the bedspread."

Edan didn't move other than to pick the pillow off the floor, tuck it behind his neck, and lay back down.

"I thank you for the gift of the earplugs. My ears hurt badly while I waited for you in the lobby. With more dogs and people tomorrow, I am grateful for something to help block all the noise."

"Yeah, yeah." Holly shrugged it off. "I remembered how much trouble you have when the dogs in grooming studio start barking. Saw them in the hotel's gift shop when I was getting a drink.

Holly shoved him, but he paid no attention.

She sighed. He wasn't going to move. She climbed off the bed, picked up and rolled the bedspread, and stuck it between her and Edan. A bedspread between them had worked for Claudette Colbert and Clark Gable in *It Happened One Night*. But somehow, she didn't think it was going to work for her. She doubted if she had the strength to get through the night without jumping Edan's bones and wasn't sure she wanted to. She also still couldn't think about getting naked. If, God forbid, they had to get out of the building, she didn't want to run out naked.

She propped her head on her hand. "You're welcome. You might need them tonight if we get those thunderstorms the weather people were talking about."

"Are you more comfortable now about handling Bunny tomorrow?"

"Yes, I appreciated Elliot's advice this evening. He and Madeline are nice. Tell me more about Elliot." Maybe if she talked about trivialities, she could get over her irritation and her horniness.

"As he said, he is an old friend."

Edan crawled across the rolled bedspread and nudged her. Holly didn't have the strength to resist when Edan rolled her onto her stomach. She laid her face sideways so she no longer looked at the window.

"How long have you known him?"

Edan's chuckle felt as good in her ears as his hands did on the back of her neck. "The time spans are not compatible. Since we were children."

"Is he part Elf, too? How come he doesn't have pointed ears?"

"He is currently magicked to resemble a human so he can live in this plane."

"How come your father raised him, too?"

"We did not live with my father. We grew to maturity with Sir, who is now our King."

"So, you became a Prince, not because your father is King, but because the man who raised you is King?"

Edan's palms and thumbs moved to Holly's shoulders and found the tension left from the long drive. "Sir was not King then. He was our Sir."

"I don't get it."

"'Don't get it' means you do not understand, correct?"

"Duh, yeah."

"From young Ron and Jon, I have learned that 'duh, yeah' is rude. Be polite, Holly, or I will stop this massage." Edan lightly smacked her bottom, then cupped and cuddled it.

A light shiver of heat slid through Holly when Edan squeezed her butt, but he didn't follow with anything. Holly's depression at being up so high sapped her energy, keeping her from taking it farther herself.

"I am learning your phrases. You do not understand mine. In my world, 'Sir' is someone who raises younglings. My father is currently a Sir to three younglings, two boys and a girl."

"I thought you were a Prince, like, in line to be King."

"I am a Prince, although I am under consideration to be King. I hope that I never am. It is not a responsibility I want to assume. As of now, my duties as Prince have temporarily been taken over by my father. 'King' is not a hereditary title of a ruler. The King is appointed by the Council of Elders who also appoints the Princes."

She felt Edan's hands on her shoulders; his thumbs found knotted muscles. Slowly, the tension began to ease from them.

"I'm confused. Princes usually inherit the throne and become King."

"You're still thinking in your phrases. Think of the Princes in my world as similar to a judge in this world. We hear complaints and make judgments on what we have determined to be the best course of action to settle a dispute."

"Seems a bit chauvinistic."

"I beg your–?"

"Pardon," Holly said simultaneously with him.

Holly grinned into her pillow when Edan swatted then rubbed her butt again. His thumbs dug into the small of her back and began to ease the taut muscles.

"Chauvinistic: of the opinion that only one gender can rule. Princes and Kings, but no Princesses or Queens."

"Ah. Once again, the language is not clear. I simply am using titles I learned during one of my other visits to this plane. The responsibilities of the positions can be assigned to either male or female. It is the skill of handling the responsibility of the position that is important, not the title or the gender of the office holder."

Holly's panic-induced tension, aggravated by the anticipation of handling Bunny in the morning in addition to her grooming duties, slowly unwound under Edan's massage. The buzz of sexual hunger hummed through her. It wasn't strong enough yet to overcome her depression exhaustion, but was enough to reassure her she was still healthy.

"How come your father didn't raise you and Elliot?"

"It is not the way of Elves. I cannot explain why it happens that way. It simply works for us and there is no need to change the pattern."

"You said Elliot *had* a lot of magick. He doesn't any longer?"

"Not at the moment. He has chosen to temporarily give up his Elf life for the mortal life to wed Madeline and become a father to Dora. He will go back to De'erjia once Madeline has gone Beyond. He remembers me as an old friend, not with the knowledge of being raised together."

Holly moaned in pleasure when Edan found a

muscle on her back she hadn't even realized was tight until the tension released. Despite still having her clothes on, her skin was beginning to sizzle as though his palms were kneading her bare skin.

"So, right now Elliot doesn't know he's Elf?"

"No, but he will remember when he chooses to return to De'erjia."

"That makes no sense. How can he return to some place he doesn't even know exists?"

"It is the Elven way."

"Why didn't I see that coming?" Holly muttered.

"It was a spoken sentence. How could you possibly 'see' it coming?"

"I forgot about the hearing, too," she mumbled against the pillow under her face.

"I heard that also. Oh, perhaps you meant you have the ability to foresee the future? Do you? My father can. It is not one of my gifts."

Holly knew what one of his gifts was. He kept manipulating her muscles with those gifted hands. He didn't have to remove her clothes to get her hot. She wondered why she brought such heavy cotton pajama bottoms and a thick cotton t-shirt.

"Holly? Can you foresee the future?"

I can see me getting naked and wrapping my legs around you. I can feel your mouth against my breasts. I can taste the first of your cum in my mouth, the taste of my cream in your mouth after you've eaten me. I can feel my panties getting soaked even now.

Edan's hands moved in smooth strokes to follow her rib cage in a slide around her torso from her spine to where her breasts flattened against the bed's mattress. His fingers lightly fluttered against the swell of her breasts, then his hands worked their way back to her spine.

"Can you foresee the future, Holly?"

"You're gonna keep asking until I tell you, aren't you?"

"And then I shall ask why you said I would bet my boots."

"What if I don't tell you?" Holly yawned into the pillow. "I'm pretty tired and I've got a long day tomorrow."

"Perhaps I shall keep you awake tonight."

"Oh? Do you snore?"

"I beg–"

"Your pardon?" Holly heard only her voice, then Edan's laugh.

"You bum," she turned to look over her shoulder at Edan sitting beside her. "You did that on purpose."

Edan ran a hand down the swell of her breast. The small heat pocket that had started with his massage flared into a blaze when his thumb caressed her puckered nipple. "I did that on purpose also. Shall we go farther?"

Holly smacked his hand away and sat up. She shoved her hair out of her eyes and tucked it behind her ears. Edan's hair hung in a dark curtain against the sides of his face and down past his collarbone. Holly lifted the heavy mass and pushed it behind his ears lightly brushing the ear points as gently as he once again caressed her nipple.

"What changed your mind about *Joining*?" she asked. "My performance this morning? My watching you this morning? Or did you finally realize I'm strong enough to live without you when you go back to De'erjia without me?"

Holly ignored the spurt of pain at the thought of Edan leaving her. It didn't matter though. He'd told her he was only going to be here temporarily. He'd told her he didn't want to bond firmly with her. He'd also told her he would basically wipe her memories when he left. Okay, fine. If she could only remember him as an old friend with whom she'd had fun for a time, then she'd take that.

She just wished she weren't so high in the air. But, hey, if the only way she could get down the stairs was by running to safety in her bare butt, then she'd do it. She'd grab the bedspread and Rat and be gone. Besides Edan said he'd help in an emergency and she knew he'd do it.

She wanted Edan, just like she had this morning. Had it only be this morning when she'd used her vibrator in front of him then watched him jack off in the bathroom? Wild. It felt like days ago. Time had stretched and slowed down.

If she only had Edan temporarily, then she'd take what she could get. Especially if time slowed down some more.

"Part of the reason I have not wanted to Join is I have come to believe you and I are being manipulated into Joining. I did not wish to Join with you unless you yourself wanted to Join with me."

"Manipulated?" Holly managed to shut her jaw. "Who on earth would manipulate an Elf and a human to get together. Why?"

"I do not know why. And, although they are not of Earth, the who would be Dragons."

"Dragons?" Joy bubbled in her. She knew it had nothing to do with Edan's hand sliding up her pajama leg to wrap around her calf. Well, maybe partly. "Dragons exist, too?"

"Yes, all things in legends exist. You simply have to know how to experience them. Dragons are very ancient. Sometimes they treat Elves and Humans as breeding stock, much the way Humans have bred animals such as Rat and Pook and the dogs at the Show tomorrow."

Edan said something in Elvish to a spot on the opposite side of the bed from Holly. His mouth twisted in a frown and his brows pulled together.

"What are you glaring at? I'm sitting right here," Holly waved her hand in his face. "And I'm not a dragon and have no clue what you're talking about. I hate it when you talk Elf like you're talking to somebody else in the room. What did you mean by that?"

"I am sorry," Edan turned his attention back to her instead of the pillow. "I was not speaking to you. I was speaking to your dragon."

"My?"

"Yes. Your dragon. It has been trying to push us together to Join since I first arrived in this plane. My Sir and I suspect Dragons are the ones who granted the wish for an Elf you made on the falling star. We believe Dragons pulled me from my realm to your plane. However, your dragon has been with you longer than I have been."

"Can you see him?"

"Not him. It," Edan said. "It is quite young. It has not determined its gender yet and even when it does, it will not share its gender with non-Dragons.. Its predominate color is green, although it has been with you long enough to absorb much of the yellow from your own life colors."

"I'm yellow?" Holly knew she was a wuss, she just didn't expect Edan to call her yellow. "Yellow is for cowards. Thanks a lot."

"Yellow is a good, strong color. The color of our sun, the giver of life. I do not understand why yellow is associated with being a coward."

"Go back to my dragon. Can I see him, um, it? No, never mind. I know I can't." Disappointment   slashed through Holly's joy, then a long familiar comfort wrapped itself around her as sweet as her mother's hug. She smiled at Edan. "It's leaning against me, isn't it?"

Edan nodded at her, smiling. "Yes, it is. It has given you a gift."

"Really? How wonderful."

Edan moved from the bed in one smooth motion and opened the drawer where he'd toss his clothes. From the drawer, he lifted the green velvet bag he'd given her with her necklace. He sat cross-legged on the bed and set the bag in her lap.

"What is it?"

"I have not looked at it. Your dragon gave you scales. My friend Daffodil who made your necklace fashioned the scales into a jewelry for you."

Holly untied the silver cords holding the bag shut. She pulled opened the bag and lifted out a bracelet. Multiple strands of silver were fused together at each end of the bracelet, the strands crossed and twisted around each other. Each strand pierced through at least one small chartreuse chip ranging from the size and shape of Holly's smallest fingernail to triangles half the size of her thumbnails.

Edan widened the gap between the two ends and slid it over Holly's wrist. "Ah, good. Daffodil said she would make it so it would look as though a small dragon has wrapped itself around your wrist."

"How come I can see this, but I can't see the dragon?"

"Daffodil has magicked it so you can see the scales. Others will see it also. They will think it has gemstone chips in it. Although you may meet some people who do recognize it as Dragon Scales."

"How come they can see dragons and I can't?"

"Different people see life differently. Some can see Dragons. Others cannot. I cannot explain it. Young Dora can see dragons. She also knew I am Elf."

"How?"

"She said I look like an Elf. I do not know how she knew I looked like an Elf," Edan said.

"Maybe because she's an innocent who stills believes? Like believing in Santa Claus?"

Edan looked thoughtful, then spoke Elvish. His face twisted in concentration. After a moment, he said to Holly,

"Your dragon concurs that humans who see Dragons have a special openness to the different realms. Most often it is children, but occasionally adults have kept the ability or relearned it."

Edan looked at the leather wristband he wore and turned it back and forth. Holly caught the winks of green like *her* dragon's scales on the band. Edan studied it as though looking for an answer to an unasked question.

Finally, his voice filled with thoughtfulness he said, "Since I believe Dragons are trying to manipulate us, I am now wondering if Dragons also dabbled in manipulating Elliot and Madeline because of young Dora's abilities."

Edan glared at Holly's shoulder. Holly touched her shoulder, wondering if her dragon was there.

"Dragons have much complexity in their meddling actions."

Holly heard the frustration in Edan's voice and decided some things weren't worth worrying about. At least not by her. She'd just let him handle his worry about Dragons on his own. She tilted her wrist back and forth loving the way the scales caught the light. The silver hugged her wrist like a lover's fingers.

"How can I thank my dragon?"

"It knows you are pleased. It picks up your emotions. Its color is flowing in many shades of green the way spring leaves blow in the warm breeze. Its scent is cinnamon, which is a pleasure odor."

Holly sat cross-legged and rubbed her thigh in disappointment. "I wish I saw it."

"You are petting it. It is happy."

"It's on my lap?"

Edan sat cross-legged in front of her. "Yes, for the moment. It moves frequently. You will always know when it is touching you. You touch the parts of your body it is against."

"Why did it give me a gift?"

Edan hesitated then spoke in Elvish. His face tightened in concentration, his eyes focused as though he were trying to see through a brick wall. After a moment, he looked at Holly again.

"It is as I thought. Partially, it wants to connect more with you. Since you cannot see it, the bracelet is a substitution. Partially, it wants to makes amends to you and me for interfering and disrupting our lives.

"You see," Edan held out his wrist to show Holly the two scales on his wristband, "it gave me two scales also.

"This scale," he pointed to the paler of the two, "is the most dominant shade on the dragon. It is to remind me of your dragon's Power.

"This second scale," Edan showed Holly the darker scale on the opposite side of two inscribed silver disks, "is the same shade as your eyes, to help me keep you in my memories."

"Oh. So, it's not going to interfere with us any more?"

Edan looked at the pillow behind Holly. Holly turned around and caught a brief flash, practically an illusion, of green.

"No. It's not. Whatever happens between you and I now is between us. Your dragon will no longer try to force us to Join."

"So we can do anything we want?" Holly tilted her head at Edan. "And if we want to Join anyway?"

"Do you want to?"

The hunger in Edan's voice went straight to Holly's cunt. The lust in his eyes made her skin burn. Her clothes suddenly became too tight, too constricting. She'd figure out how to get downstairs safely. She didn't need clothes. She needed Edan, hard and pounding inside her.

"Damn right. Let's get naked."

CHAPTER 10

Holly reached down to pull off her t-shirt. Edan stopped her hands before she'd done more than grasp the hem.

"Allow me."

Holly blinked once and her t-shirt landed on the floor.

"Lie down." His voice slid over her as easily as ice cream sundaes slid down her throat with the same sweetness and hunger for more.

Obediently, Holly stretched out on the bed and tucked her hands under her head. Maybe if she didn't blink this time, she could see how fast he moved. She bounced slightly, felt a draft of cool air, and realized she was naked.

"This isn't going to be a wham-bam, thank-you, ma'am fuck, is it? You're moving so fast I didn't even feel you take my clothes off."

By the time, Holly finished talking, Edan stretched out naked beside her.

"I am not even going to ask what that means," he said. He propped his head on one hand and grinned at her. The Cheshire Cat never looked so smug.

Holly turned on her side so they were face-to-face, body-to-body. Her nipples tightened almost unbearably when she saw Edan's eyes on her breasts. He tilted his head and his gaze traveled up and down her body. His jutting penis touched her bush. The contact started her cream flowing.

Edan continued to watch her. The only place their bodies had contact continued to be the small patch where his tip nuzzled against her rapidly dampening short curls.

"Where do you want to start?" Holly barely had enough breath to speak. She absolutely refused to go into orgasm with only his eyes on her.

"I am allowed to choose first?"

Holly raised her eyebrows at him. "Don't tell me it's not the Elven way. I can't believe Elf women always go first."

"No, it is usually who wants the Joining most who determines the pace."

Holly pursed her lips and pretended to consider the situation. "I do have my vibrator. You might be the one who wants this more than me. I guess I'll let you set the pace. This time. But take it slow. Don't zip through this at Elven speed."

Edan looked at her gravely. "What were you thinking while you were using your machine this morning?"

You inside me. Pounding hard. Taking me into the stars.

"Oh, not much," she teased, "just how good it felt." *How much better it would feel with my legs around you, with the hard length of you deep in me.*

"Shall I tell you what I was thinking while I watched you?"

Holly's mouth grew dry. She nodded.

"I was envious of your machine and your fingers. I wanted to taste you again, to feel your body shake while I sucked you until you screamed with pleasure. Shall I start there or would you prefer something else?"

"No-o-o," Holly moaned when a mini-orgasm shook through her. *Not yet, not yet,* she panted. A fine sheen of sweat covered her when it had finished.

Edan continued to regard her solemnly. At second glance, Holly realized he also gleamed with sweat. She felt something trickle down her belly. When she touched it, she realized it was a sticky drop of his first cum.

"Holly?"

"Start with your fantasy," she gasped.

His hand slid down her body to tangle in her nether curls. Her legs fell apart of their own accord when she rolled onto her back at his nudge. He settled between her legs.

She looked up to see his dark eyes watching her. Without taking his eyes from hers, he stroked across her nether lips with the tip of one finger. Holly began to spiral into the darkness of Edan's eyes while his finger probed firmer and deeper into her darkness. His eyes held the secrets of forever while his finger toyed with her.

Edan shifted his body and nudged her thighs with his shoulders. She lifted her knees until her feet were flat on the mattress with her calves against her thighs. He spread her thighs farther apart and draped her knees over his shoulders.

Holly felt his fingers in her labia and then his breath blew cool against her hot cream. She tried to lift herself to press her cunt against his mouth, but he chuckled and held her firm. He just kept fiddling with her with his fingers.

Damn it, with her legs in the air and his fingers spreading her, she might as well be in the damn gynecologist's office waiting for the doctor to insert the fucking specula for her Pap smear.

"Would you *just do* something?" Holly shrieked in frustration.

To her fury, Edan laughed. "You told me you believed I wanted to Join more than you did. You told me to set the pace and go slowly. I shall do as I wish. I have wanted to explore every piece of your body in the light. I shall do so at my leisure."

He continued to toy with her with his fingers. Holly pressed her knees together to try to reach his ears, but he held her at an angle and she was only able to rub her knees against his smooth cheeks.

She hadn't seen him shave, but his face held no hint of evening bristles even though she'd seen them before they'd changed to go to dinner with Elliot and Madeline.

She wondered what he'd look like with a beard. His dark hair brushed against her legs. He had just enough hair on his chest to entice a woman to twine her fingers through it before she trailed her hand down the lightly furred path to the nest that cradled his penis. She bet he'd look like a pirate with a beard.

She wanted to hold him closer, she wanted to feel his body rubbing against hers. But he continued to simply run his finger across her mound. *What can't be cured must be endured*, she sighed, and gave herself up to his languid stroking. First one finger slid down the side of her folds, then another down the other side. She floated on a cloud, her eyes closed. Nothing mattered but the feel of his fingers lightly stroking, gently probing.

Her hips started undulating. She had to get his fingers in her deeper, harder. Her clitoris ached and pulsed for his touch. She felt him insert his fingers into her vagina and begin to stroke.

Holly opened her eyes to see him watching her writhe for more. She panted and keened. She wanted to come, wanted his mouth along with his hands. Unable to reach Edan, she fisted the sheets in both hands and pushed her hips higher.

Sadistic bastard had the gall to laugh. Holly decided she'd kill him. Later.

He probed deeper, harder. She spiraled higher. Oh yes, she'd kill him later, slowly, the same way he was killing her.

Her skin overheated. Her cream flooded her legs and his fingers slipped in and out effortlessly, touching and titillating her clitoris. She climbed higher ready to reach her crest. She strained to reach the golden shimmer in her inner most being.

Just before she reached it, Holly felt Edan stretch her labia apart with his fingers, then lap her with his tongue.

She shrieked and shuddered at the explosion racing throughout her body while her clit swelled and throbbed taking on a pulsing beat that begged for more of his tongue, his teeth, his touch.

She slid down from the crest, spasms still shaking her whenever he lapped her over-sensitive clit. Holly felt Edan's body shift and dragged open heavy eyelids.

He took his mouth from her clit long enough to rise to his knees. He balanced her ass in his hands, his fingers gripping the globes of her butt. With her pale legs draped over his golden brown forearms, he looked down at her throbbing pussy. His face held joyful, almost reverent awe.

He lifted her ass higher and began to eat her pussy. Her welcoming liquid flowed heavy and sticky between her legs and down to her anus. He sucked her honey as though he'd been starving and it was manna from Heaven.

Holly's clit bloomed with unbelievable sensitivity. The womanpower swelled within her. She celebrated being the altar at which Edan worshiped. She felt treasured, the most precious object in creation. Humbleness grew in her that she had been given this body for him to enjoy. Joyfulness spread through her with the heat and shimmers from her clit that this man pleased her body so deeply.

Edan suckled her clitoris deep into his mouth and everything shattered. Her very being crystallized into pure energy fed by the unrelenting pulsating power of Edan's mouth on her. She felt like every molecule in her body exploded with heat and pleasure.

Just when she couldn't bear it any longer, Edan took his mouth away and lowered her. Holly gasped for air, then gasped again when he drove the length of his solid shaft into her.

She twisted her legs around his waist to get closer. "Harder, *harder*," she ordered.

Holly felt Edan's laugh flicker through their joined

bodies at the same time that it tickled in her ears.

He moved in and out. Each time he entered he slammed into her deeper and harder. The world narrowed to the center of their joining, the guttural moans and calls as they worked together, the slap of sweat soaked bodies coming together.

Holly twisted and got one leg braced flat against his chest. Edan came into her tight and hard. She twisted again, brought that leg down, and the other up.

"Yes!" Edan yelled in pleasure.

Their bodies strained and writhed and they started the climb together. Hunger for their own pleasures, for each other's delight set them on fire. They sparked. They burned. No longer could they tell where one separated from the other. They were a beast that lived for this moment, this fire, this oneness with everything and everyone who ever existed. The beast flared in a screaming conflagration of heat, fire, and pure sensation, then slid away to give Holly and Edan back their bodies, still joined into one. The fire slowly died, leaving them exhausted, drenched with sweat, the trickle of Holly's cream, the stickiness of Edan's semen.

Edan kept himself joined deep inside Holly while he lowered her limp body to the bed. He rolled her with him to lie on his side. She slid one arm under his neck and the other around his torso, her legs still around his waist. Her breasts flattened gently against his chest. Her soft roundness pillowed his tired body with more comfort than the hotel's mattress and pillows ever could. He ran his hand over the globes of her sweet rear once again marveling at their curved perfection. From comments she'd made, he knew she thought her rear and thighs were too big, but he loved holding them. He couldn't comprehend bedding some of the bony females he saw on Holly's television and in the stores he and Holly went to. Holly had a body a male liked to hold and caress.

Edan felt something solid along the side of his neck. He reached a hand up and fingered the dragon bracelet on Holly's wrist. The dragon had not returned, which reassured him Holly's passion had not been artfully enhanced by it. He was still puzzled about why Dragons wanted him and Holly to join, but for the time being he accepted it and relished Holly's body lax against his.

He listened to her soft breathing, still slightly labored from their exertions. He'd heard Pook whining earlier and suspected she might have been concerned that Holly was attacking him. Then he'd heard her snuffling and she settled down as though his and Holly's scents had registered in her small brain as mating, not anger. Rat had simply huffed and gone back to sleep.

Edan controlled the sudden surge of envy. Rat was too familiar with Holly's mating scents. Edan firmly told himself he had no right to be envious of other males plundering Holly's body, tasting her sweetness, hearing her gasps and keens. He did not know how many lovers he'd taken, enjoyed, or been pleasured by. He had no right to be jealous of Holly's lovers. If Holly were Elf, lovers would stand in line for the honor of her pleasure.

It must be the human part of him that selfishly wanted Holly all to himself, he thought. *Elves always shared lovers. It was impractical to attempt monogamy with the life span of an Elf.*

On the heels of that thought came the realization that his father had stayed with Edan's mother, his human lover, throughout her entire life. By human standards, she had lived a long time, over 90 human years. He remembered Elliot standing firm before him in his court while he probed Elliot over his intention to remain with Madeline and the baby Dora. After Judgment, Edan had given recommendation to Council and the King that Elliot's commitment was unshakeable and must be honored. He knew both his father and Elliot had committed to monogamy while their human lovers lived.

For the first time, he understood why. One couldn't demand a lover take no other lovers if one were not willing to make the same commitment.

Holly's breathing slowed to the regular rhythms of light sleep. He tugged the bedspread over her cooling body, wanting to keep her warm and comfortable while he held her. He'd become used to the quiet of Holly's home. Here, many different noises throughout the hotel and outside resonated through his ears.

He sorted through the conflicting sounds. In the room behind his head, he heard the stilted conversations of television shows and the music of various commercials. Somewhere across the hallway, a child awakened by a nightmare wailed, then was comforted by a woman's soft voice. A baby cried in the room next to them. A man's voice rumbled while he soothed the squalling baby, a woman sleepily spoke, then Edan heard the soft suckling of the baby rooting for milk at the mother's breast while the man's voice crooned a low melody.

He heard the faint rumble of thunder and the splashing of water. With a word, Edan opened the drapes to see the rain. Yet, the rain hadn't begun although Edan heard water splashing. In the far distance, he saw lightning streak across the sky. The thunder was still too distant to hurt his ears.

Edan realized the splashing came from a shower in the room above his and Holly's. He sharpened his hearing when he heard a female call and immediately relaxed when he realized the call came from the pleasure of a Joining. He heard her call again and a male's answering call.

Edan began to harden inside Holly. She slept so peacefully as part of him that he didn't want to wake her. The shower splashed again and the mating couple's celebration echoed in their shower. Edan grew thicker and harder.

Holly sighed and opened her eyes. Edan lost himself in the dark pools of green that twinkled at him in the lamplight. He could swim in their depth and lose himself and have no regrets.

Holly shifted and rolled on top of him to straddle his body. Her inner muscles flexed against his penis further stiffening him. She placed her palms on his chest, her belly a soft mound against his hard stomach. Her fingers feathered through the hair on his chest and rolled his flat nipples into tight buds while she gently shifted against him, his shaft sliding up and down her passage.

He cupped the bounty of her breasts and thumbed her nipples. He eased her downward and lifted his head to lap his tongue across their creamy beauty. He traced the faint webbing of blue lines, the pulse of her lifeblood separated from him by such a fragile barrier of skin and soft tissue.

He forced away the thought of a baby suckling these generous breasts the way the baby in the room next to them suckled its mother's milk. A baby to suckle on these nipples would come from the seed of a human male, not him. And he didn't want to think of Holly having another man deep in her vagina and planting his seed in her womb. No, this time was for him and Holly, not the future.

He took a nipple deep in his mouth. It was taut and firm. It tasted of Holly, sweetness and light. He rolled it around his tongue hungry to memorize its shape and texture. He felt the softness of her breast, then the tiny beading of the deep pink that bordered her nipple, finally he again felt the hard, raised flat knot of her nipple. It bloomed in his mouth offering itself to him for his pleasure, for him to savor.

Edan manipulated the other breast with his hand, relishing its silky heaviness in his palm. His fingers were callused and covered with scars from nicks and cuts. Holly made no complaint when his harsh hands circled her skin as smooth as fragile porcelain. Instead, she moved closer silently encouraging him to clasp her fullness tighter and rub the extended nipple.

She moved up his body and ran her tongue over his ear, suckling it the way he suckled her nipple. He surged upward and deeper into her. She pushed her body down hard onto his, meeting his upward thrust.

A flash of light caught Edan's eye. He glanced toward the window he'd freed of its draperies earlier. The lightning flashed again and thunder rumbled closer. He still had time to enjoy Holly.

In the window's glass, the outside dark from the brewing thunderstorm, he saw Holly's body folded over his.

She shifted to suckle his other ear and Edan concentrated on her second breast. Even the thunder faded from Edan's hearing when he heard Holly's breathing change to the frantic pants of hungry desire.

Holly sat up and tightened herself more solidly around Edan's bucking body. She flexed her fingers across his nipples and through his chest hair while she rode him.

Edan filled his hands with her breasts and thrust upward, matching each of her downward plunges. He glanced at the mirrored window glass again. Between flashes of lightning, he watched the beautiful arch of her back while she pushed her body down to stay joined to his.

The friction of her tight passage holding his shaft while they moved up and down started to send him beyond the here-and-now. He caught the rainbow spiral of the upward journey to the peak of pleasure. He grew harder the closer he got to his impending release. He wanted Holly with him. He took his hands from her breasts and gripped her soft round rump to hold her in place while he thrust higher and deeper. Her essence joined his. Her slick, hot passage started to shudder and spasm around his shaft, pulling him in deep, milking him to free him of this reality to join into the heat and light

With Holly's body encouraging him, with her voice urging him, the glory of being One in Joining slipped the bounds of this reality. Light, sound, heat, smell, hunger blended into one sense. Edan caught a glimpse of the Beyond then coasted back into his own being with final small shudders.

Holly released a final whimper of joy then collapsed across Edan. She melted against Edan's hard abs, firm muscles, and long strong bones. She thought how good it felt to lie against him and feel his hands stroke and pat her butt and thighs like they were his special pets.

Through her closed eyelids, light flashed, then she heard thunder rumble. She opened her eyes to see lightning streak across the sky followed by a thunder boom. Edan flinched underneath her.

"I'm sorry," Holly rolled off him. "I'm too heavy."

"No, you are not. You are comfortable to hold."

Lightning snapped and thunder rolled. Edan grimaced in pain.

"Hey, how'd the drapes get opened?"

"I opened them while you slept the first time. I wanted to gauge how far away the storm was." Edan winced in concert with the thunder rattling the glass. "This storm hurts my ears. I must move you and get the earplugs you bought me."

He eased out from under Holly. Holly enjoyed the view of his naked body, gleaming with sweat, while he found and inserted the earplugs.

"Can you please shut the drapes, too?" she called..

With a word, Edan sent the drapes sliding shut. Then he stretched out beside her and pulled her close to him.

"How come you can shut the drapes with a

command, but you had to look for the earplugs?"

Edan pulled out an ear plug. "What?"

Holly repeated her question.

Lighting and thunder crashed.

At Edan's grimace of pain, Holly said, "Never mind. I bet it's an Elven thing. Put the earplug back in."

She laid her head against his shoulder and felt him flinch when thunder boomed.

"Earplugs not helping?"

"A bit."

Holly heard Rat whimper and felt him paw the bed. Her heart overruled her previous firm instructions. She sat up and patted the bed. "Up, Rat."

Rat snuggled his shaking body between her and Edan with both of them stroking him, trying to calm him.

On his side, facing her, Edan touched Holly's hair and then splayed his fingers across her belly. "Your skin is so soft."

"So is my belly. Sit-ups are so not my thing."

"How many times must I tell you I like your body as it is? It's soft and comfortable and fits against mine. I wish you'd like your body as much as I do."

"It's just..."

"It's just that you have a warped view of how your body is supposed to look. You are lovely."

Edan sprang upright and cursed in Elvish. Pook's head jerked up and, through the cords across her face, she looked sorrowfully at Edan

"What on earth?"

"I am sorry I yelled. Pook, your nose was cold against my back." Edan reached down to pet Pook. "Pook is afraid of the storm also. She must have decided if Rat could be in bed with us, so could she. She stuck her nose on my back to get my attention."

"It's a big bed. Let her up." Holly shouted over the

storm. She scooted to the far side to make room for Edan to allow Pook to join them.

Once Pook had settled, Edan lay down with one hand patting Pook and the other again resting on Holly's stomach. With each closer crack of lighting, each louder boom of thunder, Edan's body jerked as badly as the dogs trembled.

"Edan?" Holly sat up so he could read her lips. "Maybe you should go back to Deergeea."

"I promised you I would stay."

"Edan, it's a storm. You're in pain," she shouted. "Go to Deergeea and wait it out. I'll be okay."

"De'erjia." He pulled the pillow around his head to press against his ears. "I promised to stay with you."

"I'll be fine. When the storm ends, you come back. It's stupid for you to be in this much pain. I'll be fine."

"I do not wish you to be alone."

"I've got the dogs," Holly yelled over the storm's fury. "My dragon will probably be back soon. You go on back."

"Are you positive?"

"Yes." Holly pushed at him. "Go. We'll be here waiting for you. Go."

Edan brushed a kiss across her lips. "You are like Mother Earth, everything wise and good. I will be back."

Edan got off the bed and stood at the foot of it. With a hand held in farewell, he faded from Holly's sight.

Holly buried her nose in the sheets that still held his imprint. Both the dogs trembled against her. Finally, she forced herself to the bathroom to get cleaned up. Afterwards, again clad in her pajamas, she opened the drapes and watched the storm. She fiddled with the necklace Edan gave her. It and the dragon's bracelet brought her joy and comfort.

She'd forgotten how much she loved the views from

up high. She'd been so afraid of getting trapped, she'd
sacrificed the joy of city views from tall buildings. She'd
loved the view of New York City from her office in the
North Tower.

The terror when she saw the plane come straight at
the building sent her and a couple of her co-workers to the
emergency exits even as the building still shuddered. They
ignored people who called building security and family to
find out what was going on. Holly didn't even trust the
elevators, knowing they'd stop and lock in a fire. She kicked
off her Manolo Blahniks and scrambled down the stairs as
fast as she could with firefighters coming upward even
before she and other workers got to the bottommost floors.
She'd listened to one of her fellow runners, who was
convinced that the top of the building would sheer off, and
kept on moving.

When her cell phone rang, the Caller ID identified
one of her apartment building neighbors who also worked in
the North Tower. Even at that point he knew he was trapped
on one of the topmost floors and, yet, he celebrated that
Holly had made it out. In the relative safety of the street,
dodging running firefighters and police, she had wept while
he calmly asked her to take his Chihuahua because his dad
and mom couldn't keep a dog in their retirement complex.

Holly made it to her apartment building just as
police were ordering people to evacuate. She ran upstairs,
shoved on her battered running shoes, grabbed some water
bottles, and got Rat from the neighbor's apartment. She
shoved him in her knapsack with her water bottles and ran
again. The dust cloud from the collapsing South Tower
caught them, but she ducked underneath a car with a few
others and prayed.

Now she picked up Rat, trembling from the storm's
fury and continued to watch through the window. Pook, also
shaking, moved and leaned against her.

She didn't regret quitting her job and leaving the City behind. Even before the Towers fell, she'd begun to look at less stressful, more fulfilling avenues of work than investment decisions.

But looking at the lightning-lit skyline, she did resent the power she'd given those asshole terrorists over her. She knew she wouldn't be afraid anymore. Life was too short, too fragile to be frightened of heights, closed doors and being trapped – or even of frogs.

It was even too short to worry about dying. She realized she'd wanted an Elf because Elves were immortal and lived forever. But she wasn't. She looked back through her life and realized her major regret was all the fears and worries that shortened her days and drained the joy from life. She'd like to have a husband, children, but she had family and close friends. She'd made a difference in other people's lives, helped them to be happy. Anything else in life would just be the icing on the cake.

Life was definitely too short to worry about whether or not someone would be around to bail her out when she had a panic attack or needed help if she were trapped. She could accept Edan for the time he gave her. He was definitely icing on the cake for the short time she knew him. She didn't need to go whining to him in fear the way the dogs whined at her now.

Lightning snapped and thunder rattled the window simultaneously. The lights went off in the entire area around the hotel. The smoke alarm shrieked and Holly calmly located the dogs' leashes, commanded them to sit to give her time to snap the leads in place. She dropped her keycard in her purse and called the dogs to heel to leave the room. She knew where the stairwell was. She'd get out. She'd done it before.

CHAPTER 11

Holly's dragon exploded into Edan's abode. The dragon didn't have the blue color tones it used when trying to manipulate. Instead, it held the purples of anger and the reds of worry. The dragon's worry, combined with his own sense of shame at leaving Holly when he had promised to stay, was enough to make him return to Holly's plane, even though he didn't feel any panic or fright from his bond with Holly's essence. It mattered not that the storm still pounded. The importance was returning to Holly.

Edan arrived in their hotel room to find himself alone. He had no idea where the dragon had gone. He clamped his hands over his ears. The earplugs Holly had given him helped muffle the noise, but the small machine above the door screamed worse than a banshee. The sound stabbed like swords into his eardrums. Blinking away tears of pain, he surveyed the room by the weak light from the screaming machine. Holly and the dogs were definitely gone.

He opened the door to see people in various stages of dress hurrying to the area where Holly had found the stairwell when they first came onto the floor. He debated returning to the room and trying to link to Holly's essence, then crossing the realms and reappearing closer to her. With so many people milling about, he doubted he'd find a quiet place to reappear. Instead, he decided to follow the others.

The stairwell filled with babbling people, some frightened, some annoyed, all of them rapidly heading down.

Using the thin bond-line between them, Edan cast a thought for Holly's essence. Far below, he picked up her Being, relaxed and serene. Intent on reaching her, he weaved his way through the crowd. At the doorway to one of the floors, an elderly man, leaning on a cane, stood beside an equally elderly woman in a wheelchair. Two younger men were bent over and breathing heavily.

Holly's dragon materialized, fluttered in his face, and demanded he immediately go to Holly. He reached for Holly's Being, Edan found her tranquil and comfortable. Even the blue line of grief was gone. Now it shone as clear green as deep summer leaves and was loosely entwined within her instead of strangling parts of her. He knew she was safe. He sent a pulse of his Being to her and felt her answering pleasure. Edan ordered the dragon to go to Holly and stay with her while he helped the young men get the wheelchair bound woman down the stairs. .

When they reached the bottom floor and were herded into the parking garage out of the rain, Edan left his new companions. Edan didn't need the gloomy emergency lighting to find Holly among the clumps of sleepy, complaining people and dogs. Just as he found her through the realms, he easily located her in the garage. With Pook beside her, she leaned against a wall holding Rat in her arms. Her purse dangled from her elbow. Her dragon perched on her shoulder and hissed at him.

Edan ignored it and spoke to Holly. "I am sorry I was not here to help you downstairs."

"I'm fine, Edan. The dogs are fine."

"I should not have left."

An essential part of him cracked at the thought of something bad happening to Holly due to his own selfish need to be comfortable away from all the noise. He reminded himself he was not staying with her. He told himself she had to live the rest of her life without him to take care of her.

The part of him that splintered sent a spasm of pain through him. More intense, more shattering than the thunder of the now departing storm, this pain nearly sent him to his knees. Not only did Holly have to live the rest of her short

life without him, he had to live his without her. He knew
that no matter how he erased Holly's memories from
himself, part of his Being would forever feel a lack.

He took Pook's leash from Holly and held her free
hand with his. He had to leave, but not at this moment. "I
am so grateful you left the hotel room safely. For the rest of
Eternity, I will regret having left you alone."

"Edan. It's okay." Her voice caught, then continued
with confidence. "I learned something about myself while
you were gone. It's what helped me get down the stairs with
the dogs and will help me the rest of my life."

A flow of strength came from her through the hand
he held, a strength Edan hadn't felt before.

Outside the rain drummed, lightning crackled,
thunder roared. Inside people grumbled, hotel staff tried to
placate, babies and small children cried, dogs whined and
howled.

Edan managed, just barely, to ignore it and
concentrate on Holly. In her, a new color emerged. This
deep green pulsed with resolve and conviction. It overlaid
the blue grief and nearly obliterated the red fear. Whatever
had shattered Holly's life had now been accepted and the
damage had been repaired. It was Holly's private fear, and
he did not want to intrude on her privacy.

He rejoiced for her, even as he envied her. After all
these centuries, he still held much grief at the separation
from his mother.

Holly cuddled against him. The center of her
generous breast pressed in a soft mound against his bare
chest. Her nipple welcomed him with its hard knot, their
skin only separated by her cotton top. He ran his hand down
her back and inside her pajama bottoms. To his pleasure, his
hand slid against the smooth bare skin of her globes. He ran
a finger down the separation line and felt Holly's small catch
of passion.

The dragon hummed in contentment, but still didn't show the blue tones of Power.

"How are your ears?" Holly asked.

"Better, now that the storm is moving away. The earplugs help also. I thank you for them."

"Cool. Now..." Holly looped her free arm around his waist and snuggled her breast back against his chest, her back to the wall. "I'd thank you to continue what you just started."

Perhaps the earplugs and thunder garbled her voice and he had not heard her correctly. "Here? In this garage? With all these people around?"

"Duh." A flash of lightning illuminated Holly's mischievous grin. For a moment, she looked all the world like an Elf woman teasing a male that he was inadequate to pleasure her.

"Holly," he said when the thunder died, "it was just a touch because your rump is so tempting. I had no intention of taking you further."

"So, take it further. I've always wondered if I could come silently in front of a crowd. Besides, we're between two cars. I don't think anybody's going to watch."

If they were in De'erjia, elves would watch and enjoy Holly's face and her body shimmying when she crested. Edan groaned silently when his shaft pulsed hard against the blue jeans zipper at the thought of joining with Holly in the Midst. He knew with the conventions of this plane he wasn't allowed to open his jeans and have Holly reciprocate in the midst of all these humans. But he was able to give her what she wanted.

He slipped his hand inside her pajama bottoms again and maneuvered her closer to him. Slowly he slid his fingers between her globes. He moved his fingers up and down until he could feel Holly panting. She tightened her arm around his waist and pressed her body closer to his, rubbing her face against his skin and the hair on his chest.

She widened her stance and he dipped to feel her juices. He dragged her cream backwards to coat her anus and the separation. More of her honey flowed giving him a smooth pathway into her passage. He probed her passage with his middle finger while pressing his thumb hard against her anus.

Without releasing the pressure there, he slipped his finger in and out of her channel, reaching and touching her tight bud. Her body began to shake against his.

Lightning flashed and thunder rumbled, but without the intensity of moments earlier. Rat whined in her arm. Edan saw the dragon flow from Holly's shoulder to rub its head in comfort against Rat. Then it fluttered to Pook's head.

Edan pulled more of Holly's cream along her backside, wetting his thumb. He pushed his finger in deeper and pressed the swollen bud of her pleasure most point. At the same time, he used her cream to ease the tip of his thumb into her rump.

Holly's body bucked and shook against his body. She opened her mouth against his bare chest and he felt the vibrations of her moan. He reached outward and caught the wave of her orgasm. He flew with her up to the golden light of heat and satisfaction, his penis tightening unbearably against his jeans.

He drove his fingers deep into her to send her higher. His chest absorbed her pants and screams and his own body tried to pump against hers. She squirmed and wiggled against him, her vagina pulsing against his fingers while she reached the final peak of joy.

Just when Edan thought he had control, Holly's silent shriek shook her entire body. She bit him with the sucking claim of possession.

Edan exploded with his own release and took Holly

with him to reach the cosmos. He pressed his face into her curly hair to muffle his own groans. Holly's arm left his waist and her hand pressed firmly against his zipper. Her warm palm cupped his driving penis through his blue jeans.

When the long moment finally returned them to their own psyches, they leaned against the wall, barely able to stand.

"At least I'm not the only one who's going to have to walk into the hotel with soaked pants," Holly said with a laugh.

"You need not be so smug," Edan chastised affectionately since he felt pretty smug himself. Damp and sticky, but definitely smug and a trifle tired. Pook shoved her muzzle into his crotch, huffed, and lay down.

"Um," Holly sighed. "Wish I could do that."

"Feel free to stick your nose in my crotch at any time."

"I meant lie down, doofus," Holly twisted and tugged his chest hair until he yipped.

Edan unwound his hair from Holly's fingers and placed her hand back on his crotch. "If you twist my hair again, I might have to spank you." He didn't want to pull his hand from her silky bottom, so he pinched one globe just to demonstrate his intentions.

"Ow. That hurt. You'd better kiss it and make it better."

"I can do that." Edan grabbed the back of her pajamas and pulled it down.

Holly yelped and grabbed at the pajamas front to keep it in place.

Edan didn't care. He stretched the elastic waistband and held it in place below her globes. He leaned down behind her and kissed where he'd pinched. He licked between her globes, tasting her drying cream. He moved her further away from the wall and knelt behind her to suckle each round buttock, then moved her legs further apart to lap her honey flowing again. Just when he'd reached his tongue to her center, the parking garage lights came on.

Edan rose and tugged up Holly's pajama bottoms. "Later," he promised, "when we return to our room."

******

A week later, Holly's thighs ached from being stretched to wrap around Edan's body so many times. Even the excitement of being in the Best of Show ring with Bunny paled in comparison to the way her body thrilled at the sight of Edan standing outside the ring watching her and Bunny go through their paces.

Bunny's confidence soared and fairly vibrated through the leading leash, especially when applauded by Edan and his entourage of Junior Handlers, whom he'd befriended during the early shows. The kids and Dora followed Edan like the Pied Piper, with Edan as fascinated by them as they were by him.

Her own confidence had been enhanced by the occasional pressure of warmth and caring on her neck and shoulders. Since Edan made her aware of the dragon, she'd been able to feel it pressing with joy against her skin. Her bracelet glittered giving her a visual reminder of its care.

But, mostly, Edan's gaze on her, reminding her of the way he watched her naked body in their room, boosted her adrenaline and sent the heated flush throughout her. From the time they walked into the room until they needed to take the dogs out or go to work at the Show, they stayed naked.

They'd gotten little sleep since that long weekend. On the drive home, they found an overgrown back road. Edan took her with her leaning over the front hood of her car.

During the days, they tended to keep their clothes on, mostly. But as soon as they were inside her house, both of them got and stayed nude.

Amazing to have a lover who'd been around for so many centuries. She'd learned positions she'd only seen in the *Kama Sutra*.

There was also the way Edan helped her in her grooming studio and around the house. He watched and learned how to cook, then preened when he fixed a full meal for their supper. She found herself tickled explaining television shows to him and annoyed at his pre-emption of the remote control. Sometimes he acted just like a man. She was fascinated watching the care and precision with which he shaped the boots he was making. Yet he told her seeing her knit a strand of yarn into a sweater was magical.

Now she knelt in her herb garden, grubbing weeds. Her long cotton skirt brushed against the backs of her calves, the front of her skirt mounded in front of her knees. An evening breeze blew sweetly across her back and molded the skirt to her bare butt. Holly smirked to herself. It was only a matter of time before Edan realized she was naked under her skirt.

From the far back part of the yard, Edan watched her come from the house. She'd waved, then labored in her herb garden while he worked on Pook's training. She'd seen his face brighten while he looked at her and she wondered if he'd been able to see her breasts swinging loose under her t-shirt.

Holly shooed a lizard away from under her basil. She certainly didn't want Crush, prowling the back of the yard for rabbits, to catch it and eat it. Idiot cat would puke on her bed. The mighty hunter always did after he ate his catch. Cleaning up cat barf was not in Holly's plans for her bed.

She had a four poster bed in her bedroom and ice cream in the freezer. Maybe she wouldn't make supper, but just go straight for dessert. She wondered how much shrinkage factor, if any, Edan would have if she used him for her ice cream platter.

Then again, maybe she'd just torture him and make him wait. The dough was rising for pizza. She had fresh basil and tomatoes to put on it. If she made pizza, they'd eat it with their fingers and maybe, accidentally on purpose, smear it on each other. Then, gosh, oh, golly, they'd just have to lick that mess away.

Holly finished the last of the minor weeding and gathered basil. She stood and placed her fists on her back and arched to stretch. The setting sun kissed her face and showed blood red behind her closed eyes. Around her neck, she felt the now familiar warmth of the dragon. Relaxed and at peace, Holly reached to pick a ripe tomato and another lizard, or maybe the same one, jumped at her.

Silly creature must have a death wish, she thought. She flapped her hand at it to get it out of Crush's hunt zone. It darted away when Edan's dog galloped up from the back of the yard.

"Pook. No. Stop."

At Edan's fierce command, Pook skidded to a halt just before she ran into Holly's garden after the lizard.

"What a good girl," Holly crooned to her. She ruffled her hand through Pook's forming cords and looked into the dog's happy eyes. "You stopped just in time."

"You're doing a great job with her," Holly told Edan who had caught up to Pook and was praising her.

"I do a good job with you also." Standing behind her, Edan's brought his arms around her, cupping her breasts with his hands.

"Do you want a fresh tomato?" Holly asked. She held one up to his face then caught her breath when Edan bit it. The juice ran down her fingers and arm. Edan licked the trickling juice before taking the tomato from her.

He pulled her t-shirt from her skirt's waistband and

off her, coming to stand in front of her. He pressed the cavity left in the tomato from his bite against her breast until the juice flowed down. Then he lapped the juice from her skin. Each time he caught a rivulet of tomato juice, he licked it back up the slope of her breast to suckle her nipple. She crushed the basil she had gathered in her hand and dropped it to hold him closer to her.

Dazzled by the setting sun, caught in the heat of Edan's mouth, Holly closed her eyes. She moaned, glad she lived in the country and her nearest neighbor was a mile down the road.

Something shoved Holly. She opened her eyes to see Pook sitting calmly between her and Edan.

"Pook, go. Deck," Edan commanded with dignity, despite Pook's nose in his crotch.

Pook thumped her tail against Holly's calves begging to stay.

"No, Pook. Deck."

Her ears drooping, Pook followed the direction of Edan's pointing finger and climbed to join Rat watching them from the deck.

"Now," Edan's mouth curved around the tomato when he took another bite. He chewed and swallowed without taking his eyes off Holly. "Where were we? Ah, yes." He placed the tomato's cavity on her other breast and squeezed the tomato until the last of the juices ran in sticky ribbons down her body.

Holly untied his hair and ran her hands through its heavy mass while he licked her breasts clean. She palmed his ear points the way he palmed the nipple he wasn't sucking. They grew warm under her hands and fingers, the way her breasts and nipples pulsed under his mouth and hands.

The grass edging her garden curled between her bare toes. The breeze whispered around her ankles and slithered upward to cool the moisture gathering between her legs. Basil and rosemary scented the air along with the clean smell of the freshly turned soil from her weeding.

"I believe," Edan's dusky, harsh voice sent ripples of anticipation flooding Holly, "some of the juice has gotten underneath your skirt. Perhaps I should remove it and clean you there also."

"Perhaps you should," Holly murmured.

Edan pushed the elastic band of her skirt down. He stepped back and raised an eyebrow after the skirt dropped past her hips and drifted to the grass.

"Ms. Tate," he said formally, "you are not wearing panties."

Holly put her knuckles on her pelvis bones, thrust out her hips, took a deep breath, and lifted her breasts with her pectoral muscles. "Prince Fariss, you are wearing too many clothes."

"That can be remedied." With a snap of his fingers and a word, Edan's clothes disappeared.

Afterwards, Holly lay against Edan's chest picking tomato seeds out of his chest hair. "Your knees are green."

"So is your rump." Edan patted it, once again delighting in its round softness.

"You know, I kind of like it when you say 'rump' instead calling it a fat ass."

Edan eased her off his chest and rolled on top of her to cup her face in his hands. "You say that in such a derogatory tone. You have a wonderful body, the kind of body a male likes wrapped around him. And I like your rump. I love how it mounds in my hands when I'm deep inside you and your hips are pounding against mine. I love how your thighs grip my body with strength and softness. I love your generous breasts in my hands and your soft stomach pressed against mine. You are as beautiful and warm and generous as this earth that nourishes us. Three thousand years ago you would have been revered for having the body of a fertility goddess. I will thank you not to denigrate your body again. I treasure it as I do you."

Edan saw tears shimmer in Holly's eyes. Frantically, he thought back over what he'd said. He did not remember saying anything that hurt her feelings or mad her mad. "Do not cry, Holly, please."

He wiped the tears from her eyes and grabbed her t-shirt to wipe her smeary face.

"Did I say something wrong? I am sorry. I did not mean to hurt your feelings."

"You didn't. You didn't.." Holly snuffled. "It's just that I haven't even known you a month. You make me feel all gooey inside. Nobody's ever told me they treasure me before."

"Males in this plane are – what was that phrase the young handlers used? Ah, yes, 'not the brightest bulb in the chandelier'."

"Thank you. You make me feel so good." Holly mopped her face and stared at her messy shirt. She huffed in disgust at it. "You make your clothes disappear in a snap, but you couldn't conjure up a handkerchief or tissue for my snotty face? You had to give me my own shirt? Gross."

"You shall simply have to walk back into the house naked then." Edan sat back on his heels, embraced by Holly's spread legs. He drew a finger across her folds, exploring the smooth texture, feeling her hot moisture once again flow.

He smiled at her body's shiver. "Now, since I like your lovely rump so much, I believe this time you shall be on your knees so I can hug your rump to me when we join. And you will have green knees to match mine."

In the last of the evening glow, Holly lay with her face mashed into her filthy t-shirt, her head pillowed on her arms. She imagined her knees were green by now and probably her boobs and elbows, too. Edan lay draped across her back, partially supporting his weight on his hands and knees.

Holly giggled at the pop-eyed lizard balefully watching them from under the thyme. At her giggle-vibrations, Edan's finally limp penis slid from her vagina.

"Damn. Go back in," Holly demanded.

"You were the one who shook me out. What made you laugh?"

Holly giggled again and pointed at the lizard. "That. The critter is glaring at us like we've invaded its private space."

Edan slid off Holly and stood up in one smooth movement. He stalked into the herb garden then got on his hands and knees. Holly stuffed both fists in her mouth to keep from laughing as her dignified Elf Prince crawled in the dirt, with his ding-dong dangling.

Edan pounced, sprawled on the dirt before rising to his full height. Stiff-legged, he stamped back to Holly. He held his arm straight out, his fist clamped around the tail of the struggling lizard.

Pook, with Rat at her heels, came charging from the deck. Both dogs tried to jump for the lizard. Rat couldn't get the height, but made up for it in twice as many enthusiastic jumps as Pook. Edan held the lizard above his head and ordered both dogs to Sit, Stay.

Holly rolled on the grass unable to do anything but laugh. Edan glared at her.

"I'm sorry," she sputtered between giggles. "Your knees are green and have grass stuck on them. You've got dirt all over your calves and hands. And your dong is at half-mast and has leaves and dirt stuck to it."

"Holly?"

Something in Edan's voice stopped her giggles cold. Holly's skin shivered when Edan's dread slid through their bond. She stood to peer at the lizard.

"Do you remember the nucklelavee?"

"Nucklelavee, nucklelavee." Where had Holly heard that term before? Her memory sent her a stale mucky pungent scent. That triggered the memory of the washroom's tiled wall, cold, slick, unyielding against her back while a frog jumped at her. "Oh. You said that gawd-awful ugly frog wasn't a frog but a nucklelavee. Some kind of cruel faery."

"Yes. And this is not a lizard anymore than the nucklelavee was a frog. This is an attorcroppe."

"Huh?"

"Notice the shape of the legs? They are longer and straighter than a lizard. It is a very malicious faery. One of the prominent legends of the beginnings of human tells of an attorcroppe. It persuaded the humans to eat a fruit the creator told them was forbidden. The humans then had to learn to survive outside of the creator's home. The attorcroppe does not care who or what it harms. It exists only to harm."

Holly looked more closely at it. Its beady little eyes didn't have the darting roll of a lizard's eyes or the flat, blankness of a snake's. Instead it glared at her with total malevolence.

"Why's it in my herb garden?"

Edan focused his attention on the weird lizard, uh, attorcroppe. He said something in Elvish. The attorcroppe froze, then disappeared.

"I shall return to De'erjia for help." Edan moved closer to Holly. He stroked her hair then the warmth behind her neck vanished.

To Holly's shock, Edan stood in front of her, both arms firmly gripping nothing.

"Is that my dragon?" Holly yelled over the dogs' barking.

"Yes," Edan said between gritted teeth while he struggled to contain the emptiness. "Now I'm going to take it to De'erjia and discover exactly why Dragons are meddling in our lives. Neither a nucklelavee nor an attorcroppe comes without help from another Being. Since I know of no Elves who wish us harm, I am only guessing Dragons sent them for some obscure reason. Now I will use this small dragon to make Dragons answer my questions."

Seemingly from nowhere, Crush gave his battle meow just before he launched himself at Edan's hanging penis.

Without letting go of his fighting burden, Edan sidestepped Crush. His dong waved proudly.

Pook broke Stay to lunge at Crush followed immediately by Rat.

"No. Pook." Edan's voice thundered in command. "Stay."

"Sit, Rat. Stay," Holly ordered.

The dogs stopped and whined at the base of the tree to which Crush had retreated. Crush dropped from the branch and crouched. His tail twitched and back flanks wiggled in preparation to rush Edan again. The dogs whimpered in eagerness to get him. Crush flattened his ears and hissed at the dogs.

Holly took advantage of the cat's momentary distraction and swooped over him with her skirt. With the skill gained at the cost of scratches and bites when she groomed the few cats in her care, she mummified the squalling cat.

His breathing labored with the strain of holding the dragon, Edan said, "I will not allow either of us to be manipulated by Dragons. I will take this one to De'erjia and demand an audience with Dragons. They should not have sent the nucklelavee or attorcroppe after you. I will not permit you to be harmed."

"I don't think my dragon would have harmed me." Holly held the wrapped, screaming cat as tightly as Edan held the invisible dragon.

"Nevertheless, this dragon knows things. It shall lead me to Dragons who will answer my questions."

Edan stood in the dusky light with green knees and dirt liberally coated down his calves the tops of his feet. The leaves, grass clippings, and dirt caught in the drying cream liberally decorating his shaft after their lovemaking were nowhere near as effective as the proverbial fig leaf. Even while Holly watched his muscles strain and bunch with the effort it took to contain the squirming – if invisible – dragon in his arms, his penis started to rise again.

Instead of looking insanely ridiculous, Edan looked more like a warrior at the end of a battle. He held the dignity of the original Greek runners to Marathon and back. Every molecule of his being beat with the satisfaction of a job accomplished

It took all Holly's physical strength to hold the yowling Crush. It took all her emotional strength not to lie down on the grass and open her knees wide to him again the way women throughout the centuries welcomed home their warriors.

But she knew this warrior had only completed a minor skirmish. His features were set in the grim lines of battles yet to come before this war was finished.

"I promise you I shall return," Edan told her, his voice deep and penetrating, almost as satisfying as when he thrust deep and solid into her body. "Pook. Protect Holly."

Edan held the vision of Holly's face lit by the glowing pinks and golds of the setting sun while he struggled through the mists and planes to return to De'erjia with the enraged dragon. He materialized outside the King's chambers and roared for admittance. The King's entry host clucked and sputtered at his appearance. Since nakedness was commonplace in De'erjia, Edan knew it was the dragon still staining to be free that triggered the chatter.

He ignored it the way he ignored the dragon's struggles. Before he'd gone to the first antechamber, his own Ta and Weg popped into the room.

"'Tis a poor reflection on us should you attend the King in bare skin, even covered with leaves and dirt," Ta scolded while magically sponging Edan clean.

"We'll not be embarrassed in front of the other Brownies that we can't take care of you," Weg added and dropped a tunic over Edan's head.

"Bah back to you." Ta stuck out his tongue at the dragon, who barely missed biting Ta's fingers as the two Brownies manipulated the sleeveless tunic and Edan's pants into place by ducking and twisting under and around the dragon, distracting it from one to the other.

"Feet."

Edan lift one foot, then the other. Weg tied the soft slippers onto Edan's feet while Ta scrambled back up Edan's body to comb and pull back his hair.

Weg swatted the dragon's muzzle in passing on its climb to Edan's shoulders. Balanced carefully, with Edan and Ta holding the dragon still, Weg set Edan's Band of Judgment on Edan's head, settling the seal of Prince in the center of his forehead.

"I thank you both."

"Did you bring us more cookies?"

"Not this time. I was preoccupied."

"With Ms. Holly?"

"With the dragon."

"Hurmph, more likely with Ms. Holly. Bring us cookies next time."

Edan nodded to his Brownies and continued into the King's formal chambers.

"I crave a Favor."

Edan's demand echoed in the marble chamber despite the room being filled with Elves and other Beings. All conversations stopped and every eye turned to Edan and the snarling dragon he held.

"I will speak to Dragons. I will hold this one until the mountains crumble and the seas dry or until Dragons speak to me and answer my Query." The formal phrase sounded like an exaggeration, but Edan knew he had enough anger to hold the dragon despite the passage of the years. Holly might be a dust memory in her own plane by the time Dragons conceded to grant his Favor, but he would hold her dragon until he knew why Dragons were determined to meddle in his and Holly's lives.

The King looked solemnly from the dragon to Edan. His gray gaze held Edan's with understanding and a determination of his own.

"Have you phrased your Query to receive an answer? Will you abide by Dragon answer even though its message may not be clear?"

"I have. I will."

"In addition to me, you may choose another companion."

Edan didn't hesitate. "I choose my father."

Efran stepped to Edan's side to help carry the squirming dragon.

The King joined them forming the third side of the triangle.

"We go on the Quest to seek Dragons." The King's voice rang throughout the Hall with the authority of the Community of De'erjia. "We go Now."

CHAPTER 12

Red burned Edan's skin. Time twisted him back before his conception.

He saw a crone with Holly's green eyes drying herbs in a cavern. Yellow sang the most exquisite melody Edan ever heard, a song he wanted to listen to until Eternity crumbled. He fought nausea triggered by vertigo to see himself, a silver streak in his hair at his temple, clasp an arm around a boy with the all bone growth of a young male just before manhood.

A noxious odor from something purple made the nausea worse. It immediately eased when silver sparkled around him with the pulse of millions of stars. A maid with Holly's hair and eyes wrapped linens around a dog's leg and instructed a man with a concern-drawn face in how to administer a healing draught to the injured dog.

Blue Power tinged with gold shrieked with ear-piercing screams. He proudly watched a female just past the first cusp of womanhood speaking and knew a great number of beings accepted her as their leader. He felt Holly's essence through their Bond, but she was not where he could touch her. He missed her with an intensity that sent him to his knees in despair. Blue and green clashed in discordant time. Pressure compacted his body and pushed him from his warm, dark comfort into a cold place with bright, flickering lights and noises that hurt his ears.

His father's arm clasped one forearm, his Sir the other. Edan held onto them with all his strength.

Holly's dragon pressed against Edan's knee, lending its support. Edan picked up Holly's joy and happiness. She was gone from his life forever. He would never touch her again. Her essence remained. Her Being stayed tied to their Bond.

Noise beat against their Triangle. Colors pulsed, burned, froze them.

"Question." A bronze dragon, tall as five men, its wings as wide as ten men, demanded Edan's focus, Edan's life.

Edan looked into an indigo dragon's face. Its head was as long as Edan's body and four times his width. Eyes as deep as the darkest ocean studied Edan and dismissed him as inconsequential. Holly's dragon screamed defiance at the indigo dragon that bent again to study Edan.

A puce dragon nudged Edan, probing him. *"Question!"*

He was empty; no questions remained – or at least none that he knew how to ask, or thought he wanted to hear the answers to. Was this, then, what was meant by the human word *"despair"*, what happened when an Elf began to Fade?

Somewhere close by orange cats screamed and a kitten purred. About Edan's head, inside his ears and behind his eyelids, colors swirled and blurred together, a thin thread of green pulsed with life. Thunder beat with an under-song plucked on a gentle guitar. Plummeting air currents gave them respite from the burning heat.

A tiny star twinkled white in the black sky. It plunged to the center of their Triangle in a blinding column of white.

The journey ended with a soft jolt, and then blessed nothingness.

******

Elven time churned slowly forward, no better than human time at healing the wounded soul.

Edan didn't want to open his eyes. He felt the spider thin fingers of a Brownie tap his face, then two small fingers jerked open one of his eyelids.

"Who am I?" the squeaky voice demanded.

"Go away, Weg," Edan managed. His throat ached

as though a massive pipe had been shoved down it.

"You'll live," Weg said.

Edan didn't feel quite as certain about that as Weg did but, for now, he just wanted to lie here on this cold, solid floor, in this quiet, peaceful room. Small hands lifted his head, removed the Prince Band of Office then gently replaced his head on the cushion. Lavender drifted up from where his head rested to soothe his scorched nasal passages. The strong fingers twisted his arms into the sleeves of a warm woolen shirt and then encased his legs in warm trousers. A blanket, holding the scents of wind-blown clover and sunlight covered his body.

"Drink," Ta demanded. A drinking straw was poked at his mouth.

"Open your mouth and drink, Edan, or we'll open your mouth for you and pour it in." Weg's bony fingers were already prying between his parched lips.

Edan finally managed to open his lips enough that Ta shoved the straw in.

"Drink," Ta encouraged.

The warm wine, pungent with herbs, slid into Edan's mouth and trickled down his throat.

"More," Weg commanded.

Something else was in the wine, a bitter taste, but with Ta and Weg pestering him, he managed to swallow more. Finally they left him alone to decide if he wanted to dissolve into the Mists or sleep. Sleep finally won.

*****

Edan heard the morning birds fighting over the early worms. Damn birds should all be shot and cooked. At least the worms were quiet.

A male's voice groaned. A second male cursed.

Edan opened sand-encrusted eyes and was immediately sorry. He managed to get to the personal room before the true misery racked his body. Afterwards, he crawled back to the Hall. Crawling was better than walking. To walk meant he had to stand upright and he didn't want to risk walking because if he did, his head might finish splitting and send parts rolling across the marble floor. Brownies grumbled about cleaning blood and messes like that off the floors.

He made it to a chair, but decided trying to sit in it was beyond him. He did get upright enough to hold the cup Ta pressed into his hand. He sipped the cool fruit juice, lightly laced with wine, and again tasted the bitter herb infused through it. This time he recognized the taste of the powder used by the healers to help body aches and fevers.

"I have never had such misery," Efran's voice rasped, a harsh grating mimicry of his normal mellow tones. His head hung limply and he used both hands to hold the cup from which he took small sips.

At least his father had managed to get into a chair, Edan thought sourly. He took a couple of judicious sips from his own cup. The nausea seemed to be easing slightly.

"Now you know why we are cautious in dealing with dragons." The King coughed slightly and drank, then took the pipe his Brownie handed him.

"I think–" Efran cleared his raspy throat and drank more of the healing juice. "–I think the Dragons won."

"You're lucky they didn't eat you," Weg said.

"No ketchup," Edan managed to get out. He drank more juice.

Silence grew deep in the room. He lifted his eyes from his cup to see his father, the King, and the house Brownies staring at him.

"What is ketchup?" asked Weg.

"It is a condiment made from tomatoes," Efran said. "What has ketchup to do with dragons?"

"Holly has a shirt with a dragon on it. It carries a message that the dragons like to put ketchup on things they eat, especially crunchy things like the bones of Beings who interfere in their affairs."

To his relief, everyone shrugged that off for the nonsense it was. Dragons most certainly did not need ketchup when they ate.

"Did you ascertain an answer from all of that?" Fragrant smoke wreathed the king's head, further easing Edan's headache and stomachache. "Easy question first: Were the Dragons responsible for the nucklelavee and the attorcroppe?"

"I *think* Holly's familiar brought in the nucklelavee trying to get me and Holly to join. Often the relaxation from fear triggers the hormonal response for sex."

Edan accepted the offer of leaf and pipe from one of the King's Brownies. His father's Brownie popped into the Hall with his father's favorite pipe. The three of them sipped the healing draught and grew more relaxed with each mouthful of leaf they inhaled.

"From her familiar's reaction to the other Dragons, I *think* they sent the attorcroppe in order to take the familiar's idea a step farther."

"Let's face a fact none of us looked at when you brought the familiar into our Hall." Efran blew a long stream of smoke to the ceiling. "If the familiar had not wanted you to meet with the Dragons, even as strong as you are, you wouldn't have been able to hold it. Perhaps the familiar used the attorcroppe to entice your anger to demand an audience with Dragons. What does the familiar want? That's the question."

Edan stared into his cup. "I think the familiar's desire is to keep Holly and me together. I think Dragons might be planning to use a child of mine and Holly's to train as a Leader."

"Not the first time." The King snorted a stream of smoke through his nose all the world like an angry dragon himself reminding Edan that Sir himself was the product of just such interference.

"I will not take a child from Holly just so the Dragons can play at Kingmaker."

"Never in the length of my life has anything pained me more than having to remove you from your mother's breast."

"Is that why you stayed with her the length of her life?"

Efran blew smoke to the ceiling. "No matter how many females I have enjoyed, I have always had a special thread to your mother. She passed Beyond many centuries ago, yet her memory remains as fresh as the day I met her."

"How do you bear it?"

"By enjoying your company, by helping other younglings grow to maturity the way our Sire helped you, by seeing bits of her in you. I chose not to obliterate her memories."

"Are you considering leaving Holly?" The King tapped the leaf ashes from his pipe.

"Yes. I do not wish to father a child on her and be forced to take it from her."

His Sir harrumphed at him. "You may not have a child with her. Dragons do not predict the future. They simply see the different lines. Things change. What they showed you may not occur."

"Father, you can scry. Tell me my direction."

"I use my knife to see the future to remind myself such visions cut both ways. Should I tell you what I see? The very act of telling you will change things."

"Then what is the point of such gifts?"

His father gave him a sad smile indicating his own acceptance of the frustrations. "Like all gifts they can be as much curse as blessing."

"You need not make such a decision immediately.

There is time to consider." Smoke rings encircled the King's head. "As half-Elf, half-human, you have several human years to make your decision before it becomes irrevocable. You and Holly can still enjoy each other's company."

Edan shook his head and tapped his own pipe empty. He used the cleaning tools provided, then handed it to the King's Brownie with his thanks. He handed his cup to Weg with a bow. "I must leave Holly. It would be cruel to remain. I shall get my dog and tell Holly good-bye."

"It's quite difficult for an Elf to conceive a child."

Edan raised his eyebrows at his father. "You did. You are full Elf. Sir's mother did. She is also full Elf. It can happen. Dragons showed me two lines. One with a son and one with a daughter. In both lines Holly was their mother, yet in both lines Holly was also gone from their lives. I will not risk it. Holly should enjoy her children. If they are my children also, she will not have that joy."

He held up his hand in farewell and saw the concerned faces of the Brownies and the male Elves who loved him before they faded from his vision. He found Holly arriving home after work. He materialized on her front porch to wait for her.

Holly waved to him and released Pook from her car seatbelt. "Go to Edan, Pook."

Edan came down the steps and knelt to greet Pook. He stood and came to the car to help Holly with her groceries.

Solemnly, he shook Rat's paw. "Good afternoon to you also, Rat."

To Holly's shock, he leaned over and simply kissed her cheek, then picked up two of the bags of groceries.

"Excuse me." Holly plopped the bag she'd picked up back into the trunk. She put her hands on her hips and tapped her foot. "The last time I saw you we were both stark naked and our knees were green. And all I get is a kiss on the cheek? I don't think so, your highness."

She grabbed Edan by his ears and hauled his face down to hers. His mouth opened under hers. His tongue swept into her mouth. He tasted sweet and smoky with the slightest hint of red wine, the best of honey barbeque sauce at a Fourth of July party on a hot summer night. His ear peaks heated and pulsed under her stroking fingers. She pressed her body tighter to his, needing the pressure of his solid chest against her aching nipples. He probed and nibbled as though he were memorizing every centimeter of her mouth.

Hardly able to stand, wanting to lie down and open her legs for him, Holly took her mouth from his. "Let's go inside."

"Holly. I have to leave."

"Again? Didn't you find out what you needed to know? I think my dragon came back."

"Yes, I found out what I needed to know."

Edan's eyes looked so sad and bleak Holly's heart broke for him.

"That is why I must leave. Your dragon was here when I first came. It is gone for the moment. It should return when I leave again."

"What did you find out? Why do you have to leave?"

"Dragons have been manipulating us. They want us to breed a child to be a Leader."

"A baby?" Joy welled up in Holly. It disappeared as quickly. "But if it's Elf I can't keep it."

"Exactly. And I will not be a party to you losing a child. You deserve a husband to cherish you, a child to raise. It cannot be mine."

I don't want a man *for my husband, you stupid Elf!* Holly's heart broke, mind blazed with impotent fury. *Don't need a child. Need you. My Elf. Don't leave. Damn it.*

Don't leave.

But he was going to go. Damn, stupid stubborn Elf.

Holly took a deep breath, picked up the bag of groceries from the trunk, and slammed the lid. *Not going to cry now*, she admonished herself. Tears were for later, when she was alone. No. Not now. She forced the sadness away and focused on the joy of being with Edan again. No, she wasn't going to cry. She *wasn't*.

"I knew from the beginning you'd be leaving. Help me with the groceries, please."

"Holly, I must take Pook and leave. I do not wish to make this harder for you."

"Ah, but Edan–" Holly winked at him and rubbed her hand across his crotch. "–I want this harder for me. If we have to say good-bye, we're going to say good-bye in the best way. Memories are everything."

"I will erase your memories of me."

"You will *not*." Holly glared at him. "They're my memories and I want them. If I can't have you, I want my memories. I got through the Towers. Those miserable memories and the memories of my friends who died in the Towers have made me stronger. If I can deal with that, I can certainly live with the happy memories of this short time I with you."

"What do you mean? What Towers? Your friends died?"

"Yes." Holly softly told him what she'd never been able to tell another soul: how she'd escaped the World Trade Center bombing and the paralyzing fears that had stifled her life since. "In the hotel room after I sent you away during the storm, I realized I was not going to live my life being scared and unhappy any more. If I let myself be unhappy, the terrorists won. I won't let that happen. Not in my life."

Edan's eyes were thoughtful on her. "You are very brave. I realized when listening to you, I have let my childhood grief over the loss of my mother influence my life."

He stroked Holly's hair as if committing its texture to his memory. "Not only do I not want you to lose a child the way my mother lost me. I do not want to be responsible for another child living with grief the way I have. I think though, like my father, I can also live with the joyful memories of my time with you, the way he lives with the memories of my mother. I do not want to lose my memories of the time we spent together."

Holly finally understood the term bittersweet joy. She blinked away her tears and smiled at Edan. "Put the dogs in the backyard where they'll be fenced while I dump the meat and veggies in the 'fridge and the frozen stuff in the freezer. Then we'll make some more memories to warm us on lonely nights."

Edan bowed his head at her. "You are quite the managing sort."

"Prince, old fellow, you have no idea exactly how managing I'm about to be."

*****

The night sky was splattered with jeweled stars the way it had been when Edan first appeared in Holly's yard. Now Edan placed a hand on Pook's collar and raised his other hand in farewell. Holly hadn't been able persuade him she didn't need a baby if he stayed. Damn stubborn Elf. At least she still had her memories of him.

After he faded away, she trudged back into the house followed by Rat. Orange Crush twisted around her ankles, mewing to give her comfort.

She was not going to cry. They'd had a great time together, but she knew from the beginning their time together was limited.

She went to the freezer and pulled out the carton of chocolate chip ice cream and got a spoon from the cutlery drawer. She curled up in her favorite chair in the quiet living room.

She was not going to cry. She'd told Edan she wanted to keep her memories of him. Insisted on it, despite his initial protests. She let a spoonful of ice cream melt in her mouth. Now she had to deal with the pain of his leaving.

Holly very carefully licked ice cream from the spoon. This whole thing with Edan had started over too many margaritas with her four best friends. It ended here alone.

"Be careful what you wish for," Holly told Rat. She flipped him a doggy treat from the jar she kept on the coffee table for him and scooped up more ice cream.

Half the container later, Holly realized her stomach was full, but her taste buds were still clamoring for more, more, more. If she could have her taste buds removed, she'd probably be able to get those last mumble, mumble pounds off. Oh, well, if she couldn't have more of Edan, she might as well make her taste buds happy.

With the next spoonful of ice cream making her taste buds happy, happy as the television chef said, she wondered if the other girls' invocations had resulted in materialization of their wishes for immortal lovers. She hadn't talked to any of them since Edan landed in her life. Everyone needs friends and it was just wrong of her to ignore them just because she had an Elf in her life, or any hunky man for that matter.

She picked up the phone and dialed her best friend Isabella's number from habit. When Isabella answered, Holly forced herself to be cheerful.

"Hey, girlfriend, were you sober enough a couple of weeks ago that you can remember that drunken dance we did, naked in the woods? Well, um, it worked. I *had* an Elf."

Then she burst into tears and got the last of her ice

cream all salty and runny.

CHAPTER 13

Edan paused at the clearing, his arms filled with wild mountain thyme and fragrant flowers for the Joining Bower.

His father and Daffodil were quarreling again. This time the King was with them and also irritated.

"I tell you he's fading. The bond is too strong. He has to go back." So determined to maintain eye contact with his father, Daffodil stood on her tip-toes and held onto Efran's shirt to maintain her balance.

Efran soothed a palm over Daffodil's clenched fists, but his face was creased with worry and his eyebrows drew together as though he were trying to see the future. "He'll survive. It takes time."

Edan assumed they were yet again discussing the young boy-child in his father's care. The lad was sickly and many of the Elves were expending Power to bolster the small part-Elf's Being. He hadn't been much help with the boy. He was distracted by thoughts of Holly too frequently to keep his Power focused for healing.

But, today he was determined to add his Power to the Joining Ceremony. He and Holly did not have a life together, but he must focus to help the Joining Couple create a new Life. He owed his Community his support and his loyalty in the continuation of Life. He owed his memories of Holly to continue his own life force.

"I don't wish to have to call for Judgment," the King said. "The decision must be made willingly otherwise there may be more problems."

"Stupid, stubborn males."   Daffodil snorted in disgust. She released her hold on Efran. The King caught her to help her regain her balance. Daffodil snarled, "Get your hand off my arse, Sire. The Joining has not begun and I do not know yet if I will favor either of you."

Although he wasn't aware of it, Edan must have moved because Daffodil spotted him between the trees and called out, "Good day, Edan. What a generous armload for the Bower."

She came to him, weaved her arm through his, and led him away from his father and Sir before he could do more than greet them.

"Perhaps I shall favor you during the Joining."

Edan knew Daffodil was only joking. Or he hoped she was. He wasn't quite sure he wanted to join with her in the Midst. Sourly, he acknowledged to himself he wasn't quite sure he could join with anyone during the proceedings.

Edan glanced backwards to see his father's and the King's reaction to Daffodil's taunt. Their heads were together, worry lines deepening on both faces. The child must be more sickly than Edan thought.

Daffodil's body twined against his, hampering his movement, even as her babble grated in his ears. He laid his plant offering next to the Bower where Elves, primarily female, fussed the placement just so. Daffodil moved away with a pat on his arm and wandered not quite in the direction of his father and the King. Edan leaned against a tree, grateful for the respite before the ceremony. He'd picked and carried back more than he'd intended. He rubbed arms now aching from the strain.

Elven women in filmy gauze gowns in the multiple colors of the Earth fluttered about the clearing and woods like grounded butterflies. Their breasts hung in fruitful globes beneath the nearly invisible fabric, their nipples taut with anticipation. Elven men, clad in sheer robes of the colors of the sky and light, occasionally stopped to retie a robe so their stiffened maleness remained clad until the Joining Ceremony.

Although what the point was, Edan had never been able to understand. He looked down at his own robe, the deep blue of a summer storm, to see his chest hair, the nest of curls at his shaft, and his shaft, still lank and loose despite the tempting bodies around him and occasionally pressing against him..

He shrugged. The Power during the Ceremony would entice his shaft upright. He'd add his Power to the Fertility Couple and join in the celebration.

Energy began to hum as more Elves joined around the Bonding Trees and the Joining Bower. The energy levels soared when the Couple came into the clearing. The couple sat on the bent, entwined boughs of two trees that grew opposite the clearing from each other. The time had come.

Edan pulled himself off the tree and drifted to join the circle. He caught a flash of chartreuse. He suppressed the pang of disappointment that it wasn't Holly's dragon but simply an Elf woman in green.

As if he'd summoned her the way she'd summoned him, he saw Holly standing in front of him, smiling at him. But the transparent image dissipated when the King's voice pulled the Elves tighter into the circle.

Edan only partially listened to the ritual. He paid close enough attention to respond properly, but most of his concentration focused on gathering his Power to give it to the Couple. Efran nudged him and Edan abruptly realized the Binding Ritual was complete.

Edan joined the other males in escorting the male partner around the clearing. Each time they passed the knot of females surrounding the female partner Edan glanced through the throng trying to make a decision.

One female had ringlets of hair cascading down to her rump. The thought of that textured hair – so like Holly's – curling and tickling against his skin pooled heat into his groin.

Another female had green eyes, the brilliance of emeralds, sparkling above a cheerful mouth. He spent hours thinking about eyes exactly that shade of green. His erection stiffened more at the thought of those green eyes watching his shaft grow.

Yet another had ripe round rump cheeks – the kind of rump a male could cuddle and hold onto while he thrust deep into the cushioned hollow made to hold him alone. He grew harder. The tip of his desire peeked from his robe.

He saw another, small and round, the perfect size to tuck under his arm and cuddle. He grew hotter and discarded his robe as so many of the other males had done.

He heard a laugh, close in timber to the one that haunted his dreams. He caught the scent of lemon verbena. His body ached and burned, it demanded to be quenched in the hot wetness of a willing female.

They all circled to the Joining Bower. The females lifted *Her* and laid *Her* on the Bower. The males lifted *Him* and placed *Him* to kneel between *Her* open legs.

Edan's mouth watered at the taste and texture of *Her* nipple in *His* mouth. *His* hands filled with the bounty of *Her* breasts, the silk of *Her* wet mouth. *His* tongue battled and joined with *Her* tongue, felt *Her* teeth nip him. *Her* thighs draped across *His* arms and *His* eyes feasted on *Her* open labia, wet and gleaming with *Her* juices. *He* eagerly lapped across *Her* folds. *His* tongue probed for *Her* clitoris sucking it into *His* mouth. *His* ears rang with the pleasure of *Her* cries. *He* held *Her* body to *Him* while *She* twisted and panted on a small crest. *He* moved up *Her* body to straddle *Her*. *She* sat up and suckled *His* shaft, taking it deep into the dark wetness of *Her* mouth. *She* nibbled and sucked while *He* balanced *Her* breasts in *His* hands and thumbed *Her* nipples into tight buds. *He* began to crest and placed *His* body between *Her* legs. *He* thrust into *Her* body. *She* clung to *Him* and drove *Herself* upward to meet *His* thrusts. *Her* nails dug into *His* rump and *She* pulled *Him* closer to *Her*. *He* slammed into *Her* hot, tight, sheath. *Her* body began to shudder around *His*. The muscles holding *Him* deep inside *Her* tightened and flexed around *His* shaft. *He* lifted *Her Him*, holding *Her* by *Her* globes and as tightly as *She* held *Him*.

The Power and Energy grew and hummed around them. His shaft grew impossibly, unbearably hard. The pressure built in his loins.

Edan felt the sweetness of Holly's body around his. He felt the pleasure of her passage holding him tightly.

He grieved that he only held Holly in his memories. His consciousness sent him the memory of Holly telling him of her grief in the Towers. Abruptly, he realized he'd told Holly a falsehood. Yes, he had concerns about a child of Holly's and his, but he now knew his major distress was losing Holly to Beyond where he could not go.

Yet he was half-mortal. If he gave up his Elven life, he could go Beyond. If he could go Beyond, he might be able to remain with Holly forever, even after Eternity crumbled.

Her body shook around *His*. *He* exploded into *Her*. *Her* voice raised in a cry wrenched from the center of *Her* Being. *His* own cry came from *His* deepest Being. *His* crest caught with *Hers* and *Together They* spiraled into the Light.

Edan came back into his own Being. Around him, elves joined in couples and groups celebrating The Joining with their own. He, however, lay pressed to his belly on the spongy ground. His shaft had drained into the Earth instead of the hot body of another willing elf.

At first, he worried that his distracted thoughts of Holly might have disrupted the flow of energy in the Circle. Blurrily, he focused on the Joining Couple. Looking at them, he realized his Power had exhausted itself into the Lovers still coupling on the Bower and had indeed helped the combined Powers achieve their purpose in creating a new Life.

Relieved, he decided to return to his own abode and rest. The Joinings in the clearing had been known to continue for hours even without the celebration of a Binding and a Joining.

Slowly he made his way to his own quiet home and lay down on his own empty bed, weighing the different heartaches of choosing between Holly and his Elven life. Unlike Elliot and his father, he was not a full Elf with the ability to return to De'erjia after Holly went Beyond. He had only the ability to choose one plane or the other.

To be fully human or fully Elf, and to either fade here in De'erjia pining for Holly, or to remove himself to her plane, forget his life here and move Beyond as she did when it was time.

******

"Edan, Prince of De'erjia."

He looked up from the final polish on the last of the boots for the man who rescued Pook and into Sir's face.

Edan promptly dropped the polishing cloth, rose, and bowed. Simultaneously, he clicked his tongue at Pook and gave the "Sit, Stay" hand signals before Pook dashed up to Sir in greeting.

For at this moment, this was not his beloved Sir standing in front of him. This was his Liege Lord, the current King of De'erjia with full entourage of courtiers behind him. Edan's brain scrambled to think what he had done, or not done, to warrant a formal meeting.

"As in Tradition established during my reign as King of De'erjia, I hold as my responsibility the formal notification of Judgment being called on any of my people."

Judgment? Judgment? Someone was calling Judgment on him? Years of training kept Edan standing at respectful attention while Holly's phrase screamed in his brain: *What the fuck?*

Momentarily, he scanned the courtiers and crowd

behind them. His father gave a nearly invisible shrug and his eyes drifted to Daffodil at his side. Daffodil's hands clenched at her sides in rigid anger.

With a start, Edan realized her anger was directed at him, not at the King.

"An arbitration committee has been appointed. If the issue can be resolved to the mutual satisfaction of yourself and those calling for Judgment, Judgment will be set aside. Should the issue not come to a satisfactory conclusion, then you shall report to the Court of Judgment at the next Meeting and the Court shall determine the course of action."

The King dropped his voice from command to Sir's whisper that only Edan heard. "We'll work this out, urchin. Don't worry."

Numbly, Edan took the parchment handed him by one of the courtiers and watched the King and his entourage leave his clearing.

"Sit, Edan." Weg nudged his knees.

Edan sat heavily on his bench.

Ta pressed a cup into his hand.

His father sat beside him and took a second cup from Ta.

"Why did Daffodil call for Judgment on me?" Edan's heart hurt and the wine-laced juice did nothing to ease the bitterness in his mouth.

Ta and Weg disappeared with pops.

"I didn't think she was going to." Efran didn't bother to hide his anger. Anger that comforted Edan in his numbed misery.

"I've been trying to talk her out of it. Let me see who's on the arbitration committee." He took the parchment from Edan's slack fingers.

Pook nuzzled Edan's now free hand, asking for and giving comfort. She leaned her head on Edan's knees while he fondled her ears and cords.

"Hmm...your sword and knife tutor Costac, Goldenrod–"

"How is her pregnancy?" The last time Edan had seen her she was wrapped naked around Skyowl on the Joining Bower.

"Coming along nicely. She says the baby is a girl. Bosco," Efran continued, "nice to have the Master who taught your trade on this list. Bless the Elements, me. Oh, stars and little fishes, Daffodil is the fifth. If Daffodil is on here, then who called Judgment?"

Efran snatched the parchment from Efran's hand and skimmed through it to the Judgment Petition.

"Weg! Ta!"

"That tone of voice isn't going to bring them back." Efran's Brownie popped into the area in front of Efran and Edan. It handed Efran his pipe and leaf, then popped out of sight again.

"But why would *my* Brownies petition for Judgment on me?"

"I guess we'll discover that during arbitration."

"Or not," Edan said sourly. "Brownies are almost as bad as Dragons about not revealing their intentions."

******

Edan sat crossed-legged on the mossy ground as part of the arbitration circle. Although he tried to ignore them, and to remain angry with them, Weg and Ta only leaned closer, each tight up against one of his arms, their long fingers entwined in his.

"He's not happy," Weg said. "We can't stay with him if he's not happy."

"We thought about simply leaving his abode like Brownies usually do, but decided he needs to know why we want to leave. We want him happy again."

Edan sneered at them. "You are not Fairies to

spread happiness and joy with wishes and hopes. You are Brownies. You clean and cook and keep the abode fresh and free of dust and mites."

"Fairies are not the only ones who spread happiness and joy." Goldenrod rubbed her still flat belly where the baby's life-force visibly pulsed through her skin and the gauze of her gown.

"Think how miserable you'd be in a filthy house with no one to prepare your meals." Costac pointed a knife at Edan in emphasis. "I agree Brownies spread happiness."

"You cannot make Edan happy," Bosco pointed out. "Neither can we."

"But Edan *knows* what will make him happy," Daffodil purred. "He just won't admit it."

Edan knew that purr well. Daffodil's little purr was the equivalent of a lion's full-blown raging battle roar.

What would make him happy?

Holly. The answer smoothly slid into his Being as easily as a latte went down his throat.

"Tell us the answer, young Edan," his father cajoled. "Admit it to us. We saw your body change when the answer came to you."

"Holly."

"It is but a simple application of Power to erase the memories of your time together. We can do that now," said the battle-scarred Costac.

"I promised Holly not to take the memories away. You cannot remove mine without removing hers. And I promised I would not do that."

"Then why do you not go back to her?" Goldenrod asked.

"I do not wish to leave my home. And I will not risk fathering a part-Elf child with Holly only to have to take it from her. You have life growing in you, Goldenrod. You understand why I cannot do that to Holly."

"Yes, Edan." Her voice was as soothing as his dim remembrance of his mother's voice he heard as he grew in her womb. "But you are half-Elf. It would take great Power for you to conceive a child with Holly."

"But Dragons are interfering in our lives. They have the Power."

Bosco cleared his throat. "There are human ways to prevent a child from forming."

"Holly wants a child."

"Adopt," his father said. "Elves are always raised by others than their birth parents. It makes a stronger bond with the Community. Sir loves you as much as I do. If Holly wishes a child, you and she will love a child regardless of if it came from your bodies or not."

"But if I bond with Holly and remain with her, I lose De'erjia. I lose you, Father. I lose Sir. I lose Daffodil. I lose my Community." Edan shook his hands free of Ta and Weg's fingers and hugged them tightly to him. "I even lose these wretched Brownies who are so angry with me they've forced me into arbitration."

"You are bonded with Holly," Costac, one of the biggest, most surly of the Battle Elves, said with a gentleness as soft as dandelion fluff floating in the breeze. "We can almost see the bond. It is not as clear and strong as Goldenrod's and Skyowl's, but the bond is there. What are you afraid of, Edan?"

"Edan?" His father asked the same question without the words.

"Tell us, Edan." Goldenrod's voice filled with the comfort of Mother Earth.

"You are frightened, Edan," Bosco said. "We are your friends. We will help you."

"Like happiness," Daffodil said tartly, "fear can only be faced from the inner Being. Edan knows his fear as much as he knows his happiness. If he cannot face it and live with it, he will not live. He will only exist and fade to nothing."

As though Holly were sitting in the circle with them, Edan heard her voice: *"I realized I was not going to live my life being scared and unhappy any more."*

Edan opened the fear in his heart and looked at it. He drew on the small warm bodies of Ta and Weg for comfort. He felt the vibrations of compassion and encouragement spinning from the others in the circle.

"I am afraid that when Holly goes Beyond, the bond between us will not hold and I will not find her again."

With the bluntness of one who has lived since the first words were spoken, Daffodil said, "You will lose Holly whether you remain here in De'erjia for the rest of Eternity or accept the mortal half of your life and the ability to go Beyond at the end of that Life. Do you choose to remain and learn to live without Holly or do you return to Holly and strengthen the Bonding between you so that you might find each other in the Beyond?"

CHAPTER 14

The door chime rang in the front lobby. Rat barked and Holly heard his toenails clatter down the hallway. Abruptly, he stopped barking and gave his welcome whine. Must be one of the regulars.

"Just a minute," Holly called through the intercom in the grooming area where she was reshaping a chow's lion cut. She unhooked the stationary holder to release the dog in order to cage him while she talked to the customer.

"Hello, Holly."

Still holding the now growling chow in place, Holly whipped her head around.

Edan stood in the doorway, holding a happily, squirming Rat

"I thought you were gone for good." She refused to fan the kernel of hope that sparked inside her.

"That is what I need to talk to you about."

Holly again hooked the stationary lead around the Chow. "We can talk while I finish the dog."   Cool, she was going to be cool and not throw herself on Edan. She started the clippers and saw Edan flinch.

"Look," she said, "it's almost lunch time. Why don't you go down to the deli and get us some lunch while I finish him. Then we can talk while we eat."

After Edan left, Holly focused on the Chow. Better to concentrate on getting the dog's coat just right than to try to anticipate what Edan wanted. Her heart was still too tender to be much more than polite.

Edan came back with the food and his inevitable latte just about the time she finished the Chow. While she cleaned up, Edan settled the dog in a cage. By the time she got back to the break room, Edan was hanging up the telephone and had checked off the last phone call to the owners whose dogs were groomed that morning.

"Thanks."

"You are welcome."

Holly got a bottle of water from the break room's mini-refrigerator. She poked at the sandwich Edan bought and drank her water.

"So, why did you come back?" she asked while she concentrated on tearing the napkin into precise pieces.

"I could not get coffee in De'erjia."

Holly looked up and glared at him. His eyes twinkled like midnight stars over the rim of his cup.

"Asshole."

"Yes, I am." He set down his cup and took Holly's hands in his. "I also missed you very much. I wish to spend more time with you, if you will allow it?"

"I thought you told me once it wasn't possible for me to go to De'erjia?"

"It isn't. However, I will stay in this plane and not return to De'erjia for at least one of your years. You have a tradition called 'engagement' during which a couple decides if they truly want to go through the bonding ritual and stay mated for the rest of their lives?"

"Uh, yeah." Holly looked at him, confused. "But I think most people just use the time to plan the hoopla."

"Will you be willing to try this engagement ritual for the year? To see if we are suited for the hoopla ceremony?"

"Um." It was difficult not to laugh. Not to bubble over. Not to scream with frustration. "Are we going to live together?"

Edan's brow creased. "That is another thing. My father and Daffodil plan to spend part of this next year attending various Ren Faires. My father sells the knives he makes. Daffodil sells her jewelry. They have suggested I purchase a vehicle, and that Pook and I travel with them. They say my footwear will sell well throughout the circuit.

They believe I must live as human for a year to see if I can live without going back and forth to De'erjia. If you wish to try this engagement ritual with me, I can arrange for you to take an airplane to meet me at various festivals. I can also fly back here to visit with you."

"And if you decide you can live as a human and if we go through the hoopla, will you become temporarily human like your friend Elliot?"

Edan shook his head, his heavy hair swinging on his shoulders. "Elliot is a full Elf. When Madeline goes Beyond he, like my father and Daffodil did, will return to De'erjia. Elves cannot go Beyond. As half-Elf, half-mortal, I can only stay a limited time before I must either return to De'erjia or choose my mortal life until I also go Beyond."

Holly chewed her lip. "When you say 'Beyond', do you mean die?"

"Yes."

She looked deep into his solemn eyes. "You'd give up immortality to stay with me?"

"As I realized in De'erjia, I have a choice between living in De'erjia without you or bonding with you and possibly, hopefully, staying linked with you in the Beyond. I want to try living as human. I cannot promise I will be able to do this, but I wish to try. If I can do so, will you join me in the hoopla ritual?"

Holly stood long enough to move from her chair to Edan's lap. She wrapped her arms around him and laid her head against his heart. Languidly, she ran one finger around his ear enjoying the feel of his pulse under her finger at the tip that matched the beat of his heart.

"So you won't have your ear-peaks if you become human?"

Edan's breathing grew harsher and his hand brushed under her shirt to caress over her bra-covered nipple. "No, I will not. I must also tell you, if I become human, then like

Elliot, neither of us will remember I was ever Elf. The Powers That Be will shift our memories and give me a human history that we will remember."

Holly was having trouble with her own breathing and Edan had pushed her bra up to cradle her breast in his palm while he thumbed the nipple. "Um, can you suggest some background for a human history for you?"

"Yes. My father assures me if I become human, we will see him as my father and Daffodil as my step-mother. Sir has also said he will be part of our lives as my grandfather. I will not lose my family." Edan laughed. "My House Brownies, Weg and Ta, are trying to align some power to allow them human form. They wish to be my siblings."

"How nice. I've got a younger brother and an older sister. Family is good."

"Yes, it is."

Holly's panties were getting very wet, but Edan's hand didn't leave her breast. She nuzzled his neck, that special soft hollow of his throat below his Adam's apple.

"Um, you might suggest an ex-wife in the background. It's a weird culture. While women my age have frequently chosen to be picky about going through the hoopla—" Part of Holly giggled silently at her continual substitution of 'hoopla' for 'wedding'. She loved messing with Edan's vocabulary. "—men your age who haven't been attached to a female are looked upon as weird. Like what is wrong with that guy that some woman hasn't snatched him up. But an ex-wife is acceptable."

"That is very odd."

"I cannot explain it. It's just the human way," she said, mimicking the way Edan always told her *"It's just the Elf way"* when she questioned something.

"Are we agreed to try this engagement then?"

"Yes." Holly kissed him briefly once, then got off

his lap, and adjusted her bra. "But I'm human and I want this engagement done the human way."

"The Elf way is naked," Edan said.

A shot of heat constricted Holly's nipples unbearably.

"In front of the entire Community."

Holly's honey flowed into her panties. "Um, we're not in De'erjia."

"True, but we could pretend."

Holly sat on the chair, her legs unable to hold her. "In my human culture, you have to kneel and present me with a ring to indicate you want to be engaged."

"Ah." Edan reached into his pants pocket and pulled out a green velvet bag. "My father said as much. Daffodil made a ring. She said she will also make us binding rings should we go through the hoopla. But she called it 'wedding'."

"Hoopla," Holly said firmly as Edan knelt on the floor.

"Holly." His voice was so solemn that tears stung Holly's eyes. "Will you please Join with me, wear this ring during our engagement ritual and help me to learn to be human? And if I succeed in adapting to being human, will you bond with me in the hoopla and strengthen our threads so even going Beyond will not separate us?"

Holly's tears flowed when Edan placed the gold band made of interlaced Celtic knots and set with a deep green emerald on her finger.

******

Wearing jeans and a heavy knit sweater, her feet in warm socks and thick-soled shoes, Holly sat on her front porch enjoying a cup of coffee and the crisp autumn air. She never drank coffee any more without grinning over Edan's joy in it.

In the evening light, red, gold, yellow, and brown

leaves drifted away from the mounds Holly had raked, then swirled and danced in circles when the wind caught them. She rubbed Rat's ears and watched the green aventurine glimmer on her wrist. It always reminded her of dragon scales.

The moss agate Edan had given her hung at the base of her throat. She rubbed her thumb across the silver dragon incised in it, drawing comfort from it the same way she drew comfort from hugging Rat. Despite the new sweater she'd knitted him, Rat shivered, but she couldn't persuade him to stay in the house. Crush, perched on the porch railing, sneered at them in his already thick winter coat.

A falling star, possibly one of the first from the evening's predicted Leonid meteor shower, streaked across the sky. Holly didn't make a wish. If she was patient just a little bit longer, she would shortly have everything she ever wished for, she was sure. Her heart promised her.

The emerald ring Edan had given her over a year ago flashed green fire in the last of the evening light.

An engine rumbled on the road hidden from her porch by the trees bordering her yard. Down her driveway came a familiar old Ford F250 crew cab with an over-the-cab camper.

Holly's heart thumped, unable to believe the truck was in her driveway and its familiar driver was behind the wheel. She set her coffee cup on the step and joined Rat in racing across the yard.

Edan stepped from the truck's cab, his legs encased in blue jeans, wearing a wool shirt over a black turtleneck. Pook scrambled out behind him. She and Rat bounded through the leaves playing some doggy game.

Edan caught Holly, lifted her off the ground, and swung her in a circle. Their dizzy dance ended with them in a mound of leaves.

Holly stroked around Edan's ears. "As many times

as I've seen you without your Ren Faire Elf costume, I can still almost see the points on your ears. If I close my eyes, I can feel them."

Edan laughed. "You only love me for my Ren Faire Elf ears?"

"Well...." Happiness warmed Holly as much as Edan's nearness warmed her, as much as his hands sliding up her sweater to unclasp her bra and cradling her breasts in his palms. She shivered from the heat swamping her when he thumbed her nipples. "Those peaks were pretty sexy."

"So are these." His fingers tweaked her nipples now constricted so tightly they were pleasure to almost the point of pain.

"Mine aren't fake."

"Maybe I need to get closer to them and make sure." Edan lifted her sweater. He unsnapped the front clasp of her bra, and his mouth fastened on one nipple to suckle it deep into his mouth.

Holly spiraled upwards like the leaves around them at the wet swipe of his tongue over her cool skin.

He'd barely started when he stopped, refastened her bra, and pulled her sweater back down. His eyes were solemn on hers. "We have to talk."

"I told you how I felt."

"Are you positive you can live without experiencing a pregnancy? For all intents and purposes, my sperm count is non-existent. I wouldn't be able to deal with losing a second wife who decided she absolutely had to have a baby."

"Are you open to adoption? Not necessarily a baby?"

Edan's mouth tightened in a thin line. "I suggested adoption to my ex-wife. She didn't want a child unless it came from her own body."

"She was an idiot. I'm not. If we adopt a child, it's the icing on the cake."

"Do you still want to join with me in the hoopla?"

"I've been waiting all year for you to feel ready enough to ask me."

Edan dug in his jeans pocket and extracted one of the green velvet bags that were his step-mother's trademark packaging. "Daphne made us binding bands for the ceremony." Interlaced Celtic knots formed the bands and matched her engagement ring.

Joy filled every part of Holly being when Edan placed the rings on her palm. "What about the Ren Faire circuit? I can't leave my grooming business to follow it with you."

"My grandfather's going to join Dad and Daphne on the circuit and take measurements for the custom footwear I make and email them to me. I'm going to set up a permanent shop here. We're close enough to New York City that the town gets the high-end tourist trade so I'll sell Daphne's jewelry and my dad's knives in addition to my footwear. My family will handle the Ren Faire sales and use my shop for their own permanent base."

"It'll be so great to have your family with us when they take their breaks. Your little step-brothers are a hoot. My mom and dad had such a great time with your family, especially your dad and Daphne, when they visited. They'll be tickled to find out they're planning to be here more frequently. Can we have a Ren Faire hoopla?"

"My dad and step-mother were hoping you wanted to. They can make arrangements at the Faire they'll be at next month. My grandfather said he'll make you ear appliances and turn you into an Elf like the rest of our family for the wedding."

"Excellent. I'd love to be an Elf.

"Edan," Holly wrapped her arms around his neck, looked into his dark eyes, and saw her future. "We're going to be together forever"

"Until Eternity ends and Beyond," Edan told her while he took her sweater off.

******

Efran waved the viewing crystal to its normal opaque state.

Daffodil groaned. "Damn. Just when it was getting good."

"Give them some privacy," Efran said. "If you want public displays, I'll be happy to join with you in the clearing." He turned to the King, "What's going to happen if they do conceive a child and it is Elf despite Edan giving up his Elf heritage?"

His face tired and drawn, the King stroked his cat. "Dragons have promised they will disguise the child if it is Elf. The child will not be taken from its parents to be raised in De'erjia. Dragons keep promises."

Efran studied his King with concern. "It took much from you to negotiate a promise such as that."

"Actually, Dragons seemed to regard the idea of an Elf child of Edan and Holly's to be of little consequence." He smoked his pipe thoughtfully as though trying to remember what happened through the long negotiations. "They seemed to be more concerned that Edan return to Holly. If a promise to maintain an Elf child as human and not force it to become Elf unless it chooses to be was the key to Edan's return, they were more than willing to accept it. I think the small chartreuse dragon that remains with Holly is much more influential in Dragon ways than any of us suspected. I think because *it* wanted Edan with Holly, Dragons would have given any promise."

"Do you think Edan misconstrued his interpretation of the Dragon message to him?"

"I do not know what Edan saw, Daffodil. Efran and I were there for support, not query."

Efran snagged Daffodil to his lap. She snuggled her

bottom against his rising shaft. He asked his King, "Is it possible Dragons were talking about the chartreuse dragon as their Leader?"

Daffodil snorted. "We can sit here and discuss this until Eternity ends and probably still not come up with the right answers. The ways of Dragons are known only to Them. It matters not. Let's discuss more important things."

"Such as the three of us joining in the clearing?" the King suggested. His face brightened taking away most of the strain.

"Don't be ridiculous. We don't need to go all the way to the clearing," Daffodil sneered as Efran made her gown disappear. "When we get finished we need to discuss important things. Primarily, what am I going to wear to Holly and Edan's wedding? I don't think naked is quite appropriate."

"Damn shame. I knew there was a good reason why I prefer to remain Elf," Efran said.

******

In the yard of Holly's house, deep in the autumn leaves, Edan entered Holly. He clasped the globes of her ass and hugged her closely to him while he thrust hard into her welcoming wetness. Her fingernails dug into his butt to hold him closer to her while she arched upward to meet his thrusts. Her body began to shudder around his. The muscles holding him deep inside her tightened and flexed against his shaft.

Together they began to climb to forever. His shaft grew impossibly, unbearably hard. The pressure built in his loins. Her body shook around his. He exploded into her. Her voice raised in a cry wrenched from the center of her soul. His soul caught with hers. Together they spiraled into the Light knowing it gave them the first taste of Beyond where their bond would always keep them together.

******

Perched on the porch railing with its cat, the small chartreuse dragon watched in satisfaction. Its girl was happy. It was happy. Perhaps it might go visit the child Dora next.